FOR RICHER, FOR POORER

Kerry Wilkinson has been busy since turning thirty.

His first Jessica Daniel novel, *Locked In*, was a number one ebook bestseller, while the series as a whole has sold one million copies.

He has written a fantasy-adventure trilogy for young adults, a second crime series featuring private investigator Andrew Hunter, plus the standalone thriller, *Down Among the Dead Men*.

Originally from the county of Somerset, Kerry has spent far too long living in the north of England, picking up words like 'barm' and 'ginnel'.

When he's short of ideas, he rides his bike or bakes cakes. When he's not, he writes it all down.

For more information about Kerry and his books visit:

www.kerrywilkinson.com or www.panmacmillan.com

Twitter: twitter.com/kerrywk

Facebook: www.facebook.com/JessicaDanielBooks

Or you can email Kerry at kerrywilkinson@live.com

KERRY WILKINSON

FOR RICHER, FOR POORER

PAN BOOKS

First published 2016 by Pan Books
an imprint of Pan Macmillan
20 New Wharf Road, London N1 9RR
Associated companies throughout the world
www.panmacmillan.com

ISBN 978-1-4472-8092-7

1 3 5 7 9 8 6 4 2

A CIP catalogue record for this book is available from the British Library.

Typeset by Ellipsis Digital Limited, Glasgow
Printed and bound by CPI Group (UK) Ltd, Croydon, CR0 4YY

For my little sister.
Good job we grew up.

1

Harriet Blackledge closed the door of the children's bedroom and leant against the hallway wall, letting out a large breath. It had been another one of *those* days. Ian had been called into the office for yet another Sunday and she'd been left lugging the kids around Chester Zoo by herself. By the time she'd stopped them running off, persuaded them they weren't allowed to ride the giant tortoises, and told them that climbing into the primate enclosure wasn't a good idea, she was exhausted.

When it came to monkeys, her pair were quite enough, thank you.

Ian's voice echoed through the house from downstairs: 'Harry, where's the TV remote?'

Harriet winced. Having spent the past twenty-five minutes reading Jemma and Thomas separate bedtime stories, the last thing she wanted was her husband's booming voice to wake them up again. She made delicate shushing noises and started down the stairs.

Quite how she'd got to this, she wasn't really sure. She had a degree and wanted a career at some point . . . yet somehow she'd ended up as one of those kept stay-at-home mums she'd always ridiculed.

Tripping over the bottom step, Harriet righted herself and headed into the living room.

'. . . always in the same spot. It's not as if it's grown legs, things don't just walk . . .' Ian Blackledge was picking up cushions from the sofa, before turning and spotting his wife in the doorway. 'There you are, do you know—'

'I've just put the kids to bed. You're going to wake them.'

Ian scowled at his wife for a moment. He hated being interrupted, which was why Harriet did it as often as she could. She held his gaze until he went back to searching.

He continued as if nothing had happened, his boring voice boring into the walls, boring her. Boring, boring, boring.

'. . . I was just saying that these things don't lose themselves. Whenever I've finished watching television, I leave it on the table underneath – that way I know where to find it again . . .'

Harriet rolled her eyes behind his back. How many times had he said 'I' in that sentence? I, I, I. What a wanker. And she was married to him. Four thousand, five hundred and thirty-five days and counting: that's how long ago it was that she'd said 'I do'. Back then, there was no money, no big house, no expensive dresses and no bloody business.

'. . . I mean, it's not that hard, is it? If you use something, you put it back where you picked it up from . . .'

At least she had the kids. *She* had them. Ian had been in Johannesburg when Jemma was born and his phone had been buzzing constantly when Thomas said hello to the world. Well, gurgled a sob at the world.

'. . . I've said it before, Harry, and I'm serious this time

2

– someone's going to have to have a word with those kids. Always picking things up and not returning them. I mean . . .'

Someone's going to have to have a word: meaning her. He wasn't even subtle nowadays.

The words slipped out before Harriet even knew they were in her head. 'They've got names.'

Ian spun around again, cushion in hand. 'What?'

'Our kids. They have names: Jemma and Thomas.'

'What are you trying to say?'

'They're not *those* kids – they're *our* kids and they have names.'

Ian frowned again. He didn't like people talking back to him, which Harriet well knew because of the amount of time he spent banging on about it. Most of his complaints about work ended with: '. . . and I'm not sure who it is they think they're talking to – but I'm the boss of that company and I'll happily fire them if that's what they want . . .'

That was the clean version anyway. After a few drinks, he'd be threatening any number of anatomically awkward acts upon his workforce. Harriet suspected he was worse to work for than he was to live with – and that was saying something.

She continued holding his stare. This time Ian didn't look away. 'What are you trying to say?'

He couldn't even think of a different question but there was no going back now. Harriet felt something flare in her stomach. It had been there many times before but she always backed down, unwilling to have the argument. Always thinking of the children.

She took a deep breath. 'They're kids. Children play – they were watching "The Lion King" in here earlier while I cooked tea. Sometimes things get moved, sometimes things get knocked off. Don't you remember being young?'

'I always knew to respect my elders.'

He really was a bore. How had that skinny, smiling student who had so charmed her become this suit-wearing dullard of a man? His hair had started to go grey not long after he turned thirty, then he stopped doing anything that involved the slightest amount of exercise. Then he never wanted to do things at the weekend and the kids had come along to 'fix' their marriage. Meanwhile, everything became about 'the business', while she continued being the perfect, thin, homemaking wife.

'Didn't your dad used to hit you?' she said.

It was a low blow but Harriet wanted it to be. Ian took half a step backwards, eyes bulging. 'I . . .'

'I'm saying that "respecting" your elders didn't count for much. Kids are kids – they need discipline but they have to have space so they can be children too.'

Harriet could see Ian's shock beginning to boil into rage. The way he'd been treated by his father was something they'd spoken about years ago, when they were in love and they shared their deepest secrets with each other. They'd lain in bed, bodies entwined, and she'd listened as he cried. Different times, different people.

His eyebrow was twitching, bottom lip bobbing. His voice was low, almost a growl. 'What are you trying to say?'

Harriet felt a lump in her throat and knew she'd gone too far. She replied with a sigh: 'That being angry at them isn't going to help. It's only a remote control – if it's down the back of the sofa then I'm sure they didn't mean it.'

That wasn't what she wanted to say at all. What she should have told him was the truth – that she wasn't happy and that no amount of money was going to change that. In so many ways, she'd enjoyed herself more living in their poky old flat with noisy neighbours, a dodgy TV that needed a whack, a fridge that made a dangerous-sounding hum a couple of times a day, and a constant Friday- and Saturday-night showcase of idiots walking past their window throwing beer cans and drunkenly hurling up on the pavement. At the time she'd thought she hated it; now it seemed like living.

Ian wasn't backing down: 'Perhaps if you kept a closer eye on them?'

'I can't watch them every minute of the day – I was cooking. It's only a remote control! It's a Sunday, perhaps if you were home with them more often . . .'

Ian tossed the cushion to the floor. 'What do you think I do all day? Sit around playing games? You know how important this deal is to the business. What do you think pays for this house? Your clothes? Your car?' He threw his hands up in the air theatrically. 'Money doesn't grow on bushes, you know.'

Harriet sighed. She didn't want to have this argument because they'd only ever go around in circles. She could never tell him the truth: keep your house, your car, the clothes; keep it all. She didn't want any of it. He kept

5

bringing it up, thinking it was something he would always have over her, when the only reason she allowed him to have it was because she didn't want her kids to suffer the moneyless upbringing she'd had.

'Gone quiet now, haven't you,' he taunted.

One day she'd tell him the truth.

Harriet stepped forward, ready to help the search, when there was a crash from the kitchen. Her first thought was that the kids were going to be awoken again, then she caught her husband's eye and there was a ripple of fear. Despite what he'd become, the one thing Ian offered was security and she always felt safe around him. Seeing the confusion and anxiety in his eyes sent a shiver through her.

Ian bounded across the room, but froze next to her as the sound of heavy boots boom-boom-boomed around the walls.

There were people in the house.

Ian thrust a protective arm across her but Harriet was already heading for the stairs when a man appeared in the doorway. He was wearing black and grey camouflage-style cargo trousers, with a padded black long-sleeved top. Harriet froze, half-turning towards her husband, but there were three more identically clad men entering their living room through the other door. All four wore balaclavas and thick, dark gloves. Over their shoes were supermarket carrier bags. Harriet opened her mouth to scream to who knew who but the man was quicker, grabbing and spinning her in one movement, simultaneously putting a hand across her mouth. Harriet could taste the polyester pushing into her gums.

Ian turned from the men to her and back again. She could see the terror in the whites of his eyes. The tallest of the four men marched forward, effortlessly shoving Ian to one side and sending him sprawling towards the sofa. He kept moving until he was in front of Harriet, reaching into his pocket and taking out a pistol. Harriet felt the other man holding her tighter as she began to flail involuntarily.

An actual gun was pointing at her.

Harriet had seen them on TV, at the cinema. She'd heard the loud bangs, seen the brawny action figures with huge arms and the weedy gang members. She'd read the books and the news reports. Everyone became desensitised to the idea of guns because so many forms of entertainment put them front and centre.

But that was different to seeing an actual weapon being pointed at her. Harriet watched the man's gloved finger rest on the trigger, using the merest amount of pressure. The slightest slip and that would be it.

'Shhh,' he whispered, perfectly calmly, as if comforting a crying child. Harriet forced herself to take a breath through the man's glove, standing straighter, letting her arms flop by her side. Behind, the other figure slightly loosened his grip.

The first intruder turned towards Ian but didn't lower the angle of the gun, which was still pointing at Harriet's head. 'Where's the panic button?' he asked.

Ian was on the floor, head resting on the lip of the sofa, not knowing where to look. The thought popped into Harriet's mind that his suit was creased and she knew how much he hated that. He'd have her ironing trousers over and over, or simply drop half-a-dozen off at the dry cleaners in one go. Then she wondered why she was thinking about suits when there was a gun pointing at her.

'What panic button?' Ian replied.

Harriet coughed slightly, telling herself it was because of the fingers stuffed in her mouth and not because her husband had just lied to a man who was pointing a gun at her. He hadn't even had the good grace to do it convincingly.

The man with the weapon stepped nearer, holding the gun so close to Harriet that she went cross-eyed as she stared down the barrel. She had always thought those stylised shots in movies were completely over the top but here she was in that same position. What should she be looking for? Should she be able to see the bullet? Should his finger be twitching?

His voice sounded sort of local, not with the complete Mancunian twang that some had but there was certainly a hint. 'I don't give three chances, sonny. Where's the panic button?'

Harriet knew her husband too well. She could see his eyes darting and read his body language. He wasn't sure whether to be aggressive or deflated. He didn't accept defeats very well but this was surely different – their children were upstairs and someone was pointing a gun at her. In her mind, she screamed at him to tell them, hoping that somehow her thoughts would be projected across the room into that stupid mind of his.

'There are a few,' Ian stammered. 'In my study and—'

The gunman nodded at one of the other men, who

strode across the living room, carrier bags crackling on the carpet. He roughly yanked Ian up by the arm.

'Show my colleague where the central communications unit is,' the gunman said.

Ian was given a shove and he stumbled towards the kitchen. Harriet knew where the four buttons were around the house – one in their bedroom, one in the study, one in the kitchen and the one underneath the television cabinet she was trying not to stare at. She didn't know how they worked: all Ian had said was that pressing any of them would silently alert a security company, who would send the police around. They'd been fitted so long ago that she'd nearly forgotten about them. The gunman either knew, or he'd guessed. Based upon the area they lived in, it wasn't a big stretch – Harriet supposed most houses in this area had some sort of connection to a private security firm.

The gunman lowered the weapon until it was by his side. 'Where's your mobile phone?'

The man holding her released his fingers from her mouth but Harriet could feel the material of the gloves clutching the lower part of her neck: a warning that he could harm her at any moment.

'I . . . er . . . I think it's in my bag in the kitchen.'

He waved his hand vaguely in the direction of a third man, who scuttled away. 'Can never be too careful,' the gunman said. 'Not after . . . well, y'know.'

Harriet did know – she'd seen the other two robberies on the news. No one she knew had been targeted but they'd both occurred in south Manchester houses like theirs: big places owned by people with money. The thought had crossed her mind that perhaps it could be a pattern, as it had with the other parents she'd spoken to on the school run.

The third man re-entered with Harriet's phone in his hand, which he tossed to the gunman, who caught it one-handed. 'Nice,' he said, before dropping it on the floor and stamping on it.

'Do Jem and Tom have phones?'

Harriet started to reply before she even knew what he'd said. She ended up coughing, trying to compose herself. Somehow these men knew the names of their children. Then she remembered the website – Robert's stupid business, where there was an 'About Me' page with him fawning over the family he never saw. She'd told him at the time that she didn't want to be involved and now there was a man with a gun in *their* house speaking the names of *their* kids.

'It's a simple question,' he said, his arm holding the gun twitching slightly.

'Jemma does – Thomas is too young.' The gunman's head flickered towards the third man again but Harriet squealed. 'Please let me get it. They're asleep. I won't try anything, honestly I won't.'

Through the small slits of the balaclava, Harriet saw the gunman biting his bottom lip. As he lunged forward, she thought, just for a moment, that he was going to shoot her. A small shriek slipped from her lips before he clamped a hand across them, forcing her backwards through the door, towards the stairs.

Without a word, he pushed her upstairs, pausing at the top and waiting for her to show the way. The muzzle was pressing into her back but Harriet forced herself to stop shaking, padding as softly as she could towards Jemma's bedroom.

'Leave the door open,' the gunman whispered.

Tears were close but Harriet managed to hold on, gently easing her daughter's door open and creeping into the room. A dim orange night-light hanging above the bed shone a murky glow across the space as Harriet moved on her tip-toes.

'Mummy?'

Harriet froze, wincing at the feeling of being punched in the stomach, even though there was nobody near her. She glanced behind quickly, taking in the gunman's frame, wide and muscly underneath the padded top. He was staring towards her in silence, his chest rising almost imperceptibly.

Harriet stepped across to the bed, sweeping the phone from the bedside table into her left hand, resting her right on her daughter's forehead. 'Go to sleep, sweetie.'

'What's going on?'

'Nothing, honey. I was just checking on you.'

Even in the gloomy swathes of darkness, Harriet could see the smile spread across her daughter's face. The duvet was tucked underneath her chin, and her eyes were closed, one leg sticking out of the other side of the covers as it always did.

Harriet stood, walking carefully across the room and edging the door closed, before turning to see the gunman's outstretched hand. She placed the phone into it and then led the way back downstairs.

Ian was sitting on the sofa in the living room, elbows on knees, leaning forwards. The whites of his eyes were almost glowing, the area around them rubbed red. He gulped as Harriet was marched back in and shoved onto the sofa next to him. The gunman took Ian's phone from one of the other men and dropped that and Jemma's on the floor, before stamping on them.

Crumpled pieces of plastic, silicone and aluminium littered the carpet. Harriet found her eyes flickering towards the cordless landline phone in the corner. The gunman noticed and she could see him smiling through the bala- clava. 'Try it if you like – we're not that stupid.'

Harriet didn't move.

The gunman stood at the front, the other three behind him. He waved the gun towards Ian. 'Is there anything else I should know about?'

'Like what?'

'Do you have any other way of contacting anyone?'

'No.'

'Are you expecting visitors?'

'No.'

'Good – now open the safe.'

Harriet curled her toes, hoping Ian wouldn't be stupid. She didn't know how much money was locked away – but she did know all her expensive jewellery was in the safe. She didn't care that much about it but Ian did. On the occasions he requested that she wore it out, he would spend a large part of the evening bragging to various other people about how much it cost.

Ian's eyes darted to the floor. 'What safe?'

In one swift movement, the gunman lunged forward and cracked the butt across Ian's head. Harriet yelped but kept herself from screaming as her husband slumped sideways. Blood dripped onto their cream carpet and she again found herself drifting, thinking there was no way she'd be able to get that out. She'd once read that blood was worse than red wine. Harriet tried to blink away the ridiculous thoughts: why was she worrying about household things when her husband was bleeding? When her children were upstairs as a masked gang terrorised them? Was this normal?

'I won't ask again,' the intruder said.

Harriet opened her eyes and Ian tried to sit back up, even though he was swaying slightly. The blood drenched his hands and suit.

The gunman pointed the weapon at Harriet again. 'Don't you care about your wife? Your kids?'

The reply was low, almost a cough. 'Of course.'

'So where's the safe?'

Ian sighed. 'It's built into the wall in our bedroom.' One of the other men stepped forward but Ian held up a hand, coughing a spray of blood into his lap. 'I can't open it.'

Harriet could feel the cool ring of metal stinging her forehead as the gunman pushed the weapon into her skin.

'No, really,' Ian said, voice raised, panic making his

voice crack. 'There's a timer – it can only be opened at certain times of the day. I swear, there's no way around it.'

The pressure of the gun metal eased slightly on Harriet's forehead but she could still feel it tickling her skin. She suddenly realised her hands were balled, fingers digging into the material of the sofa. She didn't risk moving but her eyes flittered around the room as the four intruders peered at each other.

'That true?' the gunman asked.

'I don't know,' Harriet replied.

'I'll shoot her.'

The man pushed forwards again, pressing Harriet deeper into the sofa. He had one hand on her throat, the other thrusting the gun into her temple.

Ian's voice had gone up an octave, squeaking in a way Harriet had never heard before. She couldn't see him but the sofa popped up as he stood. 'No! Honestly, it's true.'

'When can you open it again?'

'Between six and eight in the morning.'

Harriet's eyes crossed again as she tried to peer at the trigger. The gunman's weight was leaning into her windpipe and she couldn't stop a gentle splutter from escaping.

'Please . . .' she whispered.

Harriet had no idea how long passed but suddenly the pressure was gone and the man stepped away from the sofa. He wafted the gun towards them, indicating the two-seater in the corner. 'Move over there – I guess we're in for a long wait.'

2

Detective Inspector Jessica Daniel listened to the hum of the radio as everyone got into position. Four officers dressed like bulked-up ninjas around the back, six at the front: no guns but batons and bloody big boots if anyone kicked off. The four tactical entry team members at the door glanced backwards through the moonlit shambles of a front garden towards Jessica.

She checked her watch, patted the incapacitating spray in her pocket for a reason she wasn't quite sure of, and then nodded slightly.

'POLICE, OPEN UP!' Bang, bang, bang, thump, crack, oof, ouch, thump, thwack, stomp, stomp, stomp.

Ouch?

The army of black-clad big bastards blasted through the house, followed by a handful of uniformed officers. Jessica stepped inside behind them, peering down at the thin, pasty figure of a girl curled into a ball in the hallway, splinters of wood on top of her, a graze across her head. The officers had thundered through the door, stepping on the teenager without even realising.

She moaned slightly as Jessica crouched. 'You all right?'

The girl uncurled herself, spitting onto the ground. 'Fucking piggy pig pigs.'

Good evening to you, too.

Jessica pushed herself to her feet and followed the noise into what turned out to be the living room. Three young men were facing the wall, being frisked, as another girl shouted and swore at a female officer, including poetic gems such as:

'You a lezzer, or what?'

'You trying to touch me up?'

'Get off my sodding tits.'

'I'm going to 'ave you, you fat bitch. And your mum.'

Jessica could only feel grateful that she no longer worked in uniform. Compared to some of the abuse hurled on a Friday night in the city centre, the young woman was positively delightful.

The girl from the hallway was led in, clutching her elbow and making oinking noises, while two more lads were frogmarched down the stairs by Greater Manchester Police's ninja squad. They were so thin that Jessica could see the outline of their ribs poking through their T-shirts, with scraggy unwashed hair hanging around their shoulders.

Jessica blinked. Neither of them was *him* but just for a moment, because of the hair, it was as if he was still with her.

The officers directed the lads to the wall where the other three were and told them to face it while they were frisked. 'This one was in the toilet,' a ninja said.

The young man flung his arms wide. 'I was taking a dump! Is that a crime nowadays? Christ's sake. Big Brother Britain where you can't even have a shite any more.'

'Shut up,' Jessica ordered sternly, creating a silence even she hadn't expected.

As the seven of them had their pockets turned out, Jessica surveyed the room. Behind and above, footsteps clunked around the dilapidated house. The walls were largely bare, with scrawny patches of ripped wallpaper clinging on for dear life. A light bulb was plugged into the fitting above, with no lampshade. The living room was sparse, with bare floorboards exposed: a television at one end with a games console and controllers on the floor in front of it, two sofas and a scuffed coffee table. Littered around the corners were empty coffee mugs, once-white plates with dried-on pieces of food, an upturned baked bean tin, cutlery, a set of speakers with a phone plugged into it, a bobble hat, a pair of dirty trainers, crumpled beer cans, empty bottles and a box of matches.

Hmm . . . not what they were expecting.

The house's inhabitants were told to sit on the sofas, which they did with minimal complaining as the search team assembled behind Jessica. Even without turning she could sense their nervousness. Eventually she spun to face Detective Constable Archie Davey but his frown told her they hadn't found what they were searching for upstairs. He was looking at his ridiculous tanned best, standing as tall as his alleged five-foot-eight frame would allow him.

Jessica nodded a silent acknowledgement to tell the ninjas they were done for the evening and then stood watching Archie, listening until the other footsteps had disappeared back into the van outside. Upstairs and in one of the other downstairs rooms, Jessica could hear the remaining officers continuing the search.

Archie strutted towards the sofa, lip curled, in his

element. This was only a few streets away from where he'd grown up as a mouthy Mancunian. He was always going to end up either sticking people behind bars, or living behind them.

His accent was as thick as ever, extending the vowels: 'Who lives 'ere?'

No one spoke.

Archie half-turned to Jessica. 'Am I speaking English? I'm not in the mood for arseing around – who lives in this dive?'

The thinnest of the males half-raised his hand. He was wearing skinny jeans, Dr Martens, what was probably a child's T-shirt and had an earring through each ear. At best he was twenty.

Jessica pointed a thumb towards the stairs. 'Right, upstairs with me.' As he started to climb to his feet, Jessica leant in and whispered in Archie's ear: 'Try not to kill anyone, please.'

The house's occupant stepped past Jessica and began creaking his way up the stairs, leading her into a bedroom with more exposed floorboards, an unmade bed and piles of clothes and shoes. He sat as Jessica tried to catch what Archie was shouting about downstairs. When she turned to him, the young man was staring up at her.

'What's your name?' Jessica asked.

'Noel.'

'I'm only going to ask this once, Noel – where are the drugs?'

He shrugged. 'What drugs?'

Jessica raised her eyebrows, not breaking eye contact. 'I told you I was only going to ask once.'

'You can ask as many times as you like – I don't know what you're talking about.'

'Come on, Noel – people coming and going all hours, loud music, empty beer bottles and cans all over; this whole place reeks of smoke. How old are you?'

A thunk erupted from the next-door room as one of the search-team officers dropped something.

Noel's eyes flittered sideways and back again. 'Old enough.'

'How old's that?'

'Nineteen.'

'Who are the people downstairs?'

He shrugged. 'Mates.'

'And what's a nineteen-year-old doing in a big house like this by yourself?'

Another shrug: 'Living.'

'*Really?*'

One more shrug: 'What about it?'

'Not too many teenagers end up living in a place like this without parents.'

The shrugs were beginning to annoy her now. 'So?'

'So, what's going on here? Is this your parents' house? Are you renting? Who's your landlord? Get talking.'

Jessica braced herself for the shrug that inevitably arrived, balling and unballing her fist. 'You got a warrant?'

'Didn't someone show you it downstairs?'

'Nope.'

Jessica stepped backwards onto the landing, not taking

19

her eyes from Noel and bellowing down the stairs for Archie. A minute later, Jessica thrust the warrant into Noel's hand as Archie continued shouting at the teenagers downstairs. As Noel read, Jessica caught the end of Archie's rant: '. . . and don't think you can get away with shoving it up your arse because we've got dirty bastards at the station who'll happily go digging . . .'

Charming.

Noel finished reading and peered up at Jessica. 'Can I keep this?'

'It's yours.'

'Good – I'm going to get it framed. It'll be something to show visitors.'

'Who's your landlord?'

'Me, I suppose. I own the house.'

Jessica thought about all the tribulations she'd had to go through to buy a house. 'You got a mortgage?'

'I bought it outright.'

Jessica couldn't hold back the cough of derision. 'You bought this house with cash?'

Another shrug: 'Gandhi once said that possession was a crime. He said "I can only possess certain things when I know that others who also want to possess similar things are able to do so". He believed the only thing we could all possess was non-possession, so that none of us had anything at all.'

Jessica's toe was tapping in annoyance. 'For someone who claims there aren't any drugs in the house, you're doing a pretty good impression of someone higher than the international space station.'

Noel's shoulders started to twitch again.

'And stop bloody shrugging!'

'What do you want me to say?'

'I want to know where the drugs are.'

'There aren't any. I just have my mates over during the week to play a few games, watch some movies, have a couple of drinks and a few fags. What's wrong with that?'

'What about the noise?'

'We have a few songs on the go: Smiths, Stone Roses, Oasis, Noel, the Mondays – not my fault if the neighbours wouldn't know a good tune if someone shoved a guitar up their arses.'

What was it with young men talking about sticking things up other people's arses?

Jessica took a moment to think and then ordered Noel to stand on the landing where she felt sure he couldn't dispose of anything without her noticing. She popped her head around the door of the adjacent room, which turned out to be the bathroom, where an officer was hunting through a cabinet.

'Anything?' she asked.

A shake of the head.

Next door was a bedroom, where a pair of officers were searching through a stack of cardboard boxes. 'Anything?'

One of them nodded towards the wall, where a red-triangle Give Way road sign was propped up against the wall.

Jessica couldn't hide her disappointment. 'Is that it?'

'So far.'

Jessica picked it up, straining unexpectedly under the weight and lugging it into the hallway. 'Whose is this?'

Noel shrugged. 'Dunno – Chris's I think.'

'Who's Chris?'

'He's downstairs.'

Jessica dropped the sign at Noel's feet. 'Tell your mate he's just cost you a front door. If we'd broken in here and not found anything, we'd have to fix it. As it is, we're going to nick him for theft – and you can pay for your own door. Now – how did a kid like you afford a house like this?'

'Inheritance – I got it at auction.'

'Who owned it before you?'

'I don't know what he's called. That lottery winner guy that was all over the news – what's his name?'

Jessica had a sinking feeling as she remembered the story. Everyone in the station had joked about it but no one would be laughing now. She sighed before answering for him. Someone had really ballsed things up.

'It's Martin Teague.'

3

Detective Sergeant Isobel Diamond perched on the edge of the spare desk in Jessica's office as Archie strode back and forth. Jessica listened to him make the same floorboard creak for the fifth time and then snapped. 'Will you sit down? You're driving me crazy.'

'*Crazier*,' Izzy corrected.

Archie flopped into the spare office chair, legs splayed wide, as ever, head bobbing up and down. 'I still say we should've ripped up the floorboards. They've probably got bricks of heroin and dead cats under that house and we've let 'em get away with it. You can't trust these student types.'

'Weren't you a student?' Jessica asked.

'Aye, but not like that.'

'What – you hung around the park drinking cider instead of trashing your own house?'

Archie stared at his shoes. 'Not quite . . .'

Jessica nodded towards Izzy. 'Haven't you got work to do now you're off probation and a proper sergeant?'

Izzy shook her head. 'I'm hiding – that pillock Franks has been trying to get me to do some work for him but he has that way of looking at you as if he's trying to chat you up.'

'What do you expect from someone known as Wanky Frankie? How's Dave?'

DC David Rowlands had been assigned to Detective Inspector Franks several months previously and hadn't escaped. Although they'd been firm friends, perhaps still were, Jessica and Rowlands had barely spoken since then.

Izzy smiled in the weary way she did when she was trying to be nice. 'He's just busy all the time.'

Jessica turned back to Archie. 'Anyway, you know I'm going to get called upstairs any minute to try to justify this balls-up, so what have you got on Teague?'

Archie clucked his tongue and straightened his suit. He replied with a twinkle in his eye: 'Too important to do your own checking?'

Jessica pointed to the papers on her desk, knowing she shouldn't really take his lip: 'Too busy.'

Archie picked up a cardboard folder from the desk and passed across a printout from a news website. Jessica scanned it, recognising the photograph. The pudgy-faced man walking out of court was bald on top but with rough stubble covering his cheeks and chin. He was wearing a thick overcoat and offering a middle-fingered salute to the camera.

'Martin Teague has been on our radar for yonks,' Archie said. 'He's lived in the area his whole life and been in trouble for most of it. He was expelled from school for threatening to burn it down and ended up in this behavioural problem place. When he was eighteen, he spent four months in prison for an assault and he's also been inside for a separate assault, handling stolen goods, as well as dealing amphetamines. In all, he has almost forty convictions for various things.'

Jessica more or less knew that part of the story – it was the later parts she was sketchy on.

'But then he turned himself around,' she said sarcastically.

'Quite,' Archie replied. 'Lucky sod won the lottery three years ago: nine point eight million quid. He bought a house out Cheadle way and set about spending it all. He bought a monster truck, a fleet of sports cars, and a non-league football team. Inside the house, he had a full-sized cinema screen installed, he bought fifty old-fashioned arcade machines, plus he'd started having a rollercoaster built that ran around his back garden and looped into the house.'

'Sounds like my place,' Izzy said.

Archie didn't miss a beat: 'He hired an entire Caribbean island on which to marry his childhood sweetheart and flew out two hundred people for a week-long celebration less than three months after winning.' He flicked to the next page and continued: 'Just over a year ago, inevitably, he was declared bankrupt. He'd been borrowing money against the interest but when the banks came calling, he'd spent it all.'

Jessica took the printout from Archie as he moved onto the next news website page. 'He burned through the lot in under three years. In the bankruptcy hearing, it came out that he didn't even have an accountant, plus he hadn't kept receipts. He'd simply spent it all. Somehow he avoided prison over the tax but he ended up moving into the old council house where his wife grew up.'

'What about the houses?' Jessica asked.

Archie passed along another sheet, saying she was best reading it herself. It was a report on Teague's bankruptcy hearing, which was mainly an account of his shambolic lifestyle. Because he hadn't kept any receipts, the only way they knew what he'd bought was because of the bank statements, credit card details and line of people asking where their money was. He'd spent the first twenty-six years of his life weaving a path of carnage through the city because of his criminal nuisance, another three by spending money he didn't have, and then the next twelve months stumbling from hearing to hearing about his bankruptcy. Finally, he'd ended up where he began: in a council house on a rough Manchester estate.

Along the line, there would be hundreds of individuals whose lives he'd trampled across – but Noel had been one of the few beneficiaries. Teague had bought twenty-seven run-down former council houses at auction for a reason no one seemed to know. Given his lack of care with money, it could be seen as an indulgence or perhaps an investment but Jessica suspected it was simply a whim. She'd spent plenty of time working with – or trying to track down – people from similar estates. The one trait they all shared, for better or worse, was a sense of pride in where they came from. It was that which led to them so despising the police and authority, wearing their underclass as a badge of honour. In some ways Jessica admired that. Owning those houses would have been a way for Teague to believe he was still a man of the people, even while blowing his money on unfinished rollercoasters.

Whatever the purpose, when the money had run out,

the houses had been seized and sold at auction again, for less than he'd paid. That was how Noel had managed to use however much he'd inherited to buy the dive Jessica and her team had raided the previous evening.

'We're screwed, aren't we?' Jessica said, looking up.

Izzy half-grinned. 'Don't bring me into this – I wasn't even there.'

Jessica nodded at Archie. 'Do you fancy taking the blame?'

'Sod off – it's not my fault every DCI has it in for you.'

Jessica laughed it off but she could tell from the way Izzy was watching her that the sergeant wasn't taken in. Archie had a habit of hitting a little too close to the truth without knowing he'd done so. The former chief inspector, Jack Cole, had retired at the end of the previous year. Despite the fact they had risen through the ranks together, their professional relationship had ended with Jessica on compassionate leave and him not talking to her anyway. He hadn't even said goodbye – not that Jessica blamed him after the way she'd behaved. As for Cole's replacement, Jessica had still been off work when he'd started and things had gone downhill from there.

Before she could reply, Jessica's desk phone began to ring: His Highness was in court and wanted a word.

DCI Lewis Topper was drumming a pen on his desk as he waved Jessica into his office on the upstairs floor of Longsight Police Station. Before she'd even closed the door behind her, his crisp accent rattled across the room: 'What went wrong?'

He'd joined from a force in Scotland – headhunted apparently – but there was a hint of Irish in his accent too. Either tone could be soft but he had the harsher elements of both, meaning he constantly sounded annoyed, like he had a mouthful of marbles.

Topper was in his mid-forties but his trim physique, clean-shaven face and abundance of dark hair – a rarity in the balding upper ranks of the police force – made him look younger.

'It was one of Martin Teague's old houses, Sir. He's—'

'You do realise how much scrutiny we're all under?'

Jessica had spent a lot of time in this office over the years but it was different now. Gone were the certificates and commendations that used to live on the wall behind the desk, replaced by a whiteboard covered with perfect handwriting that listed every ongoing investigation. DCI Cole would let his officers go out and deal with things, only getting involved if there were problems; Topper wanted details of everything.

'I know, Sir. We'd had reports of disturbances at the house and struggled to get anything from the land registry. We didn't know if there were people squatting—'

'Didn't you think to check these things? You know how damaging the fall-out from the Pratley report was.'

Jessica couldn't fail to know – it was one of the reasons why Topper was there in the first place. After a quarter-of-a-century-old false conviction had been exposed, an official investigation into Greater Manchester Police's structure and management had been launched. Although no one currently in a position of power had been drawn in, mud stuck, with the chief constable pensioned off and a raft of other management changes. The upshot from Jessica's point of view was that no one was allowed to show any initiative in case they were branded as a rogue officer.

Jessica thought Topper had paused to allow her to reply but he took a breath and continued. 'The chief constable won't be happy if there's a complaint made.'

Jessica had to stop herself from replying too quickly. In many ways it had been inevitable but the very thought that Graham Pomeroy had got the chief constable's job made her feel slightly sick. They'd only met a handful of times, the last of which being at a press conference announcing that they'd found a man who had killed two women, yet he was a constant presence in her mind. Every day she wondered how she could come to work knowing what she knew about Pomeroy without being able to tell anyone. The only other people who knew were the pair she'd barely spoken to since returning to work: DC Rowlands and her journalist friend, Garry.

'I don't think there'll be a complaint, Sir,' Jessica eventually replied. 'He was going to frame the warrant.'

She suddenly remembered how she'd told Noel they wouldn't even have to pay for his front door because of the stolen road sign. Stupid, stupid, stupid. He probably would complain now.

'What exactly happened?'

'We had some dodgy intelligence, I—'

'It doesn't sound like there was any intelligence at all – certainly not from you.'

'Sorry, Sir.'

Topper tutted, half-peering around to look at his board, where there were a disconcerting number of things on the 'unsolved' side. 'This isn't the only issue that's come up in the past couple of months.'

'We've had an unlucky run, Sir. I know the timing isn't great . . .'

Topper continued to peer at his board, rubbing his chin. 'I wonder if it's more than that.'

'Sir?'

He turned to face her, eyes narrowing like a parent questioning a naughty child. 'I read up about all of the senior officers when I started here. You have a stellar past and a record no one can quibble with but I can't help but wonder if your performance has started to dip since—'

'It hasn't.'

'You didn't have to come back. Certainly, not so quickly.'

Jessica held his gaze, not wanting to back down but unwilling to talk about it either. She'd spoken to everyone they wanted her to, done everything they said. If she wanted to return to work then it was her decision. In too many ways this was more of a home than her house was. That had too many memories attached; here she could immerse herself in the work.

'I'm fine.'

'I know you've been through a lot recently what with the car . . . accident . . . but I need all my officers to be in a good frame of mind.'

'I'm fine!'

Too forceful. With Cole, Jessica could raise her voice but Topper wasn't one to allow any questioning of the way he worked. He began tapping his pen again, biting his bottom lip.

'If that's the case then you need to start showing it.' He pointed to the whiteboard. 'Something needs to be done about this lot.'

Jessica managed to calm her tone again. 'I know, Sir.'

Topper was still biting his lip when his desk phone rang. He picked it up, listened, wrote something on the pad in front of him, and then turned to Jessica: 'Now's your chance: there's been another burglary.'

4

The site of the third burglary was similar to those of the first two: an expensive house, slightly set back from the road towards the end of a street lined with similar properties. Jessica knew they were intelligent choices – not mansions because the security would be too tight, but houses big enough to ensure there would be money and possessions inside. This area of south Manchester was far enough outside the M60 ring road to avoid the noise, yet close enough to ensure its residents weren't cut off. The area was occupied by those who didn't want to live on a Manchester housing estate but who weren't quite sufficiently rich to move across the county border into Cheshire.

Ian and Harriet Blackledge's house ticked all of those boxes: clean red-brick walls, two cars on the driveway, a double garage, five or six bedrooms, vast swathes of green on one side, and a similar house twenty metres down the road.

Harriet was in her mid-thirties, only a little younger than Jessica. She sat at the dining table, eyelids heavy, struggling to make eye contact. Small flecks of dark roots peeped out from her bright blonde hair, with her skin pale except for a smattering of red blotches around her left cheek.

'I understand your children have been taken elsewhere,' Jessica said.

Harriet nodded. 'Ian's parents came and took them. Your woman said it was okay.'

'Did they see the robbers?'

A weary shake of the head: 'They slept through it all. Tom thought it was all a bit of a game when the police officers came around this morning. He's too young to understand.'

'Tell me what happened.'

'I'd put the kids to bed and come downstairs. I was in the living room with Ian when there was a bang from the kitchen. Suddenly there were men in here with masks and gloves. One of them had a gun.'

'What time was this?'

'Around eight. I don't know exactly.'

Harriet told Jessica how the robbers had smashed their mobile phones, cut the landline and disabled the panic system. She wasn't emotional, more stunned; her wide eyes fixed on the table as she spoke steadily, as if recalling something she'd seen on television. The details were similar to those of the first two robberies, although the second house hadn't had a panic system. It seemed it was something the invaders assumed, rather than them having any precise knowledge. That had thrown the police's initial theories that the robbers could have an inside link to security companies.

'Was there anything distinguishing about any of the men?' Jessica asked.

'Not really – only one of them spoke. He was slightly

taller than the other three but they were all dressed the same.'

'What was his voice like?'

'Just kind of . . . normal.'

'Did he sound British? Northern?'

'A bit local, but not over the top. He only spoke when he had to.'

That was the same as in the other incidents: aside from the main person being white with dark eyes and with a local-ish accent that could have been Mancunian, or simply northern, they had little to go on. The woman whose house had been robbed in the first incident claimed one of the balaclava-wearing men 'grunted like a European' but when asked what that meant, her only response was: 'Well, that's what they sound like, isn't it? These Polish, coming over here . . .'

It wasn't exactly something that would stand up in court.

Jessica glanced over Harriet's shoulder to the clock on the wall. 'You said the robbers broke in at eight o'clock last night – but you didn't call us for twelve hours.'

'I did try to explain to the officers who got here first. There's some sort of timer on the safe – you'd have to ask my husband about it. He told them it couldn't be opened until after six in the morning.'

'So what happened overnight?'

Harriet coughed a half-laugh, half-sob, not quite believing it herself. 'We all waited in the living room. The man who spoke had us put the TV on and we sat around watching late-night talk shows. Then they got bored, so they pointed at a few films on the rack. We ended up sitting around watching movies through the night. They even had me fetch them crisps.'

'Did they—?'

'No – the man told me to tip everything into a big bowl and they ate out of that. Then he went into the kitchen with me and watched me wash it up. I don't think they touched it but one of your people took it away just in case.'

The way Harriet described it made the previous night's events sound like the strangest house party ever: four masked men, two scared householders and a pair of kids sleeping peacefully upstairs.

'What happened in the morning?'

Harriet finally glanced up at Jessica, yawning, apologising, and then looking back at the table. She ran a hand through her hair. 'It felt as if I was watching myself. I was alert because I was thinking of the kids upstairs, hoping they didn't wake up, but my body was exhausted. I can't even remember the last time I stayed up through the night.'

'What were the robbers like?'

'Tired, I suppose. One of them was lying on our sofa, another on the floor – but the one who spoke was watching the whole time. We were in the corner and weren't allowed to move unless someone was with us. I had to go to the toilet at three in the morning and one of them . . .'

For the first time, Harriet showed a sense of emotion, choking back the start of a sentence before composing herself.

'Did he do anything?' Jessica asked.

'He just watched from the doorway but y'know . . .'

'What happened with the safe?'

'As soon as it was six o'clock, the main guy was on his feet, telling Ian it was time. You'd have to ask Ian what happened then – he doesn't even let me know the code. He took the guy with the gun and one other upstairs, leaving the other two down here with me. When they came back down, they had a rucksack taken from our spare room.'

'What did they take?'

'You'll have to ask Ian – I don't know. I didn't see inside the bag. As soon as they got downstairs, they were all on their feet and left through the back again. The guy told us there would be someone watching the house and that, if we left, they'd come back and hurt the kids. We waited until it was light and then Ian ran next door to call you.'

Jessica went over a few of the other points, at first thinking they had a lead because the robbers knew the children's names, but then being shot down by an irate Harriet pointing out that her husband had included them as part of a family profile on his 'stupid' company's website.

After talking to Harriet, Jessica was given a tour by a rather more annoyed Ian Blackledge.

'Why aren't there more police here? . . . Why didn't you anticipate something like this after the first two? . . . What are you doing to find them? . . . What do my taxes pay for?'

Jessica wondered what made people think it was a good

idea to ingratiate themselves with the police by banging on about how you paid their wages.

Not once did Ian mention his wife or children, instead asking how quickly the police report would come through so he could contact the insurance company. By the time they got to the couple's bedroom, Jessica had already had enough of him.

The bedroom itself was huge, featuring a bed as wide as it was long with a tall mirror-fronted walk-in wardrobe at the foot. On one side, an open door led into an en suite bathroom, with a gaping hole in the wall opposite where a safe door hung open. Covering it had been a painting that was connected to the wall by a hinge in a scene that lived up to every cliché ever imagined about where a safe could be hidden.

'What happened when you were brought up here?' Jessica asked, peering into the safe but not touching anything. Traces of fingerprint powder were sprinkled across the metal, with a blinking light above a keypad on the front panel.

'The man with the gun told me to open it.'

'And did you?'

Ian sat on the bed, his bulk making it sag at the bottom. As he spoke he flapped his hands around. 'I got it wrong the first time – I think my fingers must've been a bit shaky – but yes.'

'What did they take?'

'Everything!'

Jessica waited for further explanation but for a man who had apparently built a business, Ian Blackledge seemed a bit slow. Eventually she had to ask: 'What *exactly* did they take?'

'Oh . . . well, there was diamond jewellery, plus I always keep a degree of cash around the house just in case.'

'How much?'

'Around fifteen thousand.'

'You keep fifteen thousand pounds in cash at home?'

Ian shrugged as if it was the most natural thing. 'You never know when you might need petty cash for a business.'

In all, totalling the cash and jewellery, he claimed the robbers had taken more than two hundred thousand pounds. If true, it was the robbers' biggest haul yet, almost doubling the total amount taken – most of which seemed to be in jewellery. In the first two cases, the victims had been photographed at various functions showing off quite how much the jewels cost. Given the number of times Ian had mentioned how much one of the stolen necklaces was worth, it seemed likely he'd paraded Harriet around wearing it at some point or another. With that and giving his children's names out on his website, he'd not quite asked for it but he certainly hadn't helped himself. Jessica never ceased to be amazed by how stupid people were when it came to giving out private information.

She went through the same questions with Ian, even though he'd already given a statement, but he had less to say about the actual robbery than his wife did, somehow managing to spend the night not noticing anything about the people who had broken into his house.

When Jessica got downstairs, the Scene of Crime team didn't have much in the way of good news. Neither Harriet nor Ian could remember any of the robbers touching anything without their gloves on, except for the crisps – and, although the bowl had been taken away, the fact it had been washed didn't offer much hope.

'There's too much of this shite on TV nowadays,' one of the officers complained. 'Bags over their shoes, washing things up – what happened to the days of stupid criminals?'

Quite.

The method of entry was the same as in the other incidents: something bloody big and solid had been crashed into the back door. Apart from the dent indicating it had a rounded end, no one seemed to be able to give them much of a steer on what it might be – other than a vague notion that it was similar to the battering rams they themselves used. As for footprints, since the gang had covered their feet with bags, the best they'd come up with was a slight skid in the mud at the site of the second robbery.

All in all, their hunt for a white man who spoke English with a possibly northern accent and was known to have at least three mates – one with size ten or eleven feet – hadn't got them too far. The robbers knew the area well enough to get in and out without leaving anything approaching a trace. With the first and second houses, they'd disabled the private CCTV cameras; here it had been the panic buttons. Someone among the gang must have a degree of technical knowledge, which gave the police another avenue to explore. But, as had been unhelpfully pointed out by a succession of constables, anybody could do a bit of research on the Internet and find out how to incapacitate security systems. Some smart-arse had even printed off the instructions to prove it.

After a quick word with the remaining uniformed officers, Jessica headed to the driveway where Archie was leaning on the bonnet of the CID car they'd arrived in.

'Like the other houses, innit?' he said.

Jessica sighed, untying and retying her hair as she joined him, pulling her jacket tighter around herself. 'Topper's already got a strop on about everything that's unsolved. Serial burglars are the last thing we need. Did the neighbours have much to say?'

'Nowt – they're just worried they might be robbed next. That's three in five weeks. One of the houses down the road has a camera pointing towards the street but the quality's awful. A couple of cars went past at around the time our fellas drove off – but it was dark and you can only see lights.'

Jessica pointed along the road. 'Everything's too spread out. Even if a bunch of robbers had been sitting around in a van watching a house, it's unlikely they'd be spotted – especially after dark.'

As she peered along the road, Jessica saw the unlikely sight of an open-top bus turn onto the street. The bright royal blue and yellow colour scheme stood out against the sky, which was its usual wash of grey streaks. As it came closer, she could see a smattering of figures on top, scarves flailing in the wind, hats and gloves protecting them against the northern chill.

Archie offered a shrug, so Jessica moved onto the kerb where she flagged it down. Over the top of the rail on the top deck, a man wearing a deerstalker and holding a microphone peered over the edge.

'What's up?' he shouted down, as half-a-dozen people moved to the edge of the deck and began taking photographs of the police cars.

'Oi, stop!' Jessica called, pointing at them. When it was clear they weren't listening, she turned back to the man in the deerstalker. 'What's going on with the bus?'

He held up a blue clipboard with a yellow logo. 'Haven't you heard of us? This is Star Tours.'

5

Jessica and Archie sat in the dingy office down a side street opposite the Arndale Centre, staring at a black and white photo on the wall. The subject's teeth were white, his smile wide, eyes twinkling.

She frowned and turned to face the man sitting behind the desk, whose teeth were yellow, his smile nervous, eyes attempting to do everything but look at Jessica. On the desk in front of him was a metal name plate reading: 'Ace'.

'Has Tom Cruise ever been to Manchester?' Jessica asked, nodding at the photo.

Ace was wearing a cheap, ill-fitting grey polyester suit which he tugged at. 'Er . . . he was at the Manchester derby a few years ago.'

'Aye, we won.' Archie nodded approvingly. 'Last minute. Take that, you bitter bastards.'

Jessica wasn't interested in football talk. She pointed to the photo next to Tom Cruise. 'The Dalai Lama?'

The man in the suit squirmed more than before, pulling at the thighs of his trousers. 'There were rumours he's a City fan.'

'Really?'

'Well, unconfirmed . . .'

Archie muttered something that didn't sound too complimentary.

'Look Mr, er, Ace,' Jessica said, 'we're trying to establish exactly what it is you do.'

A smile finally cracked on the man's face. He swept his arm majestically, indicating the wall of photographs behind him and the blue and yellow transfer that was peeling away from the grubby window. 'I'm the owner and CEO of Star Tours.'

'What's that?'

'We offer an exclusive open-top bus tour of Manchester's rich and famous. I got the idea when I was in LA.'

'Yes but famous people live in LA. This is Manchester.'

Another sweep of the arm. 'We have our own glitterati here.'

Shitterati, more like.

Jessica recognised Tom Cruise and the Dalai Lama; beyond that, there were a few soap stars she pretended she didn't know, blokes she didn't recognise in football kit, and at least two dozen people she'd never seen before.

'And this is a business?'

'Big business! We offer a six-hour tour including soft drinks and lunch. It's only sixty quid Monday to Friday – seventy-five on a weekend.'

Ace reached into a drawer and took out a flyer, passing it across the desk. Jessica skim-read the list of famous names on the front before turning it over and taking in the route as he continued to speak.

'The Japanese lap it up,' Ace said. 'We take tourists from the centre down through Alderley Edge, towards Cheshire and back again. It's really taken off in the past six months, so we've bought a second bus. I'm looking into getting a bigger office over by Piccadilly Gardens. People can't get enough of it. We've got all the *Coronation Street* lot and the footballers, of course. Then there's the reality TV crowd. They're massive at the moment and there's something on all the time, so there are always new people being added to our maps.' He pointed to the face of a blonde woman behind him. 'You must remember her? She did that thing with the bottle on television where she stuck it up her—'

'I think the wider point, Mr, er, Ace, is that your tour is taking crowds of people along suburban streets where other *non*-famous people's privacy could be compromised.'

Ace clearly didn't get the point, still dramatically whirling his arms. 'You'd be surprised who lives where. There's some famous magician type who lives above a bookies out Stockport way. The Scandinavians love him – they all want their pictures taken next to the front door. We offer an unparalleled service, giving our customers an insight into what it's like to be famous.'

'But this is *Manchester*.'

'Yes . . .'

Jessica didn't know what confused her the most. 'Are you saying that people are seriously paying seventy-five quid to stand on the top deck of a bus and get soaked, just so they can be driven past the house of someone who was once on *Big Brother*?'

Ace shrugged. 'We've got advance bookings for the next six months. By the time the summer comes around, we might have to get a third bus.'

Jessica turned to Archie. 'We're in the wrong business.'

Archie's mouth was hanging open: 'Seventy-five quid?'

'Yes.'

'Each?'

'Yes.'

'Some people will pay for any old shite.'

Ace didn't even bother to protest, his knowing smile an admission that he couldn't believe his luck either.

'We're going to need some information from you,' Jessica said. 'From what I can tell, your bus has been regularly heading past at least one house which has later been robbed. That's a lot of potential witnesses who could have seen something suspicious. I want the names of all your tour guides – plus as many details as you have of anyone who's been on your tour since you began trading.' She nudged Archie. 'My colleague here will help to collate everything.'

Before either of them could complain, Jessica was on her feet and heading towards the door, muttering under her breath. 'Seventy-five-sodding-quid.'

Jessica sipped the foam from the top of her pint and then wiped her top lip. Archie slid onto the booth's soft bench opposite her and downed a third of his drink in one go.

'You really are a cow sometimes,' he said.

'You say the sweetest things.'

'That Ace guy's a maniac. I thought it was a nickname but he's officially changed his name because he thought "Ace Mancura" sounded more showbiz than "Clive Yates".'

'He's right.'

Jessica had never tried real ale until she started spending

time with Archie. She wasn't even sure she liked it – but at barely two quid a pint, it was like the old days of hanging around with her friend Caroline at university, getting pissed for under a tenner and then stumbling home. She took two large mouthfuls.

'It was a waste of time anyway,' Archie continued. 'His records are pretty good but his buses have only ever gone past the last house that was robbed – nowhere near either of the other places. I spoke to the tour guides but nobody remembers anything suspicious on that street.'

'I didn't think we'd get much but Topper wants to see everyone doing something. It was worth a try.' Jessica peered across to where someone on the far side of the pub had just fed a couple of pound coins into the jukebox and started up an Oasis tune. 'This is among the better places we've been to.'

As he took another large mouthful, Archie made an approving grunt.

'Where are the crisps?' Jessica asked.

'What crisps?'

'I've not had any tea.'

Archie took another sip and then climbed to his feet. 'You're so high maintenance.'

'I'm really not.'

He grinned, gave her a wink and headed back to the bar.

In an attempt to find a spot that was somewhere in between their workplace in Longsight, Jessica's house in Swinton and Archie's flat in Stretford, they had tried a succession of places along the top end of Oxford Road where plenty of student types hung around. One night they had accidentally ended up in a hole that played only dance music, another time it had been a sports bar – which was fine for Archie, but left Jessica wanting to throttle him and everyone else there. This evening, they had ventured off the main road and stumbled across a grungy-looking bar next to a curry house. Or, as Jessica saw it, they'd found the perfect combination.

Archie returned with a packet of Quavers, two bags of salt and vinegar and a cheese and onion for luck. He was also managing to cling onto two more pints as well, despite Jessica still having half of hers remaining. He plopped down all four packets and they set about opening them until the table was a mass of foil and fried potato. Over the speaker system, a second Oasis song began: whoever had fed their cash into the jukebox really knew what they were doing.

'If it's any consolation,' Jessica replied through a mouthful of Quaver, 'it's been shite at the station this afternoon.'

Archie was in the process of eating six crisps at the same time but nodded to at least acknowledge he'd heard.

Jessica tried not to grin: 'Anyway, we've got nothing back from the early test results – as with the other robberies.'

'They must be clever.'

'But are they? Everyone keeps saying that – but it's hardly the perfect crime, is it? They've watched a bit of television, perhaps read a few things on the Internet, and they know how to get in and out without leaving much of a trace – but they've still got to get rid of all this stuff. You can't just walk into a jeweller's and sell the things you've nicked. You can't go on eBay and say, "Here's a bracelet worth fifty grand, starting bid ninety-nine pence". Apart from our guy today with his fifteen thousand "petty cash", they've not got away with that much money – not when you consider the risk.'

Archie finished his first pint and started on the second. 'There's always someone who'll buy – some dodgy under-the-table jeweller or pawn shop. I know we're keeping half an eye on the ones in the city but you could go anywhere in the country to sell. Someone will always buy nicked goods.'

'Jewellery's not the same as nicking a TV or a phone though. It's not the type of thing people buy to hide away at home – they buy it to wear it, or to give to someone they're trying to impress. Someone *will* always pay – but if you're the gang who's stolen it, you're not going to get anywhere near as much money as you think. So why go to all that risk? You could ram-raid a shop, dive in and out and be done with it. You don't have to spend the night in a stranger's house – especially when the main thing you get short-term is fifteen grand. Then you've got the hassle of off-loading the rest of the jewels. Think about the difference in sentence for being caught: for a shop robbery, you might get five years if there's pre-planning. Burglary, possible kidnap charges, threats of violence and the like and you can double that at least.'

'So you don't think they're that clever?'

Jessica necked the rest of her first pint in one, realising

she wasn't explaining herself too well. 'Yes and no . . . I don't know. Obviously that only applies if we catch them – and considering we don't seem very close to doing that then they're clearly smarter than we are.' She paused: 'Well, smarter than *you*.'

Archie ignored her, working his way through the mound of crisps. 'You do know they've probably only nicked about a quarter of what this lot claim. It's like the minute there's a car accident, everyone's hobbling around clutching the back of their necks, banging on about whiplash. These rich types *dream* of a burglary – suddenly that Argos bracelet they've never worn is an antique pearl necklace that's been handed down by their grandmother's grandmother. It's all a giant insurance con – like the latest must-have accessory: designer handbag, expensive shoes, oh and we were burgled last month.'

It wasn't that Jessica disagreed with him – whenever there was an injury, theft or suspicious fire, the first thing any of them thought was 'insurance scam' – but his theory didn't feel right either.

'This is too elaborate to make a few quid off an insurance company,' Jessica said.

'You want to go through it, don't you?'

Jessica bit into a crisp, embarrassed that she'd spent enough evenings drinking with him that he could read her so easily. 'It's for your benefit, seeing as you're the young constable and I'm the . . . inspector.'

She'd almost said 'old'.

Archie snatched the final cheese and onion crisp. 'Go on then – for *my* benefit.'

'Okay, so we don't have any e-fits, obviously. We're rounding up the usual scroats to see if they know anything—'

'Whose idea was that?'

'Franks' – the idiot brought it up in our senior meeting last Friday and Topper was all over it. He reckoned that because the victims all agree the accent is "sort of local" that we should bring in anyone from around here who's ever been convicted of a robbery. I think they're up on Wednesday if we've not figured out anything before then.'

'Wanky sodding Frankie. What a knobhead.'

Jessica 'mmmed' an agreement through a mouthful of ale. It really did taste awful. 'We've been asking the victims if they can try to remember a bit more about what the gun looked like. They all say only one of the four had a weapon. We've got some firearms expert comparing the statements to see if he can find a match. I don't know what Topper thinks might happen but it's not as if they're going to be breaking into houses with a registered gun – it'll have been bought from a pub somewhere for a hundred quid.'

She stopped for another mouthful, before continuing. 'A couple of years ago, we found this guy on that council estate over the back of the station, less than half a mile away. He knew someone who worked on the Liverpool docks dealing with the container ships coming in. They had this boat arriving from Ecuador three times a year with all sorts of supplies on it – including a mini arsenal of guns. Our man in Liverpool would stick them in the back of his car, speed over here, drop them off at this housing association place and then they'd flog them to all and sundry. We only got lucky because his next-door neighbour got tired of the television being on loud late at night. It could have been a disaster because we only had two PCSOs going around to shut our arms dealer up but he got edgy, jumped ten feet over a balcony and bolted into the park. Our boys were left there with an open flat door wondering what was going on. When we went through the flat properly, we found a dozen pistols, two semi-automatics and an MP5.'

'Why didn't he put up a fight?'

'We never really found out – I think he was a bit stupid. His Scouse mate was the brains of the operation, if you can believe that. I suppose they thought they could make more money in Manchester. This guy thought he was running a shop out of his flat.'

'Are you sure the Scouse guy was the clever one?'

'Well, it certainly wasn't the Manc.'

'Bin-dipping bastard.'

'Didn't Liverpool beat Man United this season?'

'All right, sod off.'

'Home and away?'

'Blah, blah, blah. Referees in their pockets and all that.'

'I don't know why you get so upset about it – it's only a game . . .'

Jessica grinned at him, knowing there was nothing more certain to get a reaction. At first she thought he was going to storm off to the toilets but Archie took a deep breath instead. 'I'm not rising to it.'

Jessica finished the rest of her second drink. She knew

she was putting them away too quickly, that slight sense of giddiness making her giggle more girlishly and for longer than she usually would. 'Another?'

'Are you on one tonight?'

Jessica slid out of the booth. 'I was off for almost a week before Sunday night's debacle – I've got a whole week to get through.'

Archie shrugged. 'Aye, I'll have more of the same in that case – and don't forget the crisps.'

Bladder emptied, two more pints of the grim, cloudy ale in hand; Quavers, beef Hula Hoops, crispy bacon Wheat Crunchies and nice 'n' spicy Nik Naks delicately held under her armpit, Jessica arrived back at the table miraculously without dropping anything.

Without spilling a drop of their drinks, she carefully edged everything onto the table and then flopped into her seat. 'I'd like to see an Olympic gymnast show that level of control and balance,' she said.

Archie was too busy tearing into the Wheat Crunchies to notice. Jessica started on the Hula Hoops and then continued from where she'd left off. 'Anyway – aside from the fact we're not going to get much from wheeling in all the local scum and we've got no chance of finding anything from the description of the weapon, the rest of the ideas haven't been too bad.'

'Like what?'

'One of the constables is looking into similar robberies around the country – especially those where jewellery has been taken. It could be a gang who hits one area and moves onto another. The problem is talking to the other forces, of course. You'd think we were asking for a spare kidney. We're still trying to figure out if our main guy could have a link to security companies but that's not got us anywhere yet.'

'How much cash have they got away with?'

'Between thirty and forty thousand – well, according to the insurance claims. Over three hundred grand in jewellery. I don't know how people go out wearing those types of thing – I'd be terrified of breaking it.'

'How's everything else going?'

'Shite: Dave's being a moody git and—'

'I meant with the cases.'

'Oh . . . Okay. It's just one of those times where things aren't quite working out. It's not the first time. It's just unfortunate because of Topper joining and . . . me being away . . .'

Jessica tailed off. Having a few beers with Archie was fine but they both knew the one topic that was off-limits. It suited the pair of them. With Izzy having her family to look after and the fact that Jessica didn't particularly want to see much of either Dave or Garry, her evenings with Archie were one of the few times she got to relax.

Perhaps reading her mind, Archie put his glass down. 'How's your friend?'

'No.'

Archie opened his palms, leaning backwards. 'No what?'

'I know what you're thinking.'

'I didn't realise mind-reading was one of your abilities.'

'I don't need to be able to read minds to know what you're up to.'

'I'm not up to anything!'

'Either way, she's only seventeen and I'm definitely not introducing you to her.'

'This is an outrageous slander on my good name—'

'Bollocks is it – just because I'm living with her, it doesn't mean you get to be introduced.'

Archie's grin slipped as he lowered his voice. 'You must know that everyone at the station is talking about it.'

'It's not the first time people have been talking about me behind my back. I don't care anyway – she was living with me before. She's just a mate who happens to be seventeen.'

Archie shrugged. 'Maybe give me a tip when she turns eighteen?'

Jessica swallowed another crisp. 'Honestly? She'd eat you for breakfast.'

6

Jessica's key slid along the hole and scratched its way down her front door.

'Shite.'

She used a finger to trace the outline of the keyhole and then tried again, this time only succeeding in digging a pointy bit into her finger.

'Sod it.'

The hallway light switched on and Jessica could hear the female voice from inside. 'Hang on – I'm still up.'

Jessica took a final breath of the cool evening air as the door opened inwards revealing a thin young woman with long, straight black hair. She was wearing a pair of shorts, large slippers in the shape of elephant heads and a rugby shirt that could have probably fitted three of her.

'Sorry,' Jessica said, stumbling over the step.

Bex closed the door and locked it. 'It's your house.'

Jessica began fighting with the arm of her coat. 'I've told you before to treat it like it's yours too.'

'Do we have to do this again?' Finally managing to yank her arm out, Jessica dropped her jacket over the banister, where it slumped to the floor. 'Do you want something to eat?' Bex added.

'You really don't have to make food for me.'

'I'm hungry anyway – why do you think I'm up this late?'

Jessica grinned. 'What was today's subject?'

Bex returned the smile. 'What makes you think I spent the morning watching rubbish talk shows?'

'C'mon, don't tease me.'

'Fine – it was "My boyfriend wants to wear my underwear".'

'Brilliant.'

Fifteen minutes later and Jessica was on the sofa sharing a blanket with Bex, eating fish fingers on toast, drinking a mug of tea, and watching the recording of that morning's show. If all evenings ended like this, she'd be perfectly happy.

'How was college?' Jessica asked.

'All right – I thought it'd be harder though. There's nowhere near as much work as I thought there'd be.'

Jessica frowned. 'You're complaining there's not enough work? What's wrong with you?'

Bex snorted into her own tea. 'I like having things to do.'

'So go to the cinema, go bowling, hang out around the back of the offy and drink a bottle of cider with your mates. Be a teenager.'

'I don't really want to drink, I—'

'Sorry, I wasn't thinking . . .'

Bex had left home when she was barely a teenager, tired of the alcohol, drugs and men that her mother brought into her life. After a few years fending for herself – something neither of them spoke about – Jessica had given her somewhere to stay, acting more like a mate than a mother. Sometimes she wondered if that was making life better, or creating more problems.

Bex had enrolled on a course at a local college at the start of the year, with her heart set on a full-time one in September, possibly with university afterwards. For a girl who hadn't had much in the way of formal education, she had taken to it like a natural, covering her room with notes and further reading material. She wasn't even interested in something vocational – the type of course certain people would bang on about as 'cushy' – she'd gone for a five-month module in post-World War Two history. It was certainly not the sort of thing Jessica would have chosen.

For now, their strange relationship worked but there was always going to be a time when it wasn't so simple. What if Bex brought home a boyfriend Jessica didn't like? That was assuming she was into boys; another thing they'd never spoken about. It didn't matter whether she liked boys or girls – but the fact Jessica didn't know meant they were neither mother and daughter, nor friends. Instead, their relationship was something different; more than flatmates but exactly what, Jessica didn't know.

Bex moved on, not acknowledging what Jessica had said: 'Anyway, I'm happy reading and doing other things. I don't really like being out when it's . . .'

She tailed off before adding 'dark'. Before Jessica could reply, Bex added: 'Did you have a good evening?'

'Same as ever – commiserating about work.'

For a few moments, they said nothing as the husband in question on the talk show strutted onto the stage wearing his wife's underwear. The one thing Jessica could give him was that he did at least have the boobs for it. The thong was definitely a step too far though. His wife took one look at him and dashed off stage into the waiting arms of one of her friends.

Advert break: Jessica couldn't be bothered to fast-forward.

'How's your money?' she asked.

'I don't want to keep taking yours.'

Jessica finished the final fish finger. 'I don't need it – it's just money. You know this place was paid off after . . . then I had money from my dad. It's just there, not being spent. It's not as if fish fingers, crisps and tea bags cost that much.'

'I want to get a job and start paying rent.'

'I don't want your money – I won't take it.'

They'd gone around in circles on this issue before – Jessica insisting she didn't want to take anything from Bex, Bex wanting to pay her way. As yet, Bex hadn't found anyone who wanted to employ a seventeen-year-old with no experience and no qualifications. The only semi-interest she'd had was from the guy that ran the pizza shop two streets over, who asked if she was good with her hands and then – according to Bex – started foaming at the mouth when she said she was. Jessica not only advised not to work there, but vowed not to eat there either. Ugh.

They turned their attention back to the television as the wife returned to the set, mascara smeared across her face, friend patting her gently on the back. The husband was tugging up 'his' bra: 'I'm sorry but this is me. I've been denying it for too long . . .'

Bex had curled her legs underneath herself, her bony knees and elbows jutting out. She ate as much as anyone Jessica had ever met, yet didn't seem to put on weight at all. Out of the blue, she turned to Jessica. 'Can I say something?'

'Of course.'

'I know you've got money – so why don't you go somewhere and do something? Why do you work? I know you say you like it but . . . sometimes it seems that you don't.'

On screen, the husband, wife, friend, presenter and most of the audience were in tears. Jessica didn't reply for a moment. When she did, her voice cracked slightly. She didn't like talking about it, which is why she didn't hang around with Dave. Izzy and Archie knew not to ask. 'I suppose I feel I've got something to finish.'

'What?'

'I don't know . . . it's complicated.'

'Is it about . . . him?'

'You can say his name,' Jessica replied.

'Is it about Adam?'

'No.'

Bex opened her mouth as if she was going to say something but took a breath and then closed it again, focusing back on the television. Jessica was watching the screen but taking almost none of it in – somehow there was a lie detector test involved now.

In so many ways, she wanted to open up to Bex and tell her everything she thought she knew about the day her car had blown up with Adam inside but it was always in the back of her mind that the fewer people who knew, the safer it would be for everyone. As for continuing to work, knowing that Graham Pomeroy was the chief constable, she figured sometimes it was better to keep your enemies close – not that she had a speck of evidence that he was anything other than a senior police officer.

When Bex spoke again, her voice was cheerier. 'If you're staying around, perhaps you can talk to one of my college friends, Sam. She's having a few issues but doesn't want to go to the police.'

'I *am* police.'

'Yeah but you're cool.'

'Er, thanks. What sort of issues?'

'Something to do with her neighbour. She didn't really go into details. I said I'd ask you.'

'If you give me her number and address, I'll see what I can do.'

On screen, it was time for another advert as the presenter held up an envelope containing the lie detector results.

'Thank you,' Bex said softly.

'If she's having problems then it's kind of my job to sort it out.'

Bex shuffled across, resting her head on Jessica's shoulder. 'Not just that . . . everything.'

7

Jessica headed into Longsight Police Station through the main door at the front to be met by Fat Pat on the front desk crunching his way through a Danish pastry. Given the abdominal twinges she'd already had that morning, probably down to her appalling choice of food the previous day, the way Pat was licking the runny caramelised sugar from his pudgy fingers was enough to make her stomach gurgle in protest.

'Do you have to do that so openly?' Jessica said.

He swallowed the final piece and then slurped on his thumb. 'A man has to eat!'

Jessica picked up the empty paper bag with a bakery's name on the front, balled it up and threw it towards the bin behind the counter. It clipped the rim, rolled around the edge and dropped onto the floor. 'A man can eat fruit.'

'There was apple in it.' He pointed towards the paper bag. 'Are you going to pick that up?'

'What do you think?'

'I think I need to return to that bakery more often – it's this new place down by the Aquatics Centre. I saw a post about it on an Internet forum. This guy reckons he knows all the best places to eat in the city and he was saying—'

'Much as I'd love to go on a culinary tour around the north-west with you, Patrick, I was wondering if there's anything I need to know about before I go to find my office and spend the morning practising throwing balls of paper at the bin.'

'I left you a note about it.'

'You could just tell me.'

Pat frowned, making the wrinkles in his face roll together like a potato left in a darkened room for six months. 'There have been a few calls coming in from around the city. The operators don't really know what to do with them because it's so *weird*.'

'What's weird?'

'There's been three already – charity workers arriving at their shop or office to find an envelope stuffed with cash put through the door. They're asking what they should do with it. Me? I'd be on the first plane to Vegas. I've heard there's this chocolate fountain that's—'

'How much money are we talking about?'

Pat scowled more deeply, chastened by Jessica's interruptions when he was on a roll. The skin around his forehead was so saggy that it drooped over his eyebrows. Jessica hadn't thought it possible to put on weight on that area of the face, but apparently it was so.

'I'm not sure,' he said. 'Our beloved chief inspector is at HQ – there's some council function this morning so they've all been called to a briefing to make sure they don't say anything stupid. Franks is . . . well I don't know what he's up to, probably skulking around a public toilet somewhere. Two of the three parcels arrived in our district, so I suppose . . .'

'I'm guessing the charities were told not to spend it –

and that we'd either be around, or they should take it to their nearest station?'

'Probably. We really are a bunch of killjoy bastards, aren't we?'

'Speak for yourself.'

Five minutes later and Jessica was back in her car heading into the traffic she'd just spent half an hour trying to get out of. On the radio, today's phone-in subject was 'Is Britain still great?', with a succession of people whining on, apparently missing the point that bleating on the radio probably wasn't going to improve anything any time soon. The presenter sounded bored, not even bothering to talk patronisingly over people.

In the aftermath of what had happened to her previous car, Jessica couldn't bring herself to put any effort into finding a new one. She had gone to the second-hand lot on the main road closest to where she lived, picked the oldest one that didn't look like it was going to fall apart at any moment – a red Corsa – and paid for it on the spot. It sat somewhere between her old Fiat, on which nothing worked, and the car she'd bought new that had a fancy Bluetooth thing. This one got her from one place to the next, made a rattling noise when she went from second to third gear and had a radio that worked ninety per cent of the time.

The Grosvenor Street sexual health clinic was a small red-brick building wedged between a pizza shop and an old church long since converted into a bar. A small black and white sign above the unassuming doorway was the only indication it existed as it was camouflaged amid the neon signs and sandwich boards from the other shops and pubs trying to entice revellers inside.

Jessica pushed open the door and headed up the stairs to small flat-cum-office that smelled vaguely of day-old pizza. She was greeted by a woman in her early twenties wearing jeans and a loose jumper, who introduced herself as Maria. Pointing to an open envelope on a table, Maria said she was going to make some tea and left Jessica alone in the waiting room. Lining the walls were posters about sexual health, with facts and statistics on everything from diseases that caused infertility, to pregnancy. It was enough to put anyone off ever opening their legs again.

Wishing there was a way to un-see things, Jessica crossed to the table, taking a nitrile glove from her pocket and delicately re-opening the envelope. Inside, a mixture of newish and used ten- and twenty-pound notes had been neatly arranged into ten bundles of two hundred pounds. Jessica arranged the money on the table and then peered into the envelope, before turning it upside down. Nothing else came out and there was no writing anywhere on it.

Jessica placed everything into two clear bags just as Maria returned with two plain white mugs. She handed Jessica one and took a seat in an uncomfortable-looking canvas-backed chair.

'Was there any sort of note?' Jessica asked.

Maria was slim and pretty in a dressed-down, just-woke-up kind of way. She shook her head. 'It was put through the door some time overnight.'

'What time did you close yesterday?'

'Three in the afternoon.'

'When did you get in this morning?'

'A bit after eight – I was running late.'

That left a long window where anyone could have put it through the door. Even though there was CCTV on the outside of the pub, there would be hundreds of people to sift through – and that was assuming whoever had dropped it hadn't simply crossed the road, away from the camera, and headed off in the other direction.

'Was there anything else?' Jessica asked.

'No – just that. I was wary about opening the envelope. Because the word "sex" is over our doorway, you get immature kids at night putting used condoms through the letterbox. One Saturday I opened up and . . . well, you probably don't want to know what someone had pushed through. Anyway, I brought the envelope upstairs and gave it a bit of a sniff. It seemed okay, so I opened it up.'

'Did you touch the money?'

'Yes . . . I didn't know what it was at first. I thought perhaps it was a joke, or fake money. Sorry . . .'

Jessica waved a hand dismissively. The fact Maria's fingerprints were all over it didn't matter that much – she doubted the person who'd left it would have been careless anyway.

Maria apologised again before continuing: 'As soon as I realised what it was, I knew I should call the police.' She squirmed slightly, taking a sip of her tea and tugging at her jumper.

'It's okay, I would have thought about keeping it too,' Jessica said. 'You did the right thing.'

The young woman smiled slightly, embarrassed at

having her mind read but glad the fact she'd done the right thing had been acknowledged. 'I didn't know who to call – 999 is for an emergency and this isn't really urgent but what do you call for a non-emergency? I had to Google it. You really don't make it easy.'

'I know.'

'Anyway, I suppose I'm wondering if we're allowed to spend it – not me, the clinic. We do get donations but it was so much money that I wasn't sure.'

'What do you do here?'

'We're a free drop-in centre, mainly for women but a few lads come along sometimes. We offer advice about sexual issues – most of the stuff you get in schools is next to useless, plus parents don't want to talk about it.' She pointed towards a row of doors on the other side of the room. 'Those are all privacy rooms where people can wait and keep their anonymity. Some of the kids we have in are only young teenagers but they don't know who else to talk to. We're able to give out condoms and we have a nurse who can give the morning-after pill. A lot of young people don't really know what the diseases are – they hear "STI" or "STD" and switch off.'

'Where does your funding come from?'

'We get a bit from the council and a small grant from the university. We did have some money from the NHS but that was cut completely a year ago. They said they couldn't give us any more because they were already paying for a sexual health clinic over at the hospital. It's awkward, though, because a lot of the young people want to talk to others who are roughly their age. They don't want to chat about sensitive things to a bloke old enough to be their dad or granddad, or a woman twice their age – even if they are professionals. A lot of the girls don't even have a problem; they just don't know how things work. Then their boyfriends have been watching porn on the Internet and want to get up to all sorts but they don't know if it's dangerous. A fair few of us volunteer and some of the student nurses help out when they aren't busy. We were on the brink of getting one of the supermarkets to sponsor us – but a local church group organised a protest. After that, we couldn't find a company that wanted to sponsor a clinic giving away the morning-after pill, so we're reliant on donations. When I first saw that money, I thought it was a mystery donor – it'd keep us going for a few weeks – but there was no note and then I began to get worried.'

She paused, glancing at the clear bags Jessica had put the envelope and cash in, already knowing the answer but asking anyway: 'So is it ours?'

'If it was in isolation then perhaps – but you're the third place that's called in this morning. There are probably more by now.'

'Perhaps it's just a rich person who wants to give their fortune to others who need it without leaving their name?'

Jessica shrugged. 'Maybe. There have been a few burglaries recently where cash was taken. We'll have to take this away and look at it.'

Maria finished her tea and peered at Jessica, looking

disappointed. 'If you were going to go to the trouble of stealing money, why would you then give it away?'

Jessica glanced towards the pile of notes. 'I really don't know.'

8

By the time Jessica arrived back at her car and phoned the station, there had been five more calls from charities asking what they should do with the money that had been pushed through their letterbox. Officers had been sent out to pick up the packages with an estimate of around twelve thousand pounds having been given away overnight. She was about to hang up when Pat put her on hold with a gruff 'Hang on a minute'.

Jessica sat in the front seat, tapping her foot on the accelerator pedal, annoyed. Pat was someone she didn't want to get on the wrong side of, mainly because he knew something about everyone and had more to gossip about than a group of mothers standing next to the school gates. The problem was that he knew it – meaning conversations were frequently curt.

When the line cut back in, he sounded out of breath, as if he'd lifted his arm, or bent over. 'Where are you?'

'Grosvenor Street.'

'You should probably head to MediaCity.'

'Why?'

'It's probably best if you see for yourself.'

Jessica leant out of her car window to talk into the speaker. 'You called me!' she argued. 'All you need to do is raise the barrier so I can do what you wanted me here to do.'

The bored-sounding male voice echoed out of the tinny speaker. 'It's more than my job's worth, love. If you want to park up, you can walk over. It's that big glass building in front of you.'

'There are three big glass buildings in front of me.'

'It's the one on the end.'

Knowing there was little point in arguing with the type of private security Nazis who worked at places like this, Jessica did as she was told. She parked in a nearby space, wrapping a jacket around herself and then walking across the concrete-slabbed plaza as a bitter wind bristled off the canal.

MediaCity was where all sorts of television, radio and Internet companies were based, with thousands of people bumbling around awkwardly, skinny lattes thrust in front of them and ID tags dangling around their necks.

The BBC's trio of buildings soared over the water, dwarfing everything in its shadow. In the final glass building, there were half-a-dozen suited security officers waiting for Jessica, whispering into walkie-talkies and generally looking shifty. A woman ushered Jessica through a set of spinning glass doors, complained about the lifts, and then escorted her up to the third floor.

In a corner, three people wearing headphones were huddled around a table. As soon as they saw Jessica approaching, they jumped as if they'd been caught doing something they shouldn't.

They parted as the security guard eased her way into the centre, Jessica at her side. 'These are three of the production crew for the breakfast television programme,' she said.

A girl introduced herself as Pauline and then spent five minutes needlessly telling Jessica what she did. It seemed to involve a lot of showing people around, making tea and opening mail: all skills that Jessica thought were very much underappreciated and that if Pauline was ever looking for a pay-cut and far worse employment opportunities, then she could always come and work for her.

Pauline said that she had started opening the mail the show received that morning when she'd stumbled across the letter currently sitting in a clear polythene bag on the desk next to her. At first, she'd put it to one side, unsure what it meant. Then production assistant number two – Tim – had come along, got his grubby fingerprints all over the letter and envelope, before calling over production assistant three – Claire – to ask what she thought.

Jessica took a closer look at the letter – a plain white A4 sheet of paper with seven words printed in block capital letters in the centre:

'ROB THE RICH, GIVE TO THE POOR'

Pauline continued the story: '. . . we'd heard about those local burglaries and then Claire said that her sister works at a women's refuge in the city. They had eight hundred quid put through their door overnight, so we wondered if the two were linked.'

The font was something plain, the ink black, and although Jessica knew they had a geek somewhere who'd be able to tell them the make of printer and paper, she doubted it would come back as anything other than something so generic that there would be thousands in existence.

'How many other people touched this before you thought to call us?' Jessica asked.

'Six? Perhaps seven? All of our line managers spend three hours in a meeting every morning, so it's just us. We didn't know what to do at first.'

Great. How many BBC staff members does it take to open an envelope? Seven – and thirty-odd managers to sit in a meeting debating when would be the optimal time to have a separate meeting to discuss the best envelope-opening techniques. It was just like working for the police.

Jessica offered vague-sounding congratulations for managing to find the phone and dial the police's number and then headed back to her car. She wondered if she would have a better day if she left the letter and took the two grand from the clinic straight to the airport and picked somewhere warm to fly to.

Back at the station and there were now two dozen cases of charities or community projects that had been 'donated' money overnight. Unsurprisingly none of them had any sort of recording facilities near the door to catch their mysterious benefactor. The lunchtime news had reported the letter and been out to interview some of the people who had received money. Even though she was supposed to be looking into the burglaries, it was difficult for Jessica not to sympathise. Clearly people under pressure were pointing towards the community projects on which they were working and the children they were helping, explaining how an extra thousand pounds could do a lot of good. When the report cut to one of the large houses that had been robbed with police cars at the front, it didn't take much imagination to know that viewers at home would be wondering who needed the money more.

Jessica was well aware there could be other projects or charities that had kept the money and not bothered calling. In all, seventeen thousand pounds had been given away. Assuming the money was coming from the people who had burgled the houses, they had got rid of around half the money reported stolen.

Doing something she always hated herself for, Jessica visited a news website and began reading the comments underneath the article.

DazBoy1987 (84 <): 'This robbers doin evryone a favor. Robin hood had the rite idea – time 4 a revulsion.'

DykeAndProud (2 ♀): 'Though I can't condone the types of robberies described, I can't help but feel that the rich have brought this on themselves. It's simply not fair that the top 1% of society have so much of the wealth. These charities are crying out for help and I think they should be allowed to keep the money.'

BlueBoy691 (194 ♂): 'Socialist scum. String them all up and let's bring back public hanging.'

SatansGimp (287 ♂): 'Wot r the police doin in all ov this? Wot do our taxes pay 4?'

Geoff1 (No rating): 'Where do I get the free money? LOL'

Jessica closed the browser window, feeling far worse about everything – especially the public education system. The fact three families had had guns stuck in their faces should at least deserve some sympathy before even thinking about the fact they'd been robbed.

She was about to check in with Archie and the rest of the constables working on the case when the request came through for her to visit DCI Topper's office.

By the time she got to the top floor, Topper was irately changing jackets from something formal and black into a slightly more relaxed grey one. He beckoned Jessica in and started speaking before she'd closed the door. 'Bloody council things – it doesn't matter where you work, there's always some stupid civic thing you have to go to. You shake hands, nod politely and then stand around for two hours wondering what you're doing there. No wonder the country's gone to the dogs – we spend all our time fannying around gasbagging to each other.'

Jessica edged towards the seat opposite him. 'Sir . . .'

'Don't sit – this isn't a social call. Your lad with the broken-down door has put a complaint in.'

'Noel?'

'Something like that. He says we had no reason to raid his house and that if we'd just knocked, he would have let us in.'

'But you could say that about anything – we can't go knocking politely on the door of a drugs den while they flush it all down the bog.'

Topper finally finished changing jackets and collapsed

into his seat. 'Don't tell me – they want to see you at Moston Vale.'

'I have to go to HQ?'

'Professional standards want a word. It's all part of the new procedures after Pratley's report. I told them you'd be there for one, so you'd better get your skates on – and make sure you've got your story straight; the last thing I want is one of my officers being suspended. The paperwork's bad enough as it is.'

Jessica had always had a problem with authority, which made the fact that many people viewed her as someone who had it somewhat ironic. She could pretty much trace it back to the day when her entire primary school class had been kept in through their lunch break because someone had written a rude word on the blackboard and wouldn't own up. Mr Oates, a scrawny pointy-faced man, had said that if no one would tell him who'd done it, then they would all be punished. He'd made them write 'I must not harbour criminals' a hundred times each in their workbooks while he'd sat at the front of the classroom munching his way through a box of Jaffa Cakes, tutting in disapproval every few minutes. Everyone suspected the guilty party was Jamie Lambert, who was responsible for pretty much every piece of bad behaviour in their class, but because no one had seen him do it, and he wouldn't put his hand up, they were all disciplined.

Inspector Vincent was the spitting image of Mr Oates, his painfully thin body matched with a too-big head, topped with a crooked angular nose that wouldn't have been amiss if he'd been flying on a broomstick. She could easily picture him drowning a duck in his spare time, cackling away to himself and then blaming it on local kids.

Jessica took an instant dislike to him before he'd opened his mouth – and that only increased as he welcomed her into the professional standards office asking if she wanted a union representative with her.

'Should I?' she asked.

'That's up to you.'

'Am I in trouble?'

'That depends on what you say.'

Tit.

'So . . .' he said, letting the word hang and making eye contact with Jessica, apparently waiting for her to fill the gap. She let him wait. 'So . . .' he tried again, 'I suppose you know why you're here?'

'Is this the party planning committee? Christmas is a fair way off yet.'

He smiled thinly. 'They told me you had quite the sense of humour.'

'Who did?'

He peered over a set of reading glasses at her, like a doctor about to tell a patient that the cancer was terminal. 'Tell me about Noel Huntingdon.'

'He owns a house out Stretford way. I can't remember the address. We'd been getting reports over a series of weeks about people arriving and leaving in the early hours of the morning—'

'Reports from where?'

'Neighbours. They were saying there was music as well,

plus people were smoking and chatting in the back yard after dark.'

'Is that unusual?'

'Well, is it the type of thing you do around your house at three in morning?'

Another humourless smile: 'Perhaps we should stick to the activities of Mr Huntingdon and yourself?'

Jessica took a breath. 'Yes – it's unusual. From experience, the only type of houses that frequently have people coming and going at those times of the morning are places that are dealing drugs. Even the brothels shut up shop at midnight.' She raised an eyebrow as if to ask the question but the inspector seemingly didn't get the implication, so she continued. 'We've had a few successful raids in the past in similar instances – often intelligence-led starting initially with neighbour reports as per here.'

'Was the fact it could be a drugs den the only thing that occurred to you?'

Jessica nodded towards the paper in his hand. 'As detailed in the report, it wasn't entirely me – but no. We'd had a degree of surveillance on the Friday and Saturday evenings—'

'A degree?'

'That's what it's like when you actually have to do some work – it's not all sitting around in offices with your feet up drinking tea. Friday and Saturday nights are busy around the city and a full team couldn't be spared. We had marked and unmarked vehicles passing by through the evening. Between them, they witnessed half-a-dozen people arriving through until half three in the morning.'

'Was there any . . .' Vincent clucked his tongue elaborately, making a point of searching for the word, '. . . *profiling*?'

Jessica hated the term but there was no getting away from it. 'If that's how you want to phrase it. The area has a certain reputation and most of the people witnessed entering and exiting were a certain type.'

'What type?'

'Young, I suppose.'

'Just that?'

'It's hard to explain.'

'Try me.'

Jessica nodded towards the paperwork he was still holding. 'You've got the photos – they were mainly teenagers; the type that we often pick up for dealing.'

'Are you saying that all teenagers do drugs?'

'Of course not.'

'You're not explaining the reasoning very well.'

Jessica sighed in exasperation. 'I can't put it any better than that – you've got the pictures. Some people just have a "look" about them. It doesn't mean they're doing anything wrong but it sets alarm bells ringing. When you've got neighbours calling in demanding something be done, complaints about noise and then a host of people like that coming in and out, it paints a picture.'

Inspector Vincent flicked through the photos, biting his bottom lip. 'Hmmm.'

Jessica said nothing. They all knew the game – some thought it was about race, gender or age but it wasn't that, certainly not in her mind. Some people just looked shifty and, coupled with reports about misbehaviour, there was every reason to investigate.

The inspector peered over his glasses again. 'What about the house?'

'We were struggling to get a land registry reply back. It had been bought at auction, then the owner was bankrupted and it was put back up for sale again. The trail's all over the place because it was one of those old council ones which were sold off cheaply and then have been sold over and over ever since. The neighbours who complained said there were people squatting and we couldn't find anything that told us anything different. There were beer cans, a shopping trolley and all sorts of other rubbish in the front garden. It looked like a case of someone breaking into a house and then dealing drugs out of it.'

'Hmmm.' He took off his glasses and pursed his lips. 'Did you *personally* interview all the neighbours?'

'Personally? There's only one of me, so of course not. We had statements and phone records.'

'Did you *personally* check the land deeds?'

'No, this wasn't the only thing I had going on. I trusted other people – I don't see why they'd make up the fact that the deeds were hard to get hold of.'

'Did you take part in the surveillance on the Friday and Saturday evenings?'

'No, I was off. I can't be at work all of the time.'

'So exactly how much were you involved?'

'I was part of the team that examined all of the evidence, applied for the warrant, and went in.'

They went around in circles as the inspector tried to find new ways of pointing out that the decision was flawed. Quite what he wanted her to say other than 'All right, I ballsed it up', Jessica wasn't sure.

After an hour, Vincent told her she could leave, saying he'd be in contact in due course – whatever that meant. She wouldn't have been surprised if 'due course' meant she'd find him sniffing the toilet seat in the ladies' loos. If using a bit of instinct counted as 'profiling' then he'd be at the top of her weirdo list.

Jessica walked quickly through GMP's Moston Vale headquarters back to her car. As soon as she switched it on, her phone began to ring: someone at the station.

She turned it off again and threw it onto the passenger seat, Bex's words from the night before flitting through her mind: *'Why don't you go somewhere and do something? Why do you work?'*

Sometimes she didn't know either and, for now, they could all sod off.

9

Jessica sat in her car across the road from the local council's MOT-testing garage. She was watching a woman struggling to reverse through the gates. A mechanic stood on the pavement, clenched fist drawing a semicircle in the air – the universal sign for 'turn the wheel'. Eventually, she shot backwards, nearly running him over and then holding a hand up – the universal sign for 'sorry I nearly killed you'.

A minute later and the woman was hurrying towards her friend's car, still apologising as the mechanic explained to his mate how he'd nearly been wiped out by a bright pink Mini. It would have been some way to go. The day was another speckled by a nothing greyness; no rain, no wind, no anything. A different mechanic moved one car out of the garage and parked it on the road before heading towards the pink vehicle. He crumpled himself up just enough to fit inside, awkwardly easing it backwards before climbing out and leaning on the driver's-side window, staring across the road towards Jessica.

For a moment they locked eyes and then he began to walk towards her. The thought went through her mind that she should drive away, as she had in the past, but there was something that made Jessica sit tight. The man was in his early fifties, wearing dirty dark blue overalls and heavy boots. As he came closer, Jessica could see a smear of grease along his cheek. He didn't take his eyes from her until he reached the car, crouching and tapping gently on her window.

Jessica slid the window down and held his gaze.

He sighed, like a father disappointed that their child had been sent home from school with a letter explaining they were in trouble. Jessica knew that look.

'Can I help you?' he asked.

'I'm just sitting here on my lunch break minding my own business.'

'But you're here a lot – at least a couple of times a week.'

'It's a peaceful spot.'

He pointed behind her car. 'The main road's there and this is a cut-through to get to Tesco, so we both know that isn't true.'

'What do you want me to say?'

The man stood, leaving Jessica to stare at his belly. 'Do you want a tea?'

'A what?'

'Cup of tea – you are British, aren't you?'

Jessica was so surprised by the offer that she didn't know what to say. The man had already started walking away, peering over his shoulder: 'Come on then.'

She locked her car and followed, keeping her distance until he headed into an office at the side of the garage. She entered just as he was telling a younger mechanic to go and do some work. He plucked a once-white kettle from the top of a filing cabinet, filled it up from a sink, and plipped it on.

'You are allowed to sit,' he said, nodding towards a battered brown sofa underneath a calendar that had a topless woman splayed across a motorbike.

Jessica sat hesitantly, taking in the rest of the part-office, part-kitchen. A small cream-coloured dining table with matching chairs was covered with greasy fingerprints on one side but the part of the office closer to her had been kept clean – well, except for the calendar.

'I'm Keith,' the man said, washing his hands furiously at the sink.

'I know.'

He nodded. 'Course you do. It's Jessica, isn't it?'

'Yes.' He turned the water off and opened a fridge under the counter, holding up a bottle of milk. 'Milk, no sugar,' she added instinctively.

Keith poured milk into two chipped mugs, heaped four spoonfuls of sugar into his, dropped a tea bag in each, and then filled both to the brim. Squeeze, swirl, squeeze again, then he passed the mug across, before sitting on one of the dining chairs, leaving Jessica by herself on the sofa.

'You can't keep coming here,' he said, eyes fixed on her.

She stared into her mug. 'It's a free country.'

'You know what I mean. I'm an honest bloke – I do MOTs for the council. I gave the best opinion I could. It's intimidating when you come and sit opposite the garage and watch me.'

Jessica didn't reply.

Keith took a drink and then put his mug down on the

table. 'Are you here to ask me something? Or threaten me? Are you going to follow me home? Or come to my house? I've got kids – I don't know what you want from me. This is, what, the sixth or seventh time I've seen you out there?'

Jessica tried to hide behind the mug but the wave of tears hit her from nowhere. Before she knew it, she was clasping her mug with one hand, wiping her eyes with the other.

Keith leant forwards, half-stretching an arm towards her. 'Hey, I didn't mean to . . .'

Jessica shook her head, not wanting to be comforted and definitely not wanting him to touch her. He reeled back, picking up his tea again but still watching her.

Eventually, Jessica regained her voice, though she couldn't look anywhere but at the floor. 'When I first saw you at the inquest, I thought you were going to say that you'd found something different, that what happened to my car *wasn't* an accident.'

'I only testified to what I saw. They had that guy from BAE Systems too and he said the same thing. I know it's rare – it's probably the only time I'll ever see it but it was one of those things. They had that other guy from the manufacturer who said there was a similar case in South Korea. I told the court then and I'm telling you now: the circuit board which controlled the cooling system in your old vehicle failed. It was an accident that your boyfriend was in the car when it blew up. I'm not going to pretend I know what it's like when something like that happens because I don't – but it's not my fault. They asked me to examine the vehicle and then to give evidence, which is what I did. It's what the BAE guy did too.'

'Did they offer you money?'

'Who?'

'Or threaten your kids?'

'I don't know what you're talking about. The only person I feel threatened by is you.'

'I'm only a woman.'

'You're a police officer and you hang around my workplace watching me. How is that not intimidating? Am I going to have to put a complaint in?'

Jessica took a mouthful of tea. The tears had stopped but there was still a lump in her throat making it hard to swallow. Her reply was croaked: 'Please don't.'

He sounded stern now: 'Give me one reason why I shouldn't.'

'Because I'm in enough shite as it is.'

'Then what do you want?'

'I want someone to tell me that there's a chance it wasn't an accident that my car blew up.'

'Why?'

'Because I can't believe that it was. There were things going on . . . I don't know.'

Keith shuffled to the edge of his chair. Jessica could feel him watching her but knew the tears would come again if she looked up. 'I can only give my verdict on what I saw. The fire caused so much damage that it would be impossible to know anything completely one hundred per cent – but it looked to me as if there was a fault in the cooling system. I've worked with engines my entire life and know what I'm talking about. That doesn't mean I'm perfect but I do have a good idea. When they wanted a second opinion, the BAE guy said the same as me – and he knows more about engines than I do. We didn't come to that conclusion together; it was independent of each other. Until the inquest, I'd never met him. This all came out in court, so did the story about it happening in Korea.'

'But you can't be absolutely, completely certain it was an accident?'

Keith sighed. 'You're taking things the wrong way. Of course there's a chance it was something else – a tiny, minute coincidence that two experts and the manufacturer don't know anything about. But I didn't see a sign of anything other than a fault in the cooling system. I'm sorry if that's not what you want to hear.'

'But there's a chance . . .'

Jessica tailed away pathetically but Keith didn't reply this time. He finished his tea and rinsed the mug before taking his seat again. Jessica had only had a mouthful of hers.

'I can't help you,' he eventually said.

Jessica put the mug on the floor, finally making eye contact. There were tears again but this time she talked through them: 'It's just that life is full of fuck-ups. You fuck something up and then you fix it. But this . . . Adam . . . he can't be fixed. It's so final – and I can't believe it was one big accident.'

10

Jessica left the garage feeling embarrassed but thankful that Keith had finally come to talk to her. She wasn't sure that she'd ever felt anything sinister about him or his evidence but she needed someone to blame. Meeting him had made her realise how easy a target he was.

She turned her phone on briefly, ignored the missed calls, made a quick one of her own and then turned it off again. Whatever was going on at the station could wait for now.

One of the things Manchester had other than bad weather, too many traffic lights and appalling traffic jams, were long straightish streets leading directly into the centre. Jessica turned onto Oxford Road and started to follow it out of the city, crawling along in the stop-start traffic. As it passed the universities and hospital, the road widened out, turning into Wilmslow Road as she passed Whitworth Park. Jessica turned right into the tight, twisting labyrinth of side streets that were almost entirely occupied by students. Long red-bricked terraces stretched for entire streets, with cars packed nose-to-tail along either side, leaving a narrow space through the centre.

Jessica checked the address and then squeezed her vehicle in between two others in a piece of parallel parking she wished she could have recorded to show those bastards at the station that she really could drive – even if she would have had to edit out the two instances where she clipped the kerb. Bloody mirrors.

She knocked on the door of the house on the end and stepped back as it was opened by a young woman wearing bright yellow washing-up gloves, a woollen jumper with rolled-up sleeves, and skinny jeans. She had brown hair loosely tied into a ponytail. 'Jessica?'

'Sam?'

'Yep, come on in.' Bex's friend waited until Jessica was inside, peered both ways along the street, and then closed the door behind her. She led Jessica into the kitchen and then knelt next to a bucket of soapy water, dunking a sponge inside. 'I've been cleaning.'

'Bex is always cleaning too. Is this what teenagers get up to nowadays? Am I really that old?'

Sam laughed. 'I get it from my mum – I'm one of three. She's always tidying up after us.'

Jessica hovered in the doorway, trying not to get in the way as Sam squeegeed a cupboard door. 'Bex said you had some sort of problem . . .'

'Rebecca?'

'Is that what you call her?'

'That's her name . . . isn't it?'

It was another thing that Jessica and Bex – Rebecca – had never had a proper conversation about. 'Yes, sorry. Go on.'

Sam finished wiping down one door and moved onto the other, half-turning to watch Jessica over her shoulder. 'I said it wasn't a big deal. She reckoned I should contact the police but they're all twats, so I . . . oh . . . sorry. Oops – except you, obviously.'

Jessica shrugged: GMP's public relations machine was performing as well as ever.

'Bex said it was something to do with your neighbour.'

Sam stopped scrubbing, sitting cross-legged on the floor and nodding. She pointed to the wall behind Jessica. 'This was built as one house but either the landlord or a previous owner turned it into two flats. They built an internal wall behind you to seal off the stairs and then put a second door onto the outside around the side. I live at number forty-two, then there's a forty-two A.'

'Do they play their music a bit loudly?'

Sam smiled slightly. 'How long have you got?'

Jessica glanced at the clock on the wall. Technically, she'd spent her lunch break at the garage and this was work time. She was investigating a complaint, so . . . 'Maybe half an hour? I'll have to head back in a bit.'

Sam pushed herself to her feet. 'All right – how about I put the kettle on? It won't take long.'

'What won't?'

'You'll see.'

Minutes later, Jessica found herself sitting in a surprisingly comfy though rather ragged-looking armchair in Sam's living room. Sam had found a pair of fluffy boots and was looking particularly snug on the sofa. A line of wire was running around the length and width of the room with various dresses, sparkly tops and skirts hanging from it.

'Sorry about the mess,' Sam said. 'It's almost impossible

to get anything dry around here, so I end up with clothes everywhere. The radiators take ages to warm up too.'

In the corner there were three pairs of huge heels lined up next to each other: black, bright red and bright blue. Half-hidden behind one of the dresses was a black and white poster of some bloke with his top off that Jessica half-recognised.

Oh to be young again.

'Do you go to the same college as Bex?' Jessica asked, feeling slightly out of her depth.

'Sort of – I'm at Manchester Uni doing a philosophy degree but I also chose an elective history module, which is off-campus at the college where she goes. Does Bex live with you?'

'Yes.'

'And is she . . . ?' Sam tailed off, neither an expert nor particularly subtle at fishing for information.

'It's complicated.'

'I can't believe she's only seventeen. I'm nineteen and thought she was older than me. There are a few of us uni students on the module and she was helping us with the work. It's ridiculous really.'

Jessica knew the first time she'd met Bex that there was something special about her – but it felt strange to hear somebody else mention it too. 'She reads a lot – I think that helps.'

'You should persuade her to come out with us. We're not a bad a lot – I'll make sure she gets home all right, or she can kip here. I know she's not eighteen but there are loads of places that'll let you in around here – and she doesn't have to drink. One of the other girls drinks tea or water all night. I think her dad's an alky.'

'It's up to her; it's not as if I keep her locked—'

Jessica was interrupted by a thump from the other side of the wall and the sound of someone walking up the stairs. Sam gave Jessica a small nod to indicate this was what she meant.

Clunk, clunk, clunk, clunk, SLAM!

Jessica wanted to say that having noisy stairs wasn't something she could do much about but Sam held up a hand.

Muffled voices sounded from above – a female and at least one male – and then there were more footsteps. Thirty seconds later and it began: Eh-eh-eh-eh-eh-eh-eh-eh and then a screamed 'Ooooooh . . .'

The unmistakeable sound of a squeaky mattress taking a pounding and a female taking a . . . well, that was pretty obvious too.

Sam pointed overhead. 'It's like this every day and half the night. It starts around midday and goes through until one or two in the morning. Every now and then, there's shouting or banging.'

'Do you know who lives up there?'

'Only that it's a woman. I said hello once when I saw her smoking by the side door but she didn't reply. She might not speak English.'

'And it's definitely every day – it's not just an enthusiastic boyfriend?'

Sam laughed. 'If it is, she can send him down here for a couple of hours – I can't find a lad who can last longer than a minute or two. It's all, "Oops, sorry about that. I'll give you a call sometime".'

Jessica checked the pepper spray in her pocket and then told Sam to call the police if she wasn't back downstairs in five minutes.

Next to the side door was a white plastic doorbell with '42A' half-written, half-scratched over the top in blue biro next to the name 'Ana'. Jessica pressed it once, hearing the whirring from above. Thirty seconds later and there was no reply, so she tried again.

No reply.

Buzz, buzz, buzz, buzz, buzz, buzz, buzzzzzzzzzzzzzzzz.

Moments later, the door was flung open and a pasty man wearing glasses bolted out of the door, glancing momentarily at Jessica without stopping before sprinting for a green hatchback across the road. In a puff of exhaust smoke, he roared along the road, took the first left and put his foot down.

Jessica eased the door open and pressed herself to the wall, skimming along the edges of the stairs to try to stop herself making too much noise.

Creaaaaaaaaaaakkkkk.

There was another door at the top made of such thin wood that Jessica would have fancied her chances of kicking it down if need be – not that she needed to seeing as green-car-man had left it open a sliver. Jessica closed one eye and peeped through the slit. The waft of cigarette smoke was almost overpowering, even through the small gap. At first, all Jessica could see was a pile of clothes but as she adjusted herself slightly on the top step, she could see a cadaverous-looking pale blonde woman staring at something Jessica couldn't see. Aside from a pair of heels, she was completely naked, the shape of her ribs and hip bone painfully apparent. The woman bent over, giving Jessica more of an eyeful than she wanted as she slipped on underwear so small it barely counted as 'wear'.

Creaaaaaaaaaaakkkkk.

This time, Jessica had no option other than to nudge the door open. She only had a moment to take in the room: browny-grey walls, a maroon carpet covered with cigarette holes, piles of clothes and an unmade double bed with a mirror on the wall above the headboard.

The woman was wearing only her string knickers and shoes and she eyed Jessica with confusion. Her accent was Eastern European: 'Hel-lo?'

Slowly Jessica reached into her pocket and took out her identification.

The woman's eyes darted from the front door to Jessica and then to one of the two other doors next to the bed. '*Pol-iz!*'

Jessica realised too slowly what was happening. The door next to the bed flew open, revealing a hulk of a man: over six feet tall, thick, hairy arms, shoulders like a beer cask and a squat head on top. He glanced quickly away from the woman and then ran straight at Jessica.

Jessica had no idea who he was but if he was so keen to escape the flat then he was someone she should try to stop – at the absolute least he was bang to rights for pimping.

That was all nice in theory – and certainly what any future paperwork might say – but the fact he was twice the width of her and a foot and a half taller meant things weren't quite that simple. In three strides, he had crossed the room, head down, rushing for the door. Jessica had two choices, one of which involved standing still and being smashed into the wall, the second involving getting out of the sodding way as quickly as possible.

Jessica went for option two, diving to her left a fraction of a second before the man would have crashed into her. He continued moving without flinching but Jessica swung her right foot forward, connecting perfectly with the area underneath and to the side of his knee. Usually her weight would have barely moved him but she had timed it so well that his knees knocked together, sending him careering into the doorframe and then crunch, crunch, crunching his way down the stairs head-first.

Considering all she'd done was jump out of the way and swing her leg, Jessica was surprisingly tired. She hauled herself to her feet and then peered down the stairs, where the man was lying in a pool of blood, holding his head as he tried to get to his feet. Jessica was about to say something heroically hilarious about not picking on someone half your size when she heard a shriek. She only managed to half-turn before the woman was on her back, long nails of one hand digging into Jessica's shoulder, the other punching her in the back of the head.

Jessica tumbled forwards, partially breaking her fall by inadvertently smashing her face into the wall. As she crumpled, Jessica rolled, managing to land her weight on the almost-naked woman and rifling an elbow back to catch her under the ribs for good measure. She tried to stretch forward to stand but the woman grabbed her hair, yanking Jessica viciously back and hissing in her ear, sending flecks of saliva onto her skin. Jessica was pretty good at flailing herself when she wanted to, arching her knees into the air, and then bringing her weight down on her attacker and throwing two more elbows until she was finally free. In a flash, she was on her feet, pepper spray in hand. So much for the safety distance: in a flicker, the woman was howling on the floor clutching her eyes and Jessica was at the doorway, staring down at an empty stairwell, an open door and a puddle of blood.

11

Jessica felt a slight sense of déjà vu as she entered through the main reception doors at Longsight Police Station. Pat had another cake bag half-hidden next to the counter but almost choked when he saw her.

'Christ, is that what they do to you at pro standards nowadays? I thought they just had a stern word, slap on the wrists, "stop ballsing things up" and all that. I didn't realise they kicked shite out of you.'

Jessica ignored him, breezing through to the sergeant station where Izzy was on the phone to someone. She made an excuse and hung up as soon as she saw Jessica: 'What happened to you? I thought you were going to Moston Vale for a bollocking. You didn't end up getting into an actual fight with the standards guy, did you? There are scratches on your neck.'

Despite the fact that it hurt, Jessica's face cracked into a smile. 'I've got his body in my boot. Want to help me dump him in the canal?'

'Later – what's up?'

'I had to get a SOCO out Whitworth Park way. They're checking a blood sample for me – can you keep onto them about it. I'm trying to find out who the blood belongs to. I'd do it myself but my name's mud over there at the moment.'

'Fine – we've got the full list of local robbing bastards coming in tomorrow by the way.'

'That'll raise the tone of the place.'

Izzy shook her head. 'Our heating's on the blink again and there's only one interview room they'll let us use. I've had to go crawling to Bootle Street. They've got more space anyway.'

'Yes but they're also in the city centre which means any nosy git with a camera phone could get a picture of us wheeling every scumbag and his mother in for questioning.'

'Best I could do – sorry.'

'Have any other charities come forward with friendly donations?'

'Nope.'

'Any word from our lads keeping an eye on the jewellery and pawn shops?'

'Nope – though there are rumours Franks misheard the instruction and ended up in a porno shop.'

'Wouldn't surprise me, the dirty sod. Good rumour – let's keep telling people that. What else is going on?'

'Your list of similar robberies around the country would've been ready by now but I thought we should probably expand to see if there are any other robbers who've stolen something and then given it away – well, apart from Robin Hood obviously. You'll have that by morning too.'

'Do you have a twin?'

'No, why?'

'Because I don't understand how you get so much done

without battering anyone around here. It takes all my strength to walk past Pat every morning and resist the urge to pinch his pudgy cheeks and tell him to stop gossiping about me behind my back.'

'Are you sure whoever smacked you in the eye didn't hit you harder that you thought? You've gone a bit weird.'

Jessica did actually have a headache, though the combination of the fluorescent overhead strip lights, the heating which was either on full blast or not at all, and the fact her office was too close to the toxic canteen food meant that wasn't uncommon.

'Have you seen Arch?'

'Last I saw he was on the main floor moaning about Star Wars or something like that?'

'Star Tours?'

'Maybe.'

'Shite, I thought he was done with that.'

Jessica nipped into the ladies' toilets and rinsed more of the blood away from the graze over her eye. As well as the pain in her head, there was an ache at the bottom of her neck from where the woman had dug her fingernails in. People could get nicked for carrying a butter knife in their back pockets, yet women were allowed to walk around with talons on their fingers and nobody batted an eyelid. Well, unless said eyelid was ripped off their faces by an errant claw and then they'd have something to say about it.

When she was looking as if she'd gone only three rounds with a heavyweight, Jessica breezed through to the main area of the station, where most of the constables were squeezed behind overstacked desks, hammering away noisily at keyboards, talking into phones, and generally trying not to get roped into doing any more work. She found Archie at the back of the room, cowering behind a set of lever arch files. If in doubt, surround yourself with massive piles of folders – then everyone assumed you were busy. He'd learned from the best.

Jessica sat on the edge of his desk. 'Afternoon.'

'Christ, what happened to you? I thought those pro standards wankers were just calling you in for a word?'

'I headbutted the main guy and then joyrode back here in a helicopter.'

Archie squinted at her as if he wasn't quite sure whether she was joking. 'What really happened?'

'I got beaten up by a topless Eastern European prostitute with nails longer than most penknives.'

Archie's eyes narrowed again. 'You must think I was born yesterday – what really happened?'

Jessica laughed, which only made her jaw hurt again. 'You busy?'

'Just finishing wading through this Star Tours shite.'

'All right, pack it in and come with me – but keep your eyes in your head and let me do the talking.'

Archie set up the only interview room where the heater was working while Jessica downed two glasses of water and held her head in her hands. One of these days she'd learn to stop smacking her head into things. Well, maybe not – but she'd certainly think about it.

Fifteen minutes later and the woman from the flat was led into the room in handcuffs. She was shackled to the table, looking marginally worse for wear than Jessica. Her eyes were red and puffy from the pepper spray, with the fact she had kicked up such a fuss meaning the paramedics had hardly been delighted to jump in either. Her blonde hair was a mess and although she was now wearing clothes, her angled, sharp shoulders were still poking through the material. She was a walking bag of bones.

Jessica spoke slowly, not knowing whether the woman understood English. In the cells, she'd not acknowledged that she'd been offered a duty solicitor – and refused to cooperate with anyone trying to ask if she needed a translator. 'Are you named Ana?'

The woman stared blankly through Jessica, brown eyes cloudy and lifeless.

'Where are you from, Ana?'

No answer.

'If the tall man was hurting you or making you do something you didn't want to, we can help.'

The woman blinked but her eyes remained fixed on the wall behind Jessica.

'You know who I'm talking about, don't you? The hairy man who fell. We can protect you.'

For a fraction of a second, the woman's eyes flickered to Jessica and then they were gone again. It was only a moment but Jessica knew it meant she understood.

'We've taken everything from your flat – the toys, the clothes, cash. We found a phone in the room the man ran out from which we're looking at. We're going to catch him eventually. What do you think he's going to do when he finds out the money's gone?'

Another flicker of the eyes but no reply. Jessica knew she was scared. 'Talk to me, Ana. At least tell me that's your name. You're under arrest for assaulting a police officer – you've got to say something.'

Nothing.

Three minutes later and Jessica ended the interview, calling the officer back inside and sending Ana, or whatever she was called, back to the cells.

'What are you going to do now?' Archie asked.

'Time to call in a favour.'

Jessica took out her phone and dialled a number she hadn't used in a while. The female voice was half-chuckling, half-serious: 'What have you done now?'

12

Jessica arrived at Bootle Street Police Station on Wednesday morning ready for the scroat parade. She took one of the interview rooms with Archie at her side, Izzy had another with one of the other constables she insisted 'wasn't mental', while DI Franks had the third room with DC Rowlands tagging along. Dave made a point of not making eye contact with Jessica, only speaking in yes or no answers. Jessica knew it was largely her fault for barely speaking to him since her return to work – but then spending four and a bit months working closely with Wanky Frankie would be enough to send anyone a bit loopy.

Interview one – Neil Bridger, forty-four; aggravated burglary x4. Dark blue rugby shirt, ripped jeans, looks a bit like a chipmunk:

'I ain't heard nuffink 'bout no burglaries, right? I've done my time.'

Jessica glanced up from the table as Archie's pen scratched away: 'Who mentioned burglaries?'

'What?'

'I didn't say anything about a burglary and neither did DC Davey here. What automatically makes you think you've been asked to the station to tell us about a burglary?'

Bridger slumped back into the chair and started picking his nose. 'It's always the same with you lot – the minute something goes missing, one of your boys in blue come knocking on my door asking where it is.'

'Well, where is it?'

He started to answer and then stopped himself, pointing a finger at Jessica that had something suspiciously green stuck to the end of it. 'Don't think you can trick me.'

'I'm not – you're the one who brought up burglaries, I thought we were here for a chat about last night's Corrie. DC Davey here was telling me it was an absolute stormer.'

Bridger sucked the end of his finger. 'Er, was it?'

'Shall we start again?'

'Okay.'

'Right – what do you know about those three burglaries out Gatley and Cheadle way?'

'I knew it!'

Interview two – Kieran Broadheath, twenty-three; theft of a motor vehicle, theft from a shop x3. White checked shirt two sizes too big, jeans two sizes too small, keeps one hand on his crotch seemingly at all times, looks like his mum cut his hair with a pudding bowl:

'I've gotta go sign on, man. This is against my . . . what do you call them?'

Jessica kept a steady eye on him, wondering if he was ever going to stop touching himself. 'Human rights?'

'Yeah – it's against my human rights.'

'Have you got proof you're human?'

'What?'

Jessica nudged Archie. 'If you want human rights, you've got to get a card from the post office to prove you're human. There was a case in Swansea the other year of a chimpanzee trying to claim benefits.'

'Was there?'

'Of course there bloody wasn't – although it was Wales, so who knows. Anyway, the quicker you answer the questions, the quicker you can get to Greggs to spend that signing-on money.'

'What do you want to know?'

'We've had three burglaries out Gatley way – big houses; lots of jewellery nicked, big sod with a gun – tell me what you know.'

Broadheath still hadn't removed his hand from his crotch, though he was looking nervously at Archie. 'I don't know anything.'

'Bollocks do you – I can see it all over your face. DC Davey here can spot a liar at twenty paces and he saw it on you the minute you walked in the door.'

'I only know what was in the papers.'

'Now I know you're lying – there's no way you can read.'

'All right, I saw it on the telly.'

'Finally – the truth. What else do you know?'

'Nothing, I swear.'

'What about that raid on the industrial park in Reddish two weeks back? Selling nicked radios out the back of a car is right up your alley.'

Finally, he stopped cupping his genitals and put both hands on the table. 'I don't know nuffin' about it.'

'What would you say if I told you we have a bloke who reckons he saw you selling nicked goods in a pub last week?'

'Which pub?'

'Wrong answer – the correct response was "No I weren't" or, to be correct, "No, I was not". We know all about your lock-up filled with stolen goods – now are you going to tell us who did the actual raiding, or do I have to get a warrant for your flat?'

Broadheath was panicking now, looking from Archie to Jessica and back again. 'I don't have no lock-up. It was only one radio – and I bought it. I didn't know it was nicked, honest.'

'What about the jewellery?'

'What jewellery?'

'All right, sod it. Tell me who you bought the radio from and I'll see if I can negotiate the CPS down to handling stolen goods.'

'I don't remember, it was dark . . .'

Interview three – Harry Jacobs, thirty-four; handling stolen goods. Smart two-piece suit, clean shirt, smells a bit like a strip club:

'Good morning, officers.'

'Mr Jacobs, what do you know about the recent burglaries?'

'Which burglaries?'

Jessica wished she still wore glasses, because if she did, she would have peered over the top of them in a withering way. As it was, she was left with giving him a scornful glance that was definitely not withering. 'Shall we do away with the forced niceties? I'm sure you've got stolen goods to buy and I've got a sausage roll with my name on it.'

'Are you referring to the burglaries which have been in the news?'

'Congratulations – with powers of deduction like that, we should swap jobs.'

'I don't know anything about those.'

'Oh come on, an upstanding member of the scumbag society like you must know something. What was it last time? Breaking into people's homes in the week before Christmas and nicking kiddies' presents? That's low by anyone's standards.'

'I've done my time for that.'

'Yeah, yeah. You've turned over a new leaf and you only buy nicked stuff for the other fifty-one weeks of the year now. Just tell us what you know and we'll get you on your way.'

'I don't know anything.'

'You must have heard something – word on the street that someone's got a bit of jewellery to shift. All you've got to do is point the finger and we'll leave you alone for a week or two.'

Jacobs shifted backwards in the seat. 'I really don't have to sit here and listen to this.'

'True but not cooperating with the police looks a bit shifty. That suit of yours looks a bit too new for my liking – has one of your mates been nicking from Marks and Sparks again?'

'I've probably still got the receipt at home if you want to come around and check.'

He started to stand but Jessica waved him back down. 'All right, all right . . . sit down and let's go back to the beginning.'

As lunchtime approached, Jessica and Izzy sent the morning interviewees home and compared notes while DI Franks went to the toilets – presumably the men's, although no one seemed quite sure.

Jessica and Archie had spoken to six people and although they'd got a name from Kieran Broadheath of the person he bought a stolen radio from, they hadn't come up with anything in relation to the main inquiry. Izzy had gone through seven interviews, with Franks and Dave getting through five. They had a similar number to get through during the afternoon but it wasn't getting them anywhere. The people who had raided the three houses knew what they were doing, even if Jessica wasn't quite sure what their plan was in regards to the jewellery and cash. The criminals the police were getting in were those stupid enough to get caught and, in the case of Kieran Broadheath, stupid enough to keep getting caught.

Harry Jacobs was a grade-A scumbag but Jessica did believe him when he said he'd heard nothing about the burglaries. Of all the suspects they were wheeling in, it was those who had convictions for handling stolen goods that interested her the most. They were the people who knew others in 'the trade'.

All in all, a complete waste of a morning.

Jessica checked the time, told Archie she'd be back as soon as she could – and then headed off to Longsight.

13

Jessica waited in the car park at Longsight Police Station and grinned as the woman got out of her smart BMW and approached.

'Hello, stranger,' Esther Warren said, giving Jessica a hug. They had first met investigating a missing child a few years ago and, more recently, Jessica had been standing next to Esther when she was in charge of policing a public event at which a politician had been attacked. 'Why do we only ever get together when you're in trouble?' Esther added, releasing her.

'The way I remember, last time you had the Home Secretary gunning for you and I was trying to poke my nose in.'

Esther was wearing a crisp grey jacket and tight-fitting matching trousers. Her long brown hair was straight and tied back. She looked every inch the efficient, articulate modern female officer. They were a similar age yet Jessica couldn't but feel she wasn't looking quite so good, especially considering her eye was partly black and the graze above her brow had barely begun to heal.

'This is Katerina,' Esther said, turning to a slightly younger blonde woman who was walking around from the passenger's side. 'She does a lot of consulting for us over Eastern European affairs.'

Jessica led them into the station and found a corner in the canteen, warning the other two women not to try the food if they valued their health. Although, if either of them wanted to go on a crash diet, then risking anything other than toast would probably leave them spending a few days on a toilet. Jessica bought three teas from the machine and then settled back at the table, turning to Esther. 'I couldn't believe it when I saw your name on that press release about a new people smuggling division being set up. After the debacle with the public event policing, I thought you were going to find something less stressful to do – like being a drugs mule in south-east Asia.'

'I would have preferred that to continuing in my old job. I absolutely hated it.' Esther lowered her voice slightly, even though there was no one else around them. 'I heard about Adam . . .'

'It's okay.'

'Are you sure, I suppose I didn't expect you to be . . . back.'

'I'm fine.'

Jessica spoke more forcefully than she meant to, ending the conversation. Esther carried on as if it hadn't happened. 'With the whole Pratley report and me wanting to leave, it all happened at the same time. People were retiring left, right and centre trying to avoid the fallout. I heard a whisper from someone I know at Serious Crime that they were looking into setting up some sort of hybrid people smuggling-vice-exploitation thing, so I sent an email to the bloke who was putting it together. I had the panel that week and then it was all done in under a month.'

'Under a month? They can barely get the bins emptied that often.'

'I know – it must be a record. Anyway, this is Katerina and she works with me.'

Jessica explained to Katerina about the previous day – Sam's complaint, the man who had bolted out of the upstairs flat, the woman she suspected was called Ana, and the huge man who had 'fallen' down the stairs.

Katerina listened intently. 'Have you been on any of the vice courses?'

Jessica nodded.

Her accent was hard to place, slightly East European but a little more delicate than some of the Slavic ones. 'You're probably aware of how these things work then,' Katerina added. 'Girls are brought over from former Eastern Bloc countries: Poland, the Czech Republic, Hungary, Romania, Ukraine – plus some of the old Yugoslav nations: Serbia, Croatia and so on. Poland isn't so bad now because it's a full member of the EU and we have better ties with their police, plus our intelligence is stronger. There's still a problem, though. Young women are essentially groomed over there. They're promised there's a job waiting for them in the UK and then they're brought over. Some come in illegally, hidden on boats or lorries, some of the Polish girls fly in like normal visitors. They think they're coming in for a new life.'

Katerina sipped her tea and winced.

'Sorry,' Jessica said. 'The machine tea's bloody awful. I think I'm immune to it.'

'Anyway,' Katerina continued, 'as soon as they get here,

111

they find out they've been brought in by a gang. It's always a man, so it wouldn't surprise me if the person who fell down the stairs is known to us when you get your results back. Of course, knowing who someone is and stopping them are two different things. These girls are told that they owe money for being transported in and that they have to work to earn it back. They have their passports taken and then the men use them as prostitutes. They never end up repaying the money because of all the interest that gets added on. Some of them are charged for "board and keep". The gangs are never done with them.'

'What happens?'

'Sometimes they get away; sometimes we rescue them. Other times, they get sold on to other gangs around the country, or in Europe. It's a big problem in the Netherlands too. If they get too old, or if they have too many health problems, then they get dumped in the middle of nowhere. The men in charge will sometimes get them hooked on drugs, which keeps them coming back.'

'Our girl downstairs had no signs of anything in her system.'

'That's one thing. This has been going on for years but it's only now the police forces are beginning to put teams together to tackle it. If she is called Ana with one "N", then she's probably Ukrainian, perhaps Romanian. It's a common name in Serbia too – but I'd be surprised if she's found her way this far north if that was the case. London's a far bigger hotspot.'

'I said that we could protect her from whoever she's scared of.'

Katerina shook her head, giving a motherly half-smile. 'You don't understand – these girls probably trust the men more than they trust you. It's awful what they go through but at least they're getting food, water and drugs from them. The biggest problem in the Netherlands wasn't necessarily that all these young women were being brought in; it was that the local police were all using the brothels too. As soon as someone escaped and went to the police, a certain proportion would take them straight back to the gang masters in return for some freebies. Things are a lot better there now but, true or not, a lot of these girls will have a negative view of the police officers in their own countries.'

Jessica knew first-hand there were shifty officers in all countries – it wasn't a solely continental problem.

After passing across the few details they had, Jessica set up the interview room and then waited in the adjacent observation room as Esther and Katerina arranged their papers before Ana was led in, still in handcuffs. She was clearly confused, having presumably expected Jessica.

Katerina said something in a language Jessica didn't know, which made Ana sit up straighter in her chair. She glanced between the two women, wondering if she was being tricked and shaking her head. Katerina continued speaking, sometimes harshly; other times she would relax into her chair and hold her hands out as if chatting to a mate in a pub. Ana's body language altered too: at first she was pointing aggressively but she soon became more passive, holding her head in her hands.

After a few minutes, Katerina changed language. 'So

your name's Ana and you come from Ukraine. I know you can understand English, so shall we speak it for the benefit of everyone else?'

Ana didn't lift her head from her hands.

'Who was the man in your flat?'

When there was no reply, Katerina switched languages again. Ana peered through her fingers but shook her head slightly. She was shaking.

'Ana, do you know what deportation means? That's what's going to happen if you're convicted for assaulting an officer. We're going to have to check your documents anyway to see if you arrived here legally.'

Katerina repeated herself in the foreign language again – well, Jessica assumed that's what she was doing – but this time there was a reaction. Ana began shaking her head quickly from side to side, her cuffs rattling against the table.

Katerina made hushing, soothing sounds. 'Who knows where your family are, Ana?'

Jessica let things go for a few more seconds before whispering into Esther's earpiece that they should end it there. Esther tapped Katerina on the wrist and they formally ended the interview, before Ana was taken back to the cells.

Afterwards, the three women sat in the interview room. Katerina looked concerned. 'I tried to feed as much back to you as I could without disturbing her. She understands English but I'm not sure she can speak it that well. She didn't know what deport meant until I said it in Belarusian.'

'You said she was from Ukraine . . . ?'

'Oh, she is. She might not have understood my accent. A lot of the key Ukrainian, Belarusian and Russian words are interchangeable. Many Polish words too – and Serbian and Croatian. It goes back to the old Soviet Union. A lot depends on where you're born and where your parents come from originally. You can make people feel more comfortable if they realise you understand the nuances between the dialects. I suppose the nearest example is someone with a broad Scottish accent trying to speak to someone with a strong Welsh voice. They could both be speaking English but not understand what the other is saying. If you can mimic their own way of speech, the other person is more likely to open up.'

'How many languages do you speak?' Jessica asked.

'I suppose that depends on whether you count things such as Belarusian as separate from Ukrainian – or if you think the whole lot is Slavic. Seven or eight core languages, I suppose – then I'm pretty good with the subtle Eastern Bloc differences.'

'I can barely understand what half the street kids are on about nowadays, let alone knowing eight languages.'

Katerina shrugged. 'All Ana would say was that "they" knew where her family was. From what I can gather, she's here legally because she said she flew in – but it depends how deeply you want to look into things. Like I told you, it's doubtful she has her own passport right now.'

Jessica rubbed the scrape next to her eye, aware again of the gouges prickling the bottom of her neck. 'Perhaps I was mistaken when I said she attacked me. Now I think about it, I might have just been a little off-balance . . .'

14

Jessica led Esther and Katerina back through the corridors. 'What are you going to do with Ana?' Esther asked.

'I'm not entirely sure. We'll let her go this evening and I have an idea or two.'

Jessica was about to lead them through the station's front door into the car park when she heard Pat calling after her. She turned: 'What?'

'I've got something for you.'

Jessica gave Esther a quick hug and said she'd be in contact with Katerina soon and then headed back to the main desk. 'Are you sharing your crisps again?'

'No chance. I've got your blood results from that place at Whitworth Park.'

'Already? They only went off yesterday.' Jessica peered through the glass door at the front, wondering if she should call Katerina back, but she and Esther were already in their car.

Pat handed Jessica over a cardboard folder. 'I even printed them out for you.'

Jessica skim-read the top sheet but took none of it in. 'Can you do me a really, really big favour?'

Pat's eyes narrowed. 'What?'

'I've got to drive back to Bootle Street. If I put my

phone on speaker in the car, can someone read this to me down the line?'

'Do you think this is a listening library?'

'C'mon, Pat – I'm running late as it is.'

Surprisingly, he agreed – presumably collaring an unsuspecting constable and sending him into a side office to read Jessica the file.

As it turned out, the reason the blood results had come back so quickly was because the person they came from was so well known to various police forces around the continent.

Pavel Adamek was a Serbian national who had arrived in the UK four years previously and had been on the fringe of trouble ever since. First he was convicted for driving without a licence, insurance or MOT certificate but that was the only time the police had nailed him for anything. After that, he'd been arrested after a bar was smashed up as part of a brawl between football fans a couple of years back but charges had been dropped due to a lack of evidence. Twelve months ago, he'd been at a house party where the owner was convicted of dealing cocaine and amphetamines – and then three months ago he had really messed up. A known drug dealer had been beaten to death, his body dumped in an Ancoats alleyway with bleach poured over his face and his teeth smashed. Unfortunately for Pavel, scrapings of his skin had been found underneath the dead man's fingernails, meaning there was a warrant out for his arrest and a near-guaranteed conviction if they could find him.

Jessica's mind wandered to the whiteboard in DCI

Topper's office and the how good it would have been to have a nice big tick next to her name for helping their neighbouring district find a murder suspect. If only Ana hadn't jumped on her back, she'd have had him.

The drive from Longsight to Bootle Street wasn't far but Jessica hit every red light and was only halfway there. 'Does Pavel have anything else?' she shouted at her phone.

She could hear the constable flicking to the next sheet. 'A request has gone in to see if he has a separate criminal record in Serbia but that was from three months ago and it doesn't look as if we've had a response yet.'

'Can you give them a kick?'

'I, er . . .'

'Have a word with Pat – he'll know who to talk to.'

'There's something else here too – he's married.'

'In Serbia?'

'No, to an English girl. They looked into this when they were trying to find him for the murder.'

'Who is she?'

'Rosemary Dean – perhaps Adamek now, I suppose. There's an address in Abbey Hey.'

Jessica had never taken to the bells and whistles of her previous car but at least the Bluetooth had been useful. She had wedged her mobile in the grille of the heater and put it on speaker phone. As she took a corner, it slipped but just about held in place. So far, so legal.

'Can we send someone around there to make absolutely sure he's not sitting at home watching *Countdown* before we start scouring the city for him?'

'I'll ask. It does say they did all of that three months ago.'

'Which district?'

'Northern.'

'Aye, so that's not us, is it? Half of that lot couldn't spell Adamek, let alone find him.'

'Right . . .'

Jessica thanked the constable for his help and then pulled into a bus stop, making a quick call to Esther to pass on Pavel's name and ask if Katerina could do some digging among the local community. For one, she really wanted to find him in order to shut DCI Topper up; for another, she couldn't help but feel that Ana was probably one of many. If he had a host of girls holed up in dingy flats around the city and he was leeching money from them, then she wanted to put a stop to it.

Back at Bootle Street and the day wasn't going much better.

Interview nine – Janine Smith, forty-eight; theft from a shop x24, threatening behaviour x4. Dark top cut far too low for a woman of her age, skinny jeans that should only be worn by someone skinny, hint of a moustache, mullet. Quite the catch:

'What is it wiv you lot, eh? Always picking on the little person.'

Jessica really wasn't in the mood any longer: 'Aren't you the one who nicked baby's clothes from a local shop out in Hulme? Locally owned, no chain – just a poor woman trying to make a living.'

'Aye, well, I needed them.'

'You don't have any kids!'

'Yeah but our Tina, she's got this mate, right, who was having a kiddy, yeah? The council came round and said the conditions weren't good enough for a baby, right, so she were trying to sort 'erself out into this other flat, like, but then she dint 'av' no money 'cos her DSS hadn't come through. So I said—'

'All right, all right. I clock off in three hours. What have you heard about those burglaries out in Gatley?'

'Those big houses?'

'Yes.'

'Nuffin' – just that someone was giving the money away. We saw it on the news and our Tina, she was like, "I'll have some of that if it's going" and I nearly pissed myself through laughing. She's got this mate, right, whose car's on the blink. You turn the key and it just makes this sound like a fart. But her mate Pikey, right, reckons it costs two hundred quid to fix. I was like, "Two hundred quid? Is he 'aving a laugh?" So anyway, there's this other guy named Warren and he reckons he can do it for a hundred-and-twenty . . .'

By the end of the day, it was clear that the joint Franks-Topper idea of bringing in everyone who'd ever nicked anything in the Greater Manchester region was as stupid as anything anyone had ever come up with. Half of the people they'd dragged out of bed at two in the afternoon didn't know anything – and not just in regards to the burglaries, they literally knew nothing about anything other than their silly little lives.

To complete the day, Jessica's phone went with news

that two uniformed officers had been around to the house registered to Pavel and Rosemary Adamek. It wasn't a surprise to find out that the address was empty and didn't look as if it had been lived in any time recently.

Jessica said her goodbyes, turned her phone off, and then headed off for another evening of sitting in traffic that didn't move.

Wednesdays really could sod right off.

15

Jane stirred her cup of tea twice clockwise and then once the other way, before peering up at the officer opposite her in the armchair and offering him the spoon. She was trying to watch Corrie but the television had to be on silent and it was hard to make out what one person was complaining to the other about. She could never work out why the sky was blue. Anyone who lived in Manchester knew immediately there must be some sort of digital trickery going on.

The constable leant across and whispered. 'So do I call you Jane then?'

'That is my name.'

'Yes but everyone calls you . . .'

'Don't even bloody well think about it. Just because I found a few used condoms in an alley during a search once, suddenly I'm "Joy Bag Jane" for life. What's your name anyway?'

'Andy.'

'Right, how would you feel if I started calling you "Andy the Fanny" or "Bum Rapist Andy" all the time?'

'Er . . .'

'Exactly – just call me Jane and let's get this bloody thing over with.'

'Right. Do you, er, take sugar?'

'Are you calling me fat?'

'Sorry?'

After examining Andy's face for any hint that he was making a jibe, Jane decided that the young constable probably wasn't calling her fat after all; that was just her arsehole of a second husband. She changed the subject to let him off the hook, still whispering. 'I hope whoever lives here doesn't want us to keep this flat as clean as we found it – did you see the state of the cupboard doors in there? It looks like they were scrubbed this morning.'

Andy shrugged. 'It's some student's place, apparently. I dunno where they've put her for now – probably some five-star hotel while we're left here with pot noodles and crumpets.'

Jane felt her stomach grumble. 'Do you remember how to control any of this stuff? That guy who was showing us had a right "look-at-me" attitude – all press this and poke that. He's probably got a bunch of cameras in his next-door neighbour's house and spends his evenings watching them get undressed. Dirty sod.'

Andy picked up the remote control from the table and pointed it towards the two monitors sitting next to the television. 'They've put six cameras in the flat above us.' He indicated the buttons on the remote. 'Just press either one or two on the top to select which monitor you want to control, then the up or down arrows to cycle through the cameras. Everything's being recorded anyway but this lets us watch live.'

'How long ago did they release that Ana girl?'

'Two hours.'

'So why isn't she back yet?'

Andy shrugged. 'Perhaps she didn't come straight home.'

Jane eyed him. 'All right, smart-arse – why don't you make yourself useful and get some of those crumpets on the go. See if there's any real butter in the fridge – none of this low-fat shite. And if there's some Marmite then all the better. While you're in there, have a hunt around for some proper tea bags. In my day, a student flat would be full of beer cans, bongs and sex toys. Now it's all herbal teas, text-books and Disney movies. It's a disgrace.'

As he scuttled into the kitchen, Jane picked up the remote and began flicking through the cameras showing the room upstairs. Whoever this Ana girl was, her life had better be more interesting than a silent *Coronation Street* episode.

16

As Jessica turned onto the street towards Longsight Police Station, she was surprised to see the phalanx of satellite vans parked half on the pavement, half on the road. Usually the news crews only turned up if someone interesting had died or they'd nicked a footballer for peeing or shagging in the street. Again.

She edged her way slowly into the car park, managing not to run anyone over, and only having to exchange a cross word once – a new record for dealing with journalists.

Considering the melee outside, reception was surprisingly quiet, although Pat was clearly on his best behaviour, with no sign of cake bags or crisp packets anywhere near the counter.

Jessica was on the way to her office when he called after her: 'Where are you going?'

'Work.'

'Upstairs first.'

Jessica mumbled something uncomplimentary under her breath. 'What does His Highness want now?'

'A word.'

Jessica slunk back to the counter, peering over the top to see if there were any errant food wrappers that Pat had hidden. 'I could've figured that out for myself. What's going on with the satellite vans?'

'Don't you watch the news?'

'I was running late.'

'The wires finally caught up with the rob-from-the-rich-stuff and it's gone global. I think *Good Morning America* are doing a piece with one of the assistant chief constables. They reckon it's like a modern-day Robin Hood story. Sky News have been running it on a loop.'

'But it was news two days ago.'

Pat shrugged. 'Don't tell me.'

'Isn't the important part of the word "news" the fact that it has "new" in it?'

'I said don't tell me.'

Jessica headed for the stairs, still confused. At the top, she could see DCI Topper through the glass window of his office hammering away on his keyboard. Without looking up, he waved her inside and yet again began speaking before she'd sat down. 'Did you say something to a member of CBS News outside?'

'Sir?'

He glanced up from his desk disapprovingly. 'We've had a complaint that you told a member of CBS News you were going to take his microphone and shove it somewhere not very nice. Is that true?'

'It's a bit of a distortion.'

'How so?'

'For one, it depends on what you define as "nice". He might've been up for it. Secondly, I told him that if he didn't stop *waving the microphone in my face* then I'd shove it somewhere. There's a subtle difference – except that being a Yank means he wouldn't understand the word "subtle" if you took a dictionary and bashed him over the head with it. Subtly.'

Topper's expression didn't change. 'Are you done?'

'Yes.'

'Did your run-in with professional standards not teach you anything?'

'It taught me that they know how to ask the same question in a multitude of different ways.'

Topper raised his eyebrows. 'We've had this conversation – you can't live on past glories. I know you've been through a lot. If you need more time, we can talk about—'

'I don't!'

'Then start acting like it. Yesterday it was bringing in street girls and then releasing them. You stumbled across someone wanted for murder with an arrest warrant out but where is he? And where's his criminal record from Serbia?'

'We're trying – the Northern lot couldn't get it and they've been asking for three months. There are translation problems – it's coming.'

'It's not good enough.'

'I know, I was saying that yesterday. Europol's a waste of time—'

'I mean it's not good enough from you.'

'If it wasn't for me, nobody would even know Pavel was still in Manchester!'

Topper pursed his lips, like a teacher about to rip into a student for talking back at him. When he continued, his voice was lower and calmer, which only made Jessica angrier. 'We still have three outstanding burglaries unsolved, money being given away on the streets of Manchester and the world's media thinking it's one big joke.'

'What do you want me to do? We wasted a day yesterday dragging in all sorts and that got us nowhere. Forensics aren't getting anywhere – the envelopes full of money that were delivered had nothing useable on, or at least nothing yet.'

'So what have you done? Except for gallivant off to other people's flats and let suspected murderers escape.'

'He was twice the size of me, he—'

'I don't want to hear it. What else have you done?'

The reason they'd got nothing done was because of Topper and Franks' stupid idea of bringing in a host of local ne'er-do-wells.

She glanced at the Post-it note Pat had given her downstairs. 'One of the lads has found a similar case from five years ago – houses and businesses were robbed in London and then money was given to homeless people and others on the street by a man in a mask. The gang was caught and sent down but the ringleader wrote a book about it from prison and released it when he got out around a year ago.'

'So you think this could be similar?'

Jessica had no idea considering the first she'd heard of it was when she read it off the note. 'Quite possibly – I was looking into visiting him tomorrow. He still lives in London.'

Ever the bluffer.

Topper finally stopped staring at her, peering back at

his monitor. 'That's one thing at least.' Jessica stepped towards the door but was cut off by the DCI. 'One other thing – go and apologise to the CBS journalist.'

'Are you joking?'

'Why would I be?'

'He stuck his microphone through my car window – why would I say sorry?'

'Because he called our switchboard to complain and the last thing any of us wants is for you to be heading back to Moston Vale again. Either do it now, or I'll get one of the assistant chiefs on the phone and they'll tell you to do it.'

'Can't we call him inside?'

'No – go and do it in front of the other journalists. Take him a cup of tea out – and not one from the machine.'

Jessica bit her tongue, heading towards the stairs and wondering what toilet-water tea would taste like.

17

For once, Jessica kept a lid on her vindictive instincts, making the journalist a proper drink – Lancashire tea bag, semi-skimmed that wasn't out of date, two squeezes with the teaspoon – and then she 'borrowed' a Hobnob from Pat before heading out into the cold to embarrass herself in front of the media. Her only point of relief was that Garry sodding Ashford wasn't there to witness her walk of shame. The photographer from the *Manchester Morning Herald* did take a photo, however, which would no doubt find its way back to Garry at some point.

While the majority of the journalists looked on, wondering what on earth was happening, the CBS man explained how hurt his feelings were as Jessica could think of nothing other than taking that microphone of his and sticking it exactly where she'd promised. She felt slightly better as she turned to head back, empty mug in hand, when one of the Americans leant in and drawled in a beautiful southern accent: 'Don't worry about him. Everyone from New Jersey's a complete asshole.'

Back inside, Jessica didn't want to leave her office after the latest embarrassment, so she called Archie's desk phone and told him she had a packet of chocolate digestives if he had the tea. Five minutes later, he hurried into her office as if he'd just woken up on Christmas morning, plopping a steaming mug down on Jessica's desk.

'Where are the biccies?'

'Sorry, I lied. I just didn't want to leave my office.'

'Because you had to apologise to that journo?'

'How did you know that?'

Archie grinned. 'We were all watching out of the window. Izzy had a fiver on you hitting someone.'

'What do you have to do to get some respect around here?'

'Not fib about biscuits. Honestly, lie about whatever you want – but not chocolate biscuits. I'll let it go, but if you'd promised something like that out on the main floor, you'd have had a riot on your hands.'

Jessica nodded towards the empty chair. 'Have you got far with Pavel Adamek's wife?'

'I have no idea where she is if that's what you mean.'

'What do you know?'

Archie ruffled his hair and pumped his chest up. He really was a curious little man sometimes. 'Pavel and Rosemary Dean got married five months ago – only a few weeks before he apparently killed that drug dealer. Well, either that, or he stumbled across the body in the alley-way and scraped the dead man's fingernails across his skin.'

'He'd have to have a good lawyer to get him off that one.'

'You know what those slimy bastards are like – they'd probably claim Pavel was innocently walking along the alley when someone threw the body at him. He put his

131

hands up to protect himself and ended up getting his skin under the dead body's nails.'

Jessica aimed a playful kick at him. 'Don't say stuff like that out loud, you'll give them ideas. What about Rosemary?'

'She's got quite the history herself. She lived a few streets away from me, so I'm surprised I don't know her. She was excluded from school twice and ended up in this special council-run place. No GCSEs and the last we know, she was working in one of those mini-supermarkets. I put a call in earlier but the manager said she left unexpectedly about five months ago.'

'When she got married?'

'Yes, except he didn't know anything about that. She simply didn't turn up for work one day. He says it's not entirely uncommon and that they turn staff over at a reasonable rate.'

'Anyone she was mates with?'

'I've got a couple of names but he says she kept herself to herself.'

'Convictions?'

'Not really, especially considering the trouble she was in as a kid. There was a D and D but she was only cautioned for that. She's clean otherwise.'

'Someone emailed me an address in Abbey Hey.'

Archie shrugged. 'That's the only one I've seen, though I have no idea why you'd move there if you were born in God's own town of Stretford.'

'You're not one of these people who lives in one place their entire life, are you?'

Archie puffed his chest out again, like a strutting turkey looking for a fight. 'What's wrong with that?'

'Nothing – it's just there's a big world out there. On that note, are you busy tomorrow?'

'Why?'

'It's a yes or no question.'

Archie narrowed his eyes, watching her suspiciously. 'Not when you're asking. I could say "yes, I'm free" and then you're like, "oh good, you can go and help drag the canal because someone's dumped a dead cow in it".'

Jessica laughed. 'When have I ever made anyone do that?'

'Franks had someone staking out those bogs in Platt Fields Park the other month. They spent twelve hours hiding in a cubicle in case a flasher came in.'

'What is it with him and public toilets?'

'No idea. Anyway, if I was to say that I was free tomorrow, why would you be asking?'

'Fancy a trip to London?'

'Who's paying?'

'The great British taxpayer.'

Archie screwed his face up. 'On the one hand, I've got to put up with those soft southern jessies for a day; on the other it's a day out of here. What have I got to do?'

'Look threatening.'

Archie cracked his knuckles. 'For a minute there I thought it was going to be something difficult.'

The tight red-brick terraces of Abbey Hey were so similar to the row that Sam lived on close to Whitworth Park that it was as if someone had decided the only houses that could be built in the city were long dreary rows that all looked identical. Cars were parked half on the pavement on either side, just about allowing vehicles to pass each other along the centre. Each house was kitted out with a satellite dish and burglar alarm, with a huddle of grey wheelie bins arranged at the end of every street. Somewhere in the distance, the sound of a dustbin lorry chuntered.

Jessica parked outside an off-licence which had long curls of barbed wire attached to its roof and the surrounding wall. Somebody had sprayed the words 'Abbey Gay' onto a black rubbish bin in yellow paint, under which someone had written in Tipp-Ex: 'Youre mums gay'.

Jessica wondered if this was the type of insult kids would be throwing at each other in ten years' time. Or twenty? She could remember lads in her school calling everything 'gay' and that was twenty years ago. Sometimes insults lived forever.

She checked the address and then walked along the road, away from the terraces, checking the house numbers. Given Jessica's initial impression of the area, the side street that Rosemary had once lived on was a surprising change. Instead of grimy brickwork and graffiti, it was as if she'd wandered into a corner of green suburbia: low walls, leafy hedges, bay windows and patches of neatly trimmed lawn.

Jessica eased the metal gate open and went along the pathway, doing what she was sure the officers had done the previous day: knocking on the front door.

Although the street wasn't too bad, the house itself looked awful. The lawn was overgrown, the hedges had begun to encroach onto the pavement and Jessica could see the pile of mail inside the hallway through the frosted glass of the window next to the door. She'd phoned the landlord but he said that if they did run into Rosemary then he wanted a word too, seeing as she hadn't told him she was moving out. He claimed she owed three months' rent and said the first he knew of it was when he'd come around to find no one living there. Given that he'd used the word 'bitch' three times in the same sentence, Jessica didn't feel much sympathy for him.

She peered through the front window but there were no signs of life, so she climbed the back gate and dropped into the rear garden, where things were even messier. An upturned wheelbarrow had grass and weeds growing around it and the hedge at the back was so badly overgrown that Jessica had no idea where the garden ended. She again peered through the window but it didn't look as if anyone had lived there in months.

Jessica unlocked the gate and let herself out and then knocked on the house next door. After three properties with no reply, she crossed the road, knocking on the first door of the terrace. A man wearing socks, loose cotton shorts and a white vest with a blanket of grey hairs poking out answered, cigarette hanging from his mouth.

His lips barely moved. 'What?'

Jessica pointed towards the house. 'Did you know the woman who lived there?'

'Why?'

'Because I'm asking.'

'You DSS?'

'No.'

'Who are you then?'

By the time Jessica had taken out her ID card, the door had been slammed in her face.

And that was the politest it got.

The woman at number forty-two told her to piss off, the five-year-old at number forty tried to kick her in the shins, and the bloke at thirty-eight said he wasn't interested in buying anything at the door.

Jessica walked back to her car, thinking she'd wasted as much time here as she had yesterday at Bootle Street. Apparently, it wasn't just DCI Topper and DI Franks who had stupid ideas. She'd thought that at least one person might have known Rosemary, or perhaps had an idea of where she'd gone. On reflection, this didn't seem the type of area where residents poked too much of a nose into other people's business.

Back at her car, there was a pair of children sitting on the wall next to the shop, reaching up and trying to touch the barbed wire. Neither of them could have been older than ten, both with shaved heads and wearing jeans and big coats. Jessica knew she should do something – they were clearly bunking off school – but sometimes, admittedly not often, she fancied the quiet life.

As she unlocked her car, she heard one of the kids behind her: 'Oi, Miss – you got a fiver?'

For a moment, Jessica stopped, staring across the other side of the road, wishing the child hadn't spoken. After a deep breath, she turned to see the boys had climbed off the wall and were now watching her from the ground.

'Shouldn't you be at school?'

One of them was a little taller than the other and had his collar turned up. He looked every inch a skinhead in waiting, his accent like Archie's but even stronger: 'It was cancelled today.'

'Which school do you go to?'

'Can't remember.'

'Where do you live?'

'Can't remember.'

'How old are you?'

'Can't remember.'

Jessica sighed. This really wasn't what she'd signed up for all those years ago. 'What can you remember?'

He put his hand out. 'I know what five quid looks like. Ten is even better.'

'Why would I give you ten quid?'

The taller kid nudged the other one with his elbow. Reluctantly, the second lad reached into his coat pocket and pulled out something round and silver. At first Jessica had no idea what it was but she felt the sluggish realisation hitting as she walked around to the rear of her car to see the circular gap in the middle of the boot.

She turned around slowly. 'Did you nick that from my car?'

The taller one replied: 'It fell off. Finders keepers – but we're offering it back to you. We're nice like that.'

'Give it back.'

He held his hand out again. 'Tenner.'

Jessica took a step towards them. 'Give it back.'

He laughed and put on a mocking voice. 'Oooh, we're

really scared. How about you give us ten quid and a blow job?'

Jessica stared at him, unsure how to reply. He couldn't have been any older than ten. The shorter one glanced at his friend, clearly not wanting to be there. Jessica took another step forward, feeling far more nervous than she knew she should. Two days previously, she'd taken down someone twice her size, now she was feeling intimidated by two kids who weren't even old enough to be at secondary school.

'Just give it back.'

'Fuck off, you slut. It's twenty quid now, just for talking back.'

Jessica took her ID out of her pocket. 'I could just call my police mates down.'

The boy shrugged without looking at it. 'Yeah, you do that. We're not even old enough. My dad would sue the arse off you – then he'd fuck you in it, you dirty bitch.'

Jessica stopped herself again. If he wasn't old enough, that meant he was nine at the most. She could see the fury in the boy's face: his snarled top lip, half-squinting eye, the way his fists were balled. She knew it wasn't all sweetness and light on some of the estates around here but it was a big jump from that to how these kids were behaving.

Then she remembered watching through the window as her car blew up with Adam inside; the flames, the noise, the heat, the screaming, the sirens. His skin. His eyes.

She shivered.

Suddenly, this wasn't just a pair of feral kids messing around with her; this was someone who'd touched her car.

If they'd nicked the badge off the back, then what else had they done? If the tallest one could talk so confidently about the things his dad would to do her, then what else was he capable of?

Jessica locked eyes with the taller boy, who was still sneering. 'Don't look at me like that, you fat slag.'

She held her hand out. 'Give it back.'

'Twenty. Fucking. Quid.'

In a flash, Jessica lunged forward, grabbing the taller boy by the throat. He might have an attitude but he was still a kid and weighed nothing. With little effort, she lifted him off the ground, hurling him towards the wall. He landed a metre short, but skidded backwards, eyes wide, more with surprise than pain. The second boy was standing dumbstruck as Jessica snatched the badge from his hand, stuffing it into her pocket.

Slowly, the taller boy got to his feet, not taking his eyes from Jessica. 'You're going to fucking regret that, bitch.'

'Really?'

'I'm gonna sue you, your boss, your mum, your dad, fucking everyone.'

Before Jessica could say or do anything particularly stupid, an Asian man in an apron emerged from the shop. He looked nervously from one boy to the other and then Jessica. 'What's going on here?'

'That fat paedo bitch is trying to touch me up.'

Jessica turned and walked back to her car without a word, a stream of abuse disappearing into the distance behind her.

She weaved through the side streets back towards the

main road before it finally hit her. She'd never cared about cars in the past but this was more than that. It didn't matter what that mechanic said or what the British Aerospace man thought, someone had done something to her previous car and it had been meant to blow up with her in it.

Adam.

Jessica pulled over to the side of the road and closed her eyes. She could see his face, hear him laughing, picture his pasty, thin body in one of those stupid T-shirts he wore all the time. What would he think now? Beating up nine-year-olds was a new low. And for what? A stupid badge from the back of her car that she wouldn't have noticed if they hadn't called her back.

Congratulations – she'd finally hit rock bottom.

18

Jessica leant back into the train seat and closed her eyes, even though Archie was still talking from the seat opposite. 'Three hundred quid *each*?'

She pushed her head into the slot between the seat and the wall, replying without opening her eyes: 'You're not paying.'

'That's not the point – three hundred quid for a train ticket from Manchester to London?'

'It's because it was peak time.'

'Sod that, we could have flown for less.'

'Yes but we'd spend forty-five minutes trying to check in while some bored woman looked at us like we'd just insulted her mum. Then you get the security guards feeling you up. I don't know about you but that's really not my thing.'

'Depends on the security guard, I suppose. If there's any tidy twenty-somethings, I'd be up for it.'

'I'm sure that's how all the successful relationships start – being groped at an airport. It'd give a good story for the wedding breakfast anyway. But that's not even the worst part – what about the food at an airport, or on a plane? It's like eating your own feet.'

'Have you ever tried eating your own feet?'

'When I was in primary school, this Jamie Lambert kid

stole my shoes and socks and wouldn't give them back until I'd put my big toe in my mouth.'

'You're *that* flexible?'

Through her closed eyelids, Jessica could sense Archie's eyes popping out of his head. She let him have his fantasy for a few seconds and then crushed it. 'I was only about seven. I can barely touch my own toes now.'

'Oh. Anyway, three hundred quid *each* – we could've got a taxi for less than that. I could've got my mate to drive us down and back for two hundred tops. We could—'

'Can you let me sleep?'

'What am I going to do for two and a bit hours?'

'Read? Pontificate? Think long and hard about man's inhumanity to man? I don't care.'

'Pfft – some mate you are.'

Some clown on the tracks at Watford, something about leaves, a soggy sandwich and three and a half hours later the train rolled into Euston. By then, Archie was practically climbing the walls; his phone was almost out of battery, his list of ways they could've got to London for less than a combined six hundred pounds largely exhausted. Although hiring a pair of ostriches and pointing them in the right direction was something that Jessica would have certainly been up for.

Jessica checked the maps in the train station, trying to figure out the best way to get to Hackney. She turned to Archie, who was flicking up the collar on his coat and sniffing the air suspiciously. 'Aren't you going to help?' she asked.

'Help what?'

'I don't know where we're going.'

'So let's get a taxi.'

'I thought you were against spending money unnecessarily?'

'To be honest, I feel a bit dirty being this far south. It's like cheating on your missus, innit?'

Jessica leant closer, wondering if she'd heard correctly. 'It's not like that at all.'

He shook his head, pushing his top lip out. 'Nah, not for me, this place. Let's not arse about – don't wanna spend any longer here than I have to.'

'You come from Manchester!'

He rocked his shoulders forward as if he had a nervous tic. 'Aye, what's your point?'

Jessica shook her head. 'Nothing – fine, we'll get a taxi.'

Their journey across London was punctuated by the driver who couldn't stop talking about Tottenham, and Archie who was seemingly up for a ruck about anything. It ended with him slamming the door and telling the driver to 'come back when you've got as many titles as us, pal'.

He turned to Jessica, shaking his head and poking a thumb towards the departing vehicle. 'Can you believe that guy?'

'I'm just wondering how my life has come to sitting in the back of a cab listening to two blokes argue about football.'

'It's not my fault – he got my hackles up when he started talking about that ref at Old Trafford, I mean—'

'All right, United are better than Tottenham – happy? Now shut up and let me do the talking.'

Richard Froggatt wasn't exactly how Jessica would have imagined someone who'd done almost four years in prison for robbery and was still on probation. Especially given her encounter the previous day, she'd been expecting somebody with strong, battle-hardened skin, scars, short hair and tattoos. Instead, Froggatt was thin with shoulder-length hair, glasses which he wore on a chain around his neck, and a blazer with matching blue cord trousers. He welcomed Jessica and Archie into his flat and disappeared off to put the kettle on as Archie poked through the bookcases in his living room.

'London type,' he said dismissively.

Jessica sat in an armchair that had a good view of the street. 'What do you mean by that?'

Archie pulled a thick book off the shelf. 'Look at what he's reading; all people banging on about their feelings. Typical southern sort.'

'I don't think I've ever seen you like this. You're actually offended that he's chosen to live here, aren't you?'

'Well, why would you?'

'Because the sun comes out down here.'

Archie put the book back and turned to face her. 'What are you trying to say?'

'Oh for God's sake – can we stop doing this every time I point out that London isn't the hole you think it is and Manchester isn't all ambrosia and light either. They both have their good sides and they both have their bad sides. Let's leave it at that.'

Archie straightened his shirt. 'Aye, let's leave it at that. For now.'

Jessica knew Archie was proud of his area but this was ridiculous. She'd joked that he'd never left the place but the more she thought about it, the more she realised he never told stories about where he'd been on holiday. Almost every experience involved 'being out in town', while the only time he mentioned other places in the UK was when he talked about the away grounds he'd visited with Manchester United. Until she'd taken the plunge and moved into a residential home a little outside of the city, Jessica's mother had been the same, spending most of her life in the same village. With Archie, it wasn't just familiarity, it was that he was genuinely baffled why anyone would choose to live elsewhere if Manchester was an option. She'd thought he had enough of an issue with people from Liverpool but that was nothing compared to his contempt for those who lived in the south.

'Have you ever been to London?' she asked.

He nodded. 'We beat Palace down here a few years ago – plus I've been to QPR.'

'Have you ever been down for a reason other than football?'

He shrugged. 'Why would I?'

Jessica didn't have a reply but Froggatt returned shortly afterwards with a tray, teapot, three cups and six bourbon biscuits.

He might have robbed a few houses but Richard Froggatt sure knew how to entertain.

'Thanks for agreeing to see us, Mr Froggatt,' Jessica said, introducing herself and Archie.

He sipped his tea one minuscule slurp at a time. 'Not a problem, though you do realise I'm completely reformed now?'

They all say that.

'Obviously; I understand the book is going well?'

'Oh, marvellously, yes. It's a big thing now, isn't it? Write a book when you get out of prison. I wrote every word of mine – no ghostwriter needed.'

He laughed at what Jessica wasn't sure was a joke. She didn't smile either way. 'Well, I suppose everyone's got a book deal nowadays. Anyway, you've done really well for the victims not to come after you with a civil case considering it could be seen as profiting from a crime.'

Froggatt frowned but Jessica remembered she was actually here to get information from him, not wind him up, so she moved on quickly. 'I'll be honest; I've not had time to read your book all the way through but I have gone through a few passages and I was particularly interested in the fact that you gave away some of the money you stole.'

He smiled. 'Aah, chapter seventeen. One of my favourites.'

Jessica hadn't read a word of it.

'Why did you do that?'

Froggatt took another small sip of the tea, making a loud slurping noise. 'I've seen the stories in the news these past few days about someone doing the same in Manchester. Very interesting.'

'What's interesting?'

'I'd love to know what their motivation is.'

'If we catch whoever it is, I'll see if I can stick in a prison visit for you.'

Slurrrrrrrrrrrrrrrp and a thin smile.

'Do you know the truth about Robin Hood?'

'Is there one?'

He nodded, grinning. 'A very perceptive question – he was known as Robin of Loxley, of course. Loxley is a place near Sheffield, then there are all sorts of references to *a* "Robin" being in Yorkshire, not Nottingham. There are rhymes, poems, stories, all dating back to that period – but the truth is, no one can say for absolute certain whether he actually existed. There was most likely *someone* named Robin, perhaps many people. He might have even been a thief – but none of that means that the Robin Hood as people think of him is real. All of the stuff about King Richard is a twentieth-century invention.'

'What are you saying?'

Slurrrrrrrrrrrrrrrp.

'Sometimes the myth is enough. If television programmes and movies keep telling you over and over that Robin Hood robbed from the rich and gave to the poor then suddenly he's a hero in everyone's mind.'

'Is that what you were trying to be?'

Slurrrrrrrrrrrrrrrp.

He shook his head. 'You've missed my point. It's not about *being* a hero; it's about *looking* like one.'

Jessica had a drink of her own tea, wondering if Archie had got the point quicker than she had. She hoped not.

'Look at it this way,' Froggatt continued. 'We got away with a quarter of a million in cash. We gave away a tenth of that and everyone thought we were the good guys. What do you think we were doing with the rest of it?' Suddenly Jessica got it – so did Froggatt, seeing in her eyes that the penny had dropped. He grinned widely and she could see how conniving he was. 'Exactly. I was trying to buy something from a garage and only had fifty-pound notes on me. The attendant asked where it came from. I gave him a nod and a wink and that was it – he assumed I'd been one of the lucky few who'd been given money on the street. It was a badge of honour. He was turning it over in his hands.'

'How did you get caught?'

Froggatt's face fell slightly. 'That's the problem with working with amateurs. I knew what I was doing and everything was going well, then one of the others got caught drink-driving. The police had no idea who he was or what he'd done but he had a bag of notes in the back and couldn't think of a cover story quickly enough. If he'd had any sense, he would've said that someone in a mask had given the money to him in a pub. There's always one, eh?'

He shrugged at Jessica but she could hardly disagree – the truth was most of their cases were solved by someone being careless.

Froggatt didn't have a lot else to say and with Archie fidgeting endlessly, there wasn't much of a reason to stay.

After finishing their tea, they made their way back to the train station, with Archie thankfully quiet. Considering how anti-London he'd been not long before, he seemed particularly taken by the small Euston Tap pub just outside the station. Aside from a row of barrels and taps behind the barman and a list of ales and prices written on a black-board, there wasn't much to the place but it was still marvellously unique, though she doubted Archie would admit as much.

He ordered something cloudy for the pair of them and then spent five minutes whinging about 'London prices' as Jessica ummed and ahhed in the right places, thinking things through.

'. . . imagine if you were down here for a day out? Three hundred nicker on the train, then eight quid a pint – what's the world come to? I mean—'

Jessica cut across him. 'Stop moaning for a moment. Froggatt had a good point about the money but it's not quite the same with our case, is it? Our guys stole a lot less cash and they've given plenty of it away, so it still comes down to the jewellery. He's right about the smoke and mirrors. Look at all the journalists outside the station yesterday: they weren't talking about the jewellery, they were asking about the cash – and that's only a small proportion of what's been taken.'

Archie seemed slightly taken aback at being cut off mid-flow. 'I thought you said the robbers weren't very clever?'

'I don't know – maybe they are. We've still not got a clue who they are, so they're smarter than me. Do me a favour and call the station, will you? I can't bring myself to go through Pat.'

Archie held up his phone. 'No battery.'

'Sod it, I'll call Iz instead. She always knows what's going on.'

Jessica pressed Izzy's name and waited for the reply.

'How's London?' Izzy asked by means of a hello.

'Archie hates it. I think he might start a second civil war if we stay down here past tonight. What's going on up there?'

'Didn't anyone call you?'

'Should they have?'

'We got Pavel's criminal record through from Serbia.'

Jessica could tell from Izzy's tone that this wasn't a straightforward revelation. 'What's in it?'

'Are you sitting down?'

'No, Archie wanted to stand. I think he thinks it makes him look harder.' She glanced across at him, smiling. 'It certainly doesn't make him look taller.'

'Right – well, back in Serbia, Pavel did three years for breaking into houses as part of a gang. There were five of them; all wearing black, one of them with a gun. They tied the owners up, took everything valuable and made a break for it.' Jessica started to reply but Izzy cut her off: 'There's one other thing – it's what they were known for. They hardly ever got away with cash: it was mainly jewellery.'

19

Jessica sat in the Euston Station Burger King staring at the departures board, determined not to order anything unhealthy. Across the table, Archie munched his way through a Whopper, talking with his mouth full. 'It's bloody London, that's what it is. The trains are running late, the food tastes shite—'

'Is that why you've eaten two burgers?'

'I've been Hank Marvin all day – a man's got to eat.'

'You've been what?'

'Hank Marvin – starving. Haven't you picked any of this up living in Manchester?'

'No, I have this strange habit of using the actual words. Anyway – tell me what you think about Pavel.'

Mayonnaise was stuck to Archie's bottom lip and a soggy flap of lettuce dropped to the floor. 'I told you before. The victims pretty much all agree that our guy with the gun is a northerner but it could be Pavel's plan and he's one of the ones under the balaclavas. It would explain why none of them speak – the minute they open their mouths and that accent comes out, the householders would know it was someone foreign.'

'But he was a big guy – he towered over me and he had hair coming out of everywhere. Wouldn't one of the people robbed have mentioned that one of the people who broke in was a giant?'

Archie screwed three fries into his mouth. 'How long did you see him for?'

'A few seconds.'

'Perhaps he just seemed bigger because, well, you're not.'

'You're one to talk.'

'Aye, well, good things come in small packages.'

'Pavel's height is listed in his file, so it's not just me.'

Archie nodded and took a slurp of his drink. Jessica wondered if everyone was this annoying when they were eating fast food. 'I don't know – if he wasn't the one robbing those houses then it's quite a coincidence that it's on his record. People react in funny ways when they've got a gun stuffed in their face. Who knows if their memories are reliable?'

It was a reasonable point but Jessica didn't believe any of the victims would forget the huge bloke she'd seen – unless Archie was right about that too and he'd seemed more intimidating to her than he actually was.

On her phone, Jessica re-read the email Izzy had sent. The Serbian authorities had never tracked down what had happened to the items Pavel and his gang had stolen, nor recovered the money. He'd been sentenced to fifteen years in prison for the robberies, which were far more violent than the ones in the UK. After a little over three years, he'd had the conviction overturned for a reason that hadn't been detailed. The next thing anyone knew, he was in a British court for driving without a licence.

No one seemed to know how he'd got into the country, let alone how he'd managed to hang around without being deported – but therein lay the unique relationship between the police, the border authorities and the government. The border agency didn't want to admit they'd somehow let him in; the police wouldn't say they'd arrested him and taken him to court, where he'd been allowed to walk away again; while the government didn't want to know about any mistakes that could linked to the phrase 'funding cuts'. No one said a word to anyone else unless it somehow found its way into the media – and then all the talking was done through press officers with pithy soundbites and clever language to deflect the blame onto anyone who wasn't in their particular department. Jessica had seen it play out far too many times before to bother worrying about whose fault it was that Pavel was now apparently on the streets of Manchester. Regardless of whose responsibility it was, he was their problem now.

Archie continued to eat as Jessica read the email with Pavel's details another time. On the table next to them, a man was having an irate mobile phone conversation, apparently oblivious he was in a public place. '. . . you tell him I'll fly to Paris and do it myself then . . . What? I couldn't give a flying, er, hyena . . . if he's just got in from Melbourne . . . That's a complete load of bollocks. I told him not to make that payment . . . Geoff, Geoff, Geoff – will you listen to me, Geoff? All I'm saying is that I own forty-nine per cent of this company and . . . Geoff?'

Jessica rolled her eyes at Archie, who mouthed the words: 'London type'.

She peered up at the long row of orange and red on the departures board. Delayed, cancelled, cancelled, delayed, delayed . . . How hard was it to run a train on time? She didn't bother to mention it because she'd only get Archie's three hundred quid rant again – although those ostriches seemed like an even better idea now.

Archie continued eating and talking, mainly listing the ways Manchester was better than London. Jessica made a few vague half-hearted noises that sounded like they might be in agreement.

'The air's cleaner up there, innit?' (No.)

'Manchester's got this feel to it; a sort of buzz.' (No it hasn't.)

'It's all about the characters. What's a city without people? No one wants to say hello to you down here.' (Or up there.)

'Look at all the coffee shops – it's mocha-this and cappa-that. Round my way, you can still go into the local caff and ask for a white coffee and get one out of a polystyrene cup. That's what Britain was built on; none of this airy-fairy nonsense.' (There's plenty of that in Manchester too.)

'Where can I go and get black pudding in a barm around here? It's like another world.' (That did sound good right about now.)

'What's with the accents? Every other person's a bloody Aussie down here.' (He did have a point about that.)

'. . . And why's it all so expensive? If I was going to spend half-a-mil on a house, I'd want a mansion with a hot tub – not some poky shoebox.' (He also had a point there.)

'. . . Then you have all the football lot mouthing off. I mean, I hate the dippers but at least they've won a few European Cups—'

'Arch.'

'What?'

'Give it a rest. If you really want to go through all of this, put it in an email and send it to me. I promise I'll print it out, give it the briefest of glances, and then throw it in the bin.'

'All right. I was just saying . . .' He paused, eating his final chip. 'So what's going on with you?'

'Sorry?'

He shrugged. 'We've got two hours to kill and nothing to do – and that's before we get on the train. If you don't want to hear me talking then we've got to do something. My phone's out of battery and there's sod all to do around here.'

Jessica realised the biggest reason she was confused was that in all the time she'd been going out drinking with him, she couldn't ever remember him asking about her life.

'Do you really want to know?' she asked.

'Aye, why not?'

'All right, well, I have two teenage girls living in my house at the moment and—'

Archie's mouth flopped open. '*Two?*'

'Oh, for God's sake . . .'

He closed it again, suppressing a smirk. 'Sorry, go on.'

'You do realise that there's nothing at all sexual about three women living in a house together. One of them is seventeen and I'm looking after her; the other's nineteen and she's staying over temporarily because we're using her flat to stake out Ana's in case Pavel comes around.'

'If you say so.'

His lop-sided grin was so ridiculous that Jessica couldn't stop herself from giggling too.

And she continued laughing.

When Archie wasn't blathering about why Manchester was the greatest city in the world, he was quite fun to hang around with. He told her stories about the estate he grew up on, including the man who had a pet donkey and the woman who he insisted kept a partially deflated football as a hybrid pet/surrogate child. It turned out that his father had been what some would call 'a character' but which others would refer to as 'a criminal'. It seemed that a lot of delivery drivers had 'accidents' close to the Davey residence and that their evenings were punctuated by various locals popping around to see if there were any knock-off electrical items going spare.

As they finally took their seats on the train, Archie delivered the punchline: 'I spent years thinking things really were falling off the back of lorries.'

'Give over.'

'No, seriously. It's all anyone would ever say around my house. I'd come downstairs in the morning and there'd be a dozen video players. I'd ask where they'd come from and my dad or my brother would go, "They fell off the back of a lorry". I'd be at school with my mates going on about how careless drivers were round our estate. We'd sit on the edge of the main road watching the vans going past in case anything fell off.'

'Are you having me on?'

'Seriously! I really wanted a Scalextric and we'd wait on this low wall when the Woolworths and Argos vans zoomed past. I figured they were the most likely to have something fall off.'

'How old were you when the penny dropped?'

'Thirteen? Fourteen?'

'How stupid were you?'

Archie's shoulders twitched. 'All right – I was only a kid. If your mum and dad told you something every day, you'd go around believing it, wouldn't you?'

'Sorry . . .'

'Nah, you're probably right. I must've been a right thicko. One time we had five tellies in our living room and my dad said they'd come off a lorry. I was asking how they'd fallen off without smashing and he said they fell into a bush.'

Jessica laughed, just as the woman with the refreshments trolley came past, asking if they wanted anything. Considering the length of the day she'd had, plus the fact Manchester was another two and a half hours away, Jessica only had one thing on her mind: 'I'll have two mini-bottles of your rosé and one of white.'

The woman was wearing a smart dark blue suit. She pulled out a drawer, peered inside and shook her head. 'Sorry, because everything was running late, we didn't have time to do a full restock.'

'What do you have?'

'Water.'

Jessica had already taken her purse out but held it in mid-air. *'Water?'*

'Still or sparkling.'

'That's it?'

'Sorry.'

Jessica said she didn't want anything and began sulking in the corner between her seat and the window.

Archie bought a bottle of water, suppressing a grin. 'I've got booze in if you want.'

'Yeah but you live out in Stretford and I've heard that's a right dump.' Jessica couldn't keep a straight face, bursting into laughter before Archie could be offended. 'What have you got in?'

'Bit of this, bit of that.'

'Fall off the back of a lorry into a bush, did it?'

This time it was Archie's turn to laugh.

Before Jessica knew what was going on, the evening had flown by and their train had arrived at Piccadilly Station. Jessica was walking out of the front doors with Archie as he smelled the air extravagantly, waving his arms around. In the dim street lights, he didn't look anywhere near the five foot eight he claimed.

'See, I told you – the air's cleaner up here.'

'It tastes just the same.'

'Sod off, does it.'

Ahead of them was a lone black cab on the taxi rank, the driver leaning back in his seat reading the *Daily Mail*.

Archie motioned towards it: 'I'll wait for the next one if you're going home.'

'Have you seen what he's reading? He'll probably murder me and dump me in a ditch somewhere.'

'Well, I can't come back to yours – you said I was banned because there are teenagers there.'

'You've definitely got booze in?'

'Duty paid, VAT paid, not off the back of a lorry. All kosher.'

'Fine, let's go back to yours then.'

Jessica yawned her way through the journey around the descrted streets of Manchester. The nights were beginning to get warmer as winter finally gave up its grip on the city but she was still shivering on the back seat. Their train should have got in hours ago and by now she would usually be in bed, or under a blanket with Bex, watching rubbish television. She sent the girl a message to say she was running late and then told Archie to stop fussing when he offered her his coat.

Archie's story started to change the closer they got to his flat as he said he didn't quite have the 'bit of this, bit of that' booze-wise that he'd promised. Instead, he had mainly bottles of ale and one of red wine someone had given him for Christmas.

As his key hovered close to the lock of his flat's door, he apologised for the mess and then swung the door inwards directly into his living room.

Jessica stepped inside, still shivering as Archie hurried through a door to put the heating on. She sat on his sofa, taking in the room: a poster with the slogan 'FIT' above a bikini-clad model, another poster with a woman bending over a car wearing even fewer clothes and a third one of the Manchester United team with some trophy.

Underneath his television was a games console and a pile of action movies, with the bin in the corner overflowing with lager cans.

When Archie returned, he could see it in her face: 'What's wrong?'

Jessica suddenly felt uncomfortable. 'I'm . . . not sure. I suppose I wasn't expecting this.'

'What?'

'It's like a student flat. You even have jeans drying on the radiator – then there are posters of girls, action movies . . . this isn't really my thing.'

Jessica edged into the corner of the sofa as Archie sat next to her holding two bottles of ale and offering her one.

'I've lived here for years. Most of that stuff's been up since my student days.'

Jessica took the bottle and started reading the label. 'So why didn't you take it down?'

He shrugged. 'Habit? I don't know. I'm still the same bloke you've been chatting to all day.' He nudged her bottle with his. 'If you don't want that, I can get you the wine in. I found a bottle of vodka under the sink too.'

'That'll do.'

The only glasses Archie had were pint ones, so Jessica found herself drinking vodka from the bottle like a proper alcoholic. She'd been wrong about hitting nine-year-olds marking a new low – or, at the very least, this wasn't helping her rise much further.

Archie switched the TV on and they ended up watching the talk show repeat, 'I was born a man but now I'm a woman – get over it', which would have been fine morally speaking if it wasn't for the fact that the women were accusing the men they'd married of keeping it a secret. This episode wasn't even funny but the presenter was in his element, mouthing off at all and sundry.

Drink, drink, drink.

'You off tomorrow?' Archie asked.

'I'm supposed to be. I'll probably go in anyway.'

'I swapped days – in tomorrow, off on Sunday. I'm going to Old Trafford – lunchtime kick-off.'

'Can we not talk about football?'

'Sorry . . .'

Drink, drink, drink.

They had nothing left to say to each other: work was work, football was football and she didn't want to talk about any of it.

It was only when Archie checked his watch for the third time that Jessica realised this was the moment. She could kid herself all she liked but the instant she'd got into a taxi with him, she'd known it was for one reason. She put the bottle on the floor, asked Archie which room was the bedroom and then took his hand, leading the way herself, unable to even look at him.

20

Jane checked the clock on the wall and then her watch: the bloody things matched. This was her third night in this darned flat and nothing was happening. Ana was sleeping upstairs, like all normal people at four in the morning. Jane could only wait downstairs until the morning handover crew arrived and she could nick off home to get some sleep before doing it all again the next day.

Whoever's idea it was to stake out this flat needed a good boot somewhere painful.

She turned to Andy and yawned. 'Go on a chip run, will you?'

'It's gone four – nowhere's open at this time.'

'I think there's a kebab shop on the main road – those places are always open.'

'For a reason – they're the absolute last resort. When everything else is closed and everybody's gone home, they're still serving the only people drunk or stupid enough to eat there.'

'How can this be a student flat when there's no food hidden anywhere? The cupboards are full of cleaning products – but no chocolate, no biscuits, no frozen pizzas. What's the world come to?'

She turned away from Andy back towards the monitors. It felt too creepy to watch a young woman sleep when she was oblivious to their presence, so both cameras were focused on the living room.

Andy shuffled on the seat, dropping his pile of comics on the floor. 'What did the day lot say?'

'I told you earlier – if you'd been here on time, you could've asked them yourself. And aren't you too old to be reading things like that?'

'You'd be surprised how adult they can be. Anyway, you're not my mum.'

'I'm ten years too young, you cheeky sod.'

'Just tell me.'

Jane couldn't be bothered stifling any more yawns, so she let rip in full jaw-dislocating glory. 'Fine – what's the name of that PC who wears trousers that are too tight?'

'PC Prince.'

'Aye, that dirty git was here all day, probably perving. You've got to have something wrong with you to be wearing trousers that tight. I mean, where does it all go? Do you tuck it between your legs or something?'

'Don't ask me.'

'He was here all day with that Poonam girl.'

'What did he say?'

'Mind your own business – get here on time.'

Jane directed her attention back towards the television, where the twenty-four-hour news was on loop. Something had blown up somewhere that wasn't Britain but Jane had no idea what was going on, even though she'd watched the same thing half-a-dozen times now. She was waiting for the entertainment news again.

She was about to start flicking through the channels when Andy held a hand up.

She turned to him, confused: 'What?'

'Did you hear that?'

'What?'

'Listen.'

Jane put the television remote control down and picked up the one for the monitoring system. She scrolled through the six cameras fitted into the flat above, but everything looked green because of the night vision, the lights off, Ana apparently sleeping.

Andy still had his hand in the air, squinting as if that could make him hear better.

Tap-tap-tap-tap.

Jane and Andy locked eyes. 'Did you hear that?' he whispered.

'Obviously – I'm not deaf.'

'What was it?'

'I'm not psychic either. Christ's sake, where did you do your training?'

Tap-tap-tap-tap.

Andy crept towards the front of the flat. 'I think there's someone at the door.'

Jane scrolled through the cameras again, even though she knew there wasn't one pointing at the outside door. She tiptoed across to join him.

'We could try peeping through the window,' he suggested.

'What if it's that Pavel bloke we're supposed to be waiting for?'

'Why would he be knocking here?'

'I have no idea – why would you go to all of this expense and not point a camera at the door? This is bloody typical of our lot. Half of them couldn't police a christening.'

Tap-tap-tap-tap.

Andy put a hand on the door: 'Shall I open it?'

'Two ticks.'

Jane dashed off to the kitchen, returning with a frying pan.

'Seriously?' he said.

'You get the pepper spray ready and I'll batter whoever it is.'

'What if it's one of ours?'

'Come off it – which of our bunch is going to be prowling the streets at four in the morning? Well, except Franks – Christ knows what he gets up to.'

Andy pulled his pepper spray from his pocket and took a step backwards as Jane rested a hand on the door. 'Count of three, right? You spray 'im, I twat 'im.'

Andy nodded.

'One, two, three . . .'

21

Tap-tap-tap-tap.

Jessica patted gently on the glass part of the front door. After sneaking out of Archie's, she had walked for half a mile or so in the direction of what she thought was the main road until she stumbled across a twenty-four-hour taxi office. She'd thought about going home and then, for whatever reason, had given Sam's address instead. She was tired but wondering if Pavel had shown up. It would be really nice, just for once, if things came together without her having to lose her mind. It would help to get Topper off her back too; especially now Pavel was potentially tied up in the robbery case. How she'd gone from doing Bex a favour to this, she wasn't entirely sure.

And why weren't Joy Bag and Andy Whatshisface answering the door? She couldn't tap any louder, else she might disturb Ana and whoever else was upstairs – which would *really* go down well with Topper.

Tap-tap-tap-tap.

'Come on,' she muttered under her breath, wondering if she should try knocking on the window. Just as she stepped to the side, the door was wrenched open and the shape of a frying pan came careering down into the spot where her head had been moments before. Jessica ducked instinctively.

There was a blur of motion as she slipped backwards onto her arse and two heads popped out of the door at the same time, pepper spray and frying pan on hand.

Just as Joy Bag Jane looked as if she was about to take another swing at Jessica, realisation dawned on her face and she pulled out.

'Oh, it's you,' she said.

'You nearly bloody killed me!'

Joy Bag Jane shrugged. 'It's only a frying pan – it'd have been a glancing blow.'

Jessica gingerly got to her feet, trying to keep her voice low but pointing an accusing finger. 'You two lunatics have gone mad with cabin fever.'

She pushed past them into the house, taking a seat on the sofa and waiting for Andy and Joy Bag to join her – frying pan and pepper spray now conspicuous by their absence.

'We thought you were that Pavel guy,' Andy said.

He was one of the younger constables Jessica vaguely recognised: all sandy hair and enthusiasm. That'd soon drain away once he'd been on a few death knocks. As for Jane, she was looking more sour-faced than usual. She'd had it in for Jessica ever she'd been christened 'Joy Bag', even though it wasn't Jessica's fault. Well, it was a little seeing as she'd sent her out on the search but that was perhaps ten per cent of the responsibility at most.

'Why would Pavel be knocking on your door?' Jessica asked.

'I don't know – there's no camera or peephole and we couldn't exactly check through the letterbox, could we?'

Jessica turned her attention to Jane: 'What's with the frying pan?'

She shrugged. 'We didn't have much time to think – we thought we might be attacked!'

'All right, keep your voice down.' Jessica took in the surroundings – Sam must have had a proper tidy-up before she went to Jessica's house because there was no way a bunch of coppers would keep anything this clean. 'Where are the leftover chips?' Jessica asked.

Jane picked up a remote from the sofa and started changing channels on the television. 'What chips?' She waved the remote in Andy's direction. 'Everywhere's closed and *he* won't go down the kebab house.'

Jessica shook her head in utter disdain. 'Call yourself police officers – this is day one of training.' She pointed a finger towards Andy, making him shy away. 'Whoever's the most junior goes on the chip run – quarter to ten at the latest. Get double what you need and then you've got plenty left for second helpings. Don't they teach you anything nowadays?'

Jane threw both hands up. 'I told him that.'

Andy frowned. 'They told us to keep two people here at all times.'

Jessica shook her head. 'Pfft – they always say that. It's not as if you're going to the toilet together, is it? Nipping out to the chippy is exactly the same – but twice as important. Honestly, this is basic stuff. How did you ever pass anything?'

'Surprisingly, we didn't do a module on chip runs.'

'And look where it got you – hungry at four in the morning with no chips.'

'What are you doing here anyway?' Andy had clearly responded more harshly than he meant to because he cowered away slightly, lowering his voice for the final word.

Jessica could feel Jane watching her too, wondering the same thing. She looked from one officer to the other. 'I'm here because I'm a professional and I was wondering how things were going.'

She was definitely getting worse at lying – that was convincing no one. Trying to dig herself out of the hole, she kept talking: 'I've been in London all day, well, yesterday – how's it gone?'

Jane exchanged a glance with Andy that Jessica couldn't read but it looked like she was annoyed: 'The daytime crew reckon Ana spent the whole time in the flat watching television.'

'Any phone calls?'

'Nothing.'

'No visitors?'

'Not a peep – lucky girl. I'd love a day alone without people bothering me all the time. Every time I'm on a day off, I've got the kids needing this, that and the other. My other half's useless too. Then you nip into the garden for two minutes and the postman chooses that moment to try to deliver something and you have to go trekking off to the sorting office. It's a bloody nightmare.'

Jessica suspected Ana had probably had a marginally worse time of it given what she'd been through with the multitude of men passing through her flat. Although she hadn't expected the surveillance to be an immediate success, Jessica had thought *something* might happen.

She yawned, wondering if there was any coffee in the house. 'This is quickly turning into a monumental balls-up – even by our standards. We can't find his wife either and she's English.'

Jane at least knew what she was talking about: 'Is that Rosemary something?'

'Adamek or Dean – we don't really know. There's no one by that name working or claiming benefits. She's disappeared into thin air and, given who her husband is, that can't be a good thing. The last thing we need is a body showing up when we've got a warrant out for him.'

'If it's any consolation, her upstairs was acting a bit odd tonight.'

'What was she doing?'

'Nothing – that was the point. Just sitting and watching the clock – like she was waiting for something.'

Or someone . . .

22

Jessica hung around at Sam's flat for as long as she thought she could get away with while not seeming weirder than either Andy Whatshisface or Joy Bag thought she already was. A little after half six, she walked to the main road and dropped into a small grimy-looking café. She sent Bex another message to let her know she was safe and then tucked into a full English with double toast and three coffees. Her clothes felt itchy and uncomfortable seeing as she'd spent the whole of the previous day in them, with the late-night detour to Archie's seeming like more of a dream than something she'd actually done.

After debating whether she should go home for a wash, Jessica caught the bus to Longsight and did something she always hated doing – she used the staff shower. The water was never hot, the pressure was always a dribble, and she was forever in fear that someone – probably DI Franks – would wander into the women's changing rooms 'by accident'.

Despite that and her general sense of feeling partially hungover, there was some good news waiting in her email. The geeks at Bradford Park had pulled themselves away from watching *Star Trek* marathons for long enough to recover a deleted text message from Pavel's phone that had been found in Ana's flat.

'C&A at 11. Wk Weds.'

They had found the phone on a Tuesday, so it didn't take much to figure out that something was happening on the coming Wednesday at eleven – perhaps in the morning but probably at night.

That just meant they had to find out what 'C&A' referred to.

Jessica was supposed to be on a day off but reckoned it couldn't do any harm to try to work out what the note meant. She grabbed half-a-dozen constables, Izzy, a laptop, eight teas, half a packet of Pat's Hobnobs that he hadn't hidden well enough behind reception, and held a low-key morning briefing in the far corner of the canteen.

The Hobnobs barely lasted three minutes.

Aside from crumbs, the only thing they produced between them was that there used to be a large C&A department store in Manchester's Arndale shopping centre before the chain closed down. One of the constables checked the Internet to show that there had actually been two, with a second one on Oldham Street around five minutes away. They went through the maps and the handful of old photographs available but there was nothing that seemed relevant. If someone wanted to meet Pavel in the Arndale, why wouldn't he just say? As for Oldham Street, most of that area had been extensively renovated in the years since the store had closed, so how would they even know?

There was a chance that the initials could refer to something in a foreign language, even though the rest of the message was in English. Jessica said she'd give Katerina a call to see if she had any idea.

With the meeting still four days away, they at least had a little time to try to draw things together. Coupled with the surveillance of Ana, it gave them two strands in their pursuit of Pavel – but potentially a worry that whatever was planned for Wednesday was something they had no other intelligence on at all. He was a man wanted on a murder charge, with a missing wife, a young woman he was apparently pimping out, and a criminal record for burglaries that had striking similarities to the ones they were investigating. Not only that but – according to DCI Topper at least – it was Jessica's fault he had escaped. All in all, making sure they were at Wednesday's meeting, if only to nab Pavel, was an absolute necessity.

As Jessica sent everyone back to work, Izzy hung around, scraping into the bottom of the biscuit packet for a few lone crumbs. 'How was London?'

'Southern. Archie moaned the entire time.'

Izzy nodded without looking up, still delving. 'I heard you made a guest appearance in the early hours of the morning.'

'Joy Bag nearly killed me with a frying pan.'

'How come you were up so early?'

'Couldn't sleep.'

'Yet you're in a work suit, even though you didn't have to be in today – almost as if you were wearing the same one you had on yesterday.'

Izzy finally peered up, eyebrow raised imperceptibly. Jessica couldn't meet her gaze because it was so clear she knew what had happened. Her other colleagues wouldn't have seen the clues if Jessica had walked in with the word 'stop-out' inked onto her forehead. The signs were all there: slightly crumpled suit, wet hair because she'd showered at the station, unnecessary early morning visit . . . the fact she'd spent the whole of the previous day with Archie. And, of course, what had happened to Adam.

The rest of them might be oblivious but not Iz.

'I was just up and about early,' Jessica replied, refusing to give anything up that she didn't have to.

Izzy nodded, not wanting to push things. 'Are you staying around for long?'

'Why?'

'I was going through the overnights and thought there was something that might interest you.'

'I'm not here. This is a hologram.'

'Suit yourself.'

Izzy started to stand but Jessica sighed. 'Go on then, what is it?'

'Everyone's favourite bankrupt – Martin Teague.'

'What's he done now?'

Izzy held out a printout: 'The usual. If you're going home, DI Franks can sort it.'

'Sod that – he's such an idiot he'll go talk to Teague and walk away having bought a half-finished rollercoaster.'

'Want some company?'

'I thought you were busy?'

'I'm not talking about me . . .'

Jessica drove the pool car in silence through the streets of Manchester towards the area where Hulme bordered Moss Side, not far from the city centre. DC Rowlands was similarly quiet in the passenger seat. At any point over the previous few years, he would have been making cracks about her driving while she would have been having digs about everything from his hair to his latest break-up. She could still remember the moment when she thought he'd been shot: a few seconds of utter panic in which she didn't know how to react, where everything they had seen and done together seared through her mind. It had changed everything about their relationship – and then he, Garry Ashford and Jessica had sat in a café and he'd said the two sentences that she couldn't forget.

'What do you think they're going to do?' he had asked.

Jessica hadn't known what he meant. From her point of view, she had identified the person who'd killed a student and dumped him in a bin. She had dismissed Rowlands with barely a concern – *'About what?'* Even when he'd spelled it out – *'About you'* – she had thought nothing of it. Somehow, she had missed the bigger picture and then her car had blown up with Adam inside.

Her car.

'What do you think they're going to do . . . About you?'

Why hadn't Jessica listened to Rowlands when it was so obvious he had a point? After figuring out who had killed that student, she'd known there was something deeper going on – and yet she hadn't thought it could come back to her. Was it arrogance? Stupidity? Naivety?

Since then, she had little to say to Rowlands because she couldn't look him in the eye. Similarly, what could he say to her? They were strangers dressed up as people who had once been the best of mates.

After spending five minutes trying to come up with something, all Jessica could offer was: 'How are the shifts going?'

Perhaps surprised that she'd spoken, Dave took a moment to reply: 'Not too bad. The nights were awkward at first but you get used to it.'

More silence.

A minute or two later, it was Dave who tried to break it: 'Archie's on one today – worse than usual. He was sitting at his desk grumbling about various things and then saying how he hated working weekends, even though he'd swapped days so he could go to the United match tomorrow. He snapped at one of the girls just because she asked if he took sugar.'

'It's probably his time of the month.'

Dave didn't laugh and Jessica didn't feel much better either. It felt like the end of an era. Her life had changed when she'd been promoted to detective sergeant and Jack Cole had moved up to detective inspector. Since then, Cole had quit, DI Jason Reynolds had been forced out, DC Carrie Jones had died – and now the one person who'd gone through all of that with her might as well not be there either.

Trying to put it all to the back of her mind, Jessica pulled up outside Martin Teague's house and double-checked the address against what she had written down.

Archie had said that Teague now lived in the council house his wife had grown up in but this was such a far cry from a mansion with a rollercoaster that even Jessica felt a twinge of sorrow for what had happened to him, no matter how much of it was down to his own stupidity. The tight, winding road had identical houses on either side, each with a dark tiled lower half, a cream upper floor and a matching tiled roof. Everything was dull but that had nothing to do with the weather. Even from where she was standing by her car, Jessica could see two skips, three cars each with a wheel missing, a row of rusting motorbikes on someone's driveway and a vandalised green telephone exchange box sitting next to a lamppost. On the bend, there was a row of garages with its paint peeling, cars parked outside, more scrap. If an area could be judged by the number plates on the vehicles parked nearby then there wasn't a car made in the past seven years.

If he hadn't wasted all of his lottery winnings, then Martin Teague could have bought the entire street and everyone's car and still had change from his nine point eight million.

Dave offered the plainest of shrugs and they headed along the crumbling path to the faux cherry wood double-glazed door of Teague's house. Inside, a Chemical Brothers song blared to such a degree that Jessica could feel the door trembling as she reached for the bell.

After the third ring, the music went quiet and the door finally swung inwards. A thick-set man took one look at Jessica and Dave, turned around and called 'See ya, Mart', and then hurried past them without another word. Behind him was a man who was instantly familiar.

Throughout the press coverage of his rise and fall, there

had been many photos taken of Martin Teague as he went from a relatively normal-looking man to a bloated, red-faced, fat-cheeked slob. Not only had he blown his cash with a whirlwind wedding on a hired island, he'd spent it on stuffing his face and drinking to excess. By the time his bankruptcy hearing was in court, he had no clothes that fitted, his suit jacket unbuttoned, thighs battling against the material of his trousers, shirt buttons close to bursting.

Teague stood in the doorway wearing a pair of cotton trousers and a dressing gown but he had lost a lot of weight; there was an elasticity to the skin around his cheeks. The hair he'd had in court had now been shaved off and he was missing one of his front teeth.

He knew instantly who they were: 'What do you lot want?'

Jessica stepped forward so he couldn't close the door on them – well, not without smacking her first. 'We were wondering if you fancied going halves on a scratchcard? I'll put a pound in, you put a pound in, you do the scratching and we split everything down the middle if we win.'

'What?'

Jessica edged ahead again until she had one foot inside Teague's hallway, making him take a step back. 'I was thinking that if you won a few more quid, it'd stop you being such a nuisance to the rest of the community.'

Without giving him an option, Jessica skipped forward, leaving just enough room for Rowlands to edge in behind her and squeeze the door closed. Teague seemed so surprised at her audacity that he didn't point out the fact he hadn't invited her in.

He scratched his head, thick wrinkles appearing as he did so. 'Oh aye, someone been on the blower moaning again, have they? Who was it this time – that bitch next door?'

'Where's the kettle?'

'What?'

Jessica pointed a thumb over her shoulder. 'I'm milk no sugar and so's he. The quicker we get this over and done with, the quicker I can get home.'

'I don't know why you keep coming around sticking your beaks in.'

Jessica took her ID out and held it up to make things official, even though she was already inside and he didn't seem fussed who she was. 'Because you've already been bound over for breaching the peace and according to the call we had last night, it looks like you might owe the court fifty quid. At the station I'm known as Charitable Jess – well, among other things – and I thought it'd be your lucky day. Instead of coming over and making you turn your pockets out, I thought I'd pop around, have a quick brew and see if there's any way I can help. Now where's your fragrant other half?'

Teague stood staring at her. She'd spoken so quickly that he was taking a few moments to take it all in.

'Who?'

'Tania – where is she? I could do with having a word with the pair of you.'

'She's upstairs.'

Jessica pointed to the stairs he was standing next to. 'Those ones? Not quite another dimension, is it – so it should be easy enough to get her down. Now pop the kettle on and we can have a cosy little chinwag.'

Teague twisted a watch around on his wrist, the past two minutes finally catching up with him. 'You can't just come in here – I know my rights.'

'Yeah, yeah – I've heard it all before. Blah-di-blah this, I-know-my-rights that. Just stick the kettle on, or we'll get you down the station and start asking how you intend to pay that fifty quid.'

Teague looked from Jessica to Rowlands and then turned sheepishly on his tail. She heard Rowlands mutter the word '*charitable?*' and suppressed a smile. Talk quickly and sound confident – easy when you knew how, though it helped if you didn't trip over an errant gym bag when you strutted into the kitchen trying to act like a big shot.

As she righted herself, Jessica scowled at the bag, squeezing the yoga mat back down towards the bottom and re-folding a towel, then shoving it into the corner as if the incident had never happened. Teague was at least doing as he'd been told and had apparently missed her accident because of the gush of water into the kettle.

The kitchen didn't look as if it had been done up in twenty years: cracked tiles above a built-in cooker that was more brown than the white it had once been; grubby, stained counter tops; a draining board with ingrained white scum streaks and a mould-blotched roller blind. Even the slimiest of estate agents would struggle to sell this kitchen as anything other than something that needed ripping out in favour of starting again.

Teague nodded towards the open doorway where Dave was standing. 'Through there.'

Jessica led the way into a living room that was almost as out of date as the kitchen. Brown cord sofas, worn crimson carpet, peeling wallpaper with a raised flowery pattern, falling-apart flat-packed furniture – and dog hairs: lots of them. Jessica peered both ways into the room but there was no sign of the offending mongrel, so she took a seat on the sofa. Music videos were playing on the television with the sound on mute but aside from a few celebrity magazines scattered on the floor and some photographs on the wall, there was little else of anything. Nine point eight million quid and this is what they were left with.

Teague soon entered with two mugs of tea, giving Jessica one that had a large chip missing from it, and then shunting one towards Rowlands and spilling some on the floor to an accompaniment of swearing. He sat in a squeaking armchair and put his feet up on the coffee table that looked as if it could collapse at any moment, reaching down to the gap between the chair and the wall to retrieve a beer can. He popped it open, took a large swig, and leant backwards.

'What d'yer want, then?'

Jessica peered into the pale orange of the liquid in her mug, thinking it was a shocking effort at tea-making. If a constable had made one like that, it would have been a disciplinary offence. 'What happened last night?' she asked.

Teague nodded towards the wall. 'That bitch been complaining again?'

'If you call your neighbour that one more time then we'll take you down the station for threatening behaviour. Over the past few months we've had more than one complaint from more than one person – so stop moaning about other people and get talking.'

'You've got quite a mouth on you, haven't ya?'

'So I'm told.'

'There weren't owt in it. All couples have the odd barney, don't they? What's the problem?'

'If you're shouting at each other at the top of your voices and it's keeping other people awake, then there's clearly a problem. As I said – this is a conversation we need to have with your wife as well.'

Teague nodded tersely and then rocked forward: 'TANIA!'

There was a half-second pause and then a woman's voice echoed from upstairs: 'WHAT?'

'GIT DOWN 'ERE.'

'WHY?'

'BECAUSE I FUCK-ING NEED YOU.'

'WHAT FOR?'

'BECAUSE I DO.'

Jessica was getting a sense of what the complaints were about.

There was a scraping on the ceiling above and then a couple of thumps before a scratch-scrape-scramble of claws on bare-wood stairs. Moments later and a small dog skidded into the living room. Jessica had no idea of the breed, but it was white, fluffy, and had that yappy look about it as if it didn't understand the 'shut up' command.

He/she/it took one look at Jessica and then scarpered back the way it came.

Click-clack-click-clack on the kitchen floor and then Tania Teague emerged into the living room, dressed in heels, tight jeans and a tighter jumper. She had straightened bleached-blonde hair tied back into a loose ponytail and overdone eye make-up. The dog was hanging around close to her feet. She looked from Jessica to Martin and back again. 'How can I help you, love?'

She smiled slightly and it didn't even sound as if she'd said it sarcastically.

Jessica decided to respond in kind, taking her ID from her pocket and holding it up: 'It's about last night. We keep getting complaints about noise, plus there was that one from the other month about the junk left in your front garden.'

The dog crept out from under Tania's feet and edged towards Jessica. Tania slapped her husband on the arm: 'That's you, that is. I keep telling you to keep your big gob shut.'

'You can fucking talk – always at the gym and chasing around after that bastarding dog.'

Tania gasped. 'You do realise Tinkerbell can hear you?'

The dog seemed more interested in sniffing Jessica's ankles than in taking offence. Teague took another large mouthful from his can and scrunched it up. Jessica hadn't even noticed him drinking it but he'd gone through the half-litre in barely a few minutes. He dropped it on the floor and reached down for another.

Tania crouched and picked up the can: 'For God's sake,

how hard is it to pick up after yourself? And why are you drinking so early? It's not even lunchtime.'

Teague mumbled something Jessica didn't catch, although the second word was definitely 'off'. Tania turned to Jessica: 'This is what I've got to put up with. Ever since we came back here, it's been like this – well, it wasn't me who spent all the money and it's not me who's missing it.'

Using his hand, Teague simulated a mouth opening and closing. 'Always flapping on. It wasn't *your* money anyway – *I* won it. Anyway, Parky, Steve and Hamish are coming around tonight, so make yourself scarce. Either that or you can put some food on.'

'Oh, piss off.'

Jessica hadn't particularly wanted to put herself in the middle of a domestic but it was looking increasingly as if she'd done just that.

'Personally, I couldn't care less about whatever's going on between the pair of you,' Jessica said, 'but you've caused us nothing but grief over the past few weeks. If we're not getting called out here, then we're dealing with incidents at the houses that were taken off you and put up for auction—'

Teague cut her off: 'That's why I pay my taxes – so you can have a job.'

'You didn't pay your tax – that's why you're living here instead of in a mansion with a rollercoaster.'

'Well, what do you lot want? It's not my fault – I can't be expected to keep a watch on houses I don't even own.'

'Maybe not but you can keep your trap shut when it's late at night and people want to get some kip.'

'It's not my fault that nosy b—'

'Don't say it.'

Teague glanced between Jessica and Rowlands but held his tongue. 'It was only a little tiff and everyone should keep their noses out.'

'The more we keep getting called here, the more likely it's going to be that one of you gets banged up for something. Usually it's uniform, this time it's me – so I'm telling the both of you to stop pissing everyone off.'

Teague began to reply but Tania talked across him: 'We're sorry, Inspector. We don't want any trouble.'

'Good – me either. Now where's your toilet?'

'Upstairs – second door on the right.'

Jessica headed up the stairs and made a special point of peeping into each of the rooms. The first had bare floorboards and a metal-framed unmade bed, while the second must have been their room because there was a set of carpet squares pressed together around a double bed. In the open wardrobe, Jessica could see rows of dresses and shoes, with clothes that appeared to belong to Teague – jeans, tracksuit bottoms and plain T-shirts – piled on the floor.

The final bedroom was completely empty, other than a roll of carpet pushed to the side and a hammer on the floorboards. Jessica went into the bathroom and flushed the toilet to at least create the illusion before washing her hands.

Nine point eight million . . .

23

Jessica resisted the urge to go home because there was one thing she needed to deal with at the station first.

Always one thing . . .

There was marginally more chat on the journey back, with Jessica filling Rowlands in about the rooms upstairs in Teague's house but there was no depth to anything either of them had to say. He didn't even scold her or threaten to tell the rest of the station when she misjudged the speed of a cyclist and nearly gave him a friendly clip on the back wheel. The cyclist offered an angry, though justified, pair of fingers; all while Rowlands said nothing.

Back at the station, Jessica headed through to the main floor, standing over Archie's desk as he typed away. 'Got a minute?'

'I'm busy.'

'Leave it – I need a word.'

He nodded without looking up but his hair hadn't been gelled into his usual tight curls and he hadn't shaved. He didn't even have a sports website open on his monitor. He slipped his jacket on and followed Jessica off the floor, through the corridors and into the interview room. Jessica closed the door behind him and took a seat.

'Am I being interrogated?' he asked, apparently serious.

'Just sit down. No one's going to bother us here and I

don't want any nosy bastards overhearing stuff as they go past my office to the canteen.'

'What do you want?'

'Why are you acting like a dick?'

Archie peered up from the table to actually look at her: 'What?'

'I've heard you've been acting like a knobhead all morning – what's wrong with you?'

'Why are you asking?'

'Oh, for God's sake. How old are we? What are you worried about?'

'Things are different between us now, aren't they?'

'Do you want them to be?'

Archie squirmed in his seat, not wanting to give the wrong answer.

Jessica rolled her eyes – how hard was it? 'Okay, I say this with the complete admission that last night was a lot more fun than I thought it was going to be – but we're not going out, I'm not your girlfriend, you're not my boyfriend, we're not getting married and we're definitely not in a relationship. I wanted one thing from you and you weren't too bad at it. That's all. All right?'

The reply rolled slowly from Archie's tongue: 'Oh.'

'Oh what?'

'Oh . . . I thought it was going to be really awkward.'

'Do you want to be going out?'

'Er . . .'

'You can say yes or no.'

'No, then . . . sorry.'

Jessica sighed. 'Don't be sorry – I'm not. It was what it

was. I was satisfied, you seemed to enjoy your little self and now we're back at work – yes?'

Archie sat up straighter, his whole demeanour altered. 'Oh . . . right.'

'Good – then stop being a dick and come with me. I've just given myself an idea.'

Jessica and Archie followed the path through the cemetery. The constable puffed his neck up past his upturned collar meerkat-style and sniffed the air. 'This is Manchester.'

'Are you sure it's not decomposing bodies?'

He laughed. 'Aye, it's a good job we're not going out, else this would be our first date – in a graveyard.'

'Is there any chance you could just not mention it again?'

'Oh . . . sorry.'

Grr.

Jessica didn't want to admit it to Archie but the air did feel crisp and refreshing and definitely didn't smell of decomposing bodies. There was a steady hum of traffic on the breeze but otherwise the gentle walk up the slope towards the ancient church provided nothing but peace. The cemetery itself looked a little worse for wear: tall tufts of grass overgrown into the hedges around the edge and a general sense that no one was spending much time looking after it.

The church itself would have been postcard-perfect in times gone by. The sandy-grey spire towered above them, a non-ticking clock in the centre with a rusting wind gauge unmoving on top, despite the obvious draught. A huge set of double wooden doors was at ground level with a grand stained-glass window above. Stretching the length of the church was a long line of coloured windows depicting various biblical scenes. Along the bottom, weeds grew from cracks in the concrete, with the brickwork covered in a thin layer of dark dust.

For someone who wasn't particularly religious, even Jessica found the slightly sorry state of the church a little depressing. She'd enjoyed going to church as a child, especially at Christmas, mainly because of the majesty of the building. This would have once been a community hub; now it was wasting away.

The two officers eased through the creaking heavy doors into the church and onto a stone floor that smelled vaguely of incense and something burnt. Long rows of wooden pews stretched ahead of them with hard stone aisles running along the centre and down both sides. From the inside, the windows were even more impressive, scenes of Moses reading the Ten Commandments, Jacob being blessed by Abraham, Daniel in the lion's den, David defeating Goliath, and many more that Jessica didn't recognise. She took a moment to take it all in, remembering her father's funeral that had been in a place just like this.

'You all right?'

Jessica didn't know if Archie had taken the edge from his local twang just for her or if it was a coincidence but she didn't like it anyway.

'Fine.' She cupped her hands to her mouth. 'Hello?'

The 'O' echoed its way into the distance, reverberating around the ancient walls. At the front, off to the left, there was a clunk and a short grey-haired man emerged from the side room wearing dark robes but no collar. He smiled slightly as Jessica and Archie made their way along the aisle.

'Can I help you?' he asked softly.

Jessica showed him her ID. 'We'd like to talk to you about a wedding.'

He glanced between the two of them. 'You want to get married?'

Jessica couldn't believe how badly she'd phrased things. 'Sorry, no. We're here on official business about a wedding you conducted around five months ago. I've got the date if that helps.'

He pouted out his bottom lip. 'I'll do my best to help. All the records are in the back room. Can I check your identification again?'

Almost nobody ever asked to check it properly but Jessica handed her card over, watching as the priest read every word, made sure she was the person in the photograph and then examined the back. He then did the same with Archie's. She supposed she didn't blame him – they were asking to talk about private details, after all. It would probably be better if more people actually checked these things.

Satisfied, the priest told them to call him James and then led them into a back room which smelled of dust and was littered with books and papers. He hefted a bulky, wide hardback onto the largest desk, showing a strength that wasn't initially apparent from his slightly hunched figure and greying hair combed across the top of his balding head.

'Obviously the official certificates are taken away but we tend to keep our own records too,' he said. 'We have marriage archives dating back almost three hundred years.'

Archie sniggered: 'I feel sorry for the poor sod who's been married for three hundred years. Imagine the nagging.'

Neither Jessica nor the priest laughed.

James turned to Jessica, realising she was the sensible one. 'Which wedding are you interested in?'

'I'm more interested in your recollections than in the specific times and details – Pavel Adamek and Rosemary Dean.' She gave him the date and he found the page in his book.

The crinkles around the priest's eyes folded into each other as he nodded slightly. 'That's a fairly recent one.'

'What do you remember about it?'

He puffed out a large breath and pinched the top of his nose. 'My memory's not what it was. I think it was a small affair.'

'How small?'

'I really don't remember. Perhaps a dozen people? Maybe fewer?'

'Pavel is Serbian – does that help? Were there any other members of his family here?'

The priest shook his head. 'I really don't remember. The bigger services happen on a Saturday but the date here is a Tuesday. I've perhaps only conducted half-a-dozen weddings on a Tuesday during the last twenty-eight years I've been doing this.'

'So it stood out?'

'I suppose – it's all about the donations, of course. Obviously if people want to get married on a weekend then the amount would usually be higher.'

'Do you have an attendance requirement?'

'We would usually ask for people who want to marry here to attend for sixteen weeks. If they are asking for God's blessing, then it's important they understand what that means.'

'Obviously – but if Pavel and Rosemary were attending here for four months then you must have come to know them reasonably well . . . ?'

The priest stumbled over his words, seeming a little confused by everything. Given his age and the number of people he must have had through his doors over the years, it wasn't necessarily a surprise. 'Serbia . . . Serbia . . . yes, no, yes . . . sorry – I remember. Pavel seemed very committed, certainly. Rosemary was very nice but I suppose I always had the sense her heart wasn't in it.'

'The marriage?'

'No, no . . . sorry, forgive me. The church. I'm not naive – I realise some people will come along for those months and then they won't return.'

'Have you seen either of them since the wedding?'

'I'm afraid not.'

'Did they make friends with any of your other parishioners?'

The priest sat and loosened the top part of his gown. 'I can perhaps ask a few questions for you but I don't really know. I don't think I ever saw them talking to anyone.'

'How many people do you have attending services each week?'

He smiled sadly. 'Far fewer than we used to. It's not the done thing today, is it? Everyone's more interested in their phones and gadgets.'

'How many would that be?'

Another deep breath: 'Forty to fifty? When I began here, the church would be full for two services every Sunday.'

'Do you have an address for Pavel and Rosemary?'

The priest seemed flustered again, flicking through a Rolodex and then opening a drawer and removing a box filled with notecards. He sorted through them all and then gave Jessica one that listed the address they already knew about: the one around the corner from where she'd assaulted a nine-year-old.

After thanking him for his time, Jessica and Archie left, meandering through the cemetery back towards the car.

Archie didn't waste any time in getting to the point: 'He was bloody useless, wasn't he? I'm surprised he knew his own name. Imagine being in one of his services – it'd go on for hours because he'd forget where he was up to.'

'All right, give him a break. He's old. I've got another idea anyway but—'

Her phone interrupted her yet again. She listened, told the caller to send the details to the car and then hung up.

Archie read it in her face: 'Trouble?'

'Another robbery – I'm going to drop you back at the station though. I've got an important job for you – and it's not even sweeping dead cows out of the canal.'

24

The site of the fourth burglary was worryingly similar to the first three: a house that was large but not too big, just outside the M60 ring road, an expansive back garden, two cars on the drive and neighbours who were just beyond shouting distance away. Jessica didn't need to bother checking the address because there were already three media vans and two cars outside. She walked the gauntlet of radio microphones and suited tall men doing pieces to camera as a slightly constipated-looking officer leant to one side, trying to enforce a police line that didn't need enforcing.

'You all right?' Jessica asked him as she passed.

He glanced nervously towards the cameras and then covered his mouth: 'I've been out here for over an hour.'

Jessica pointed a thumb over her shoulder towards the vans. 'How long ago did this lot turn up?'

'They were here when I got here.'

'Were you first on scene?'

'Second.'

Jessica took a couple of steps towards the house and then changed her mind, heading for the journalists. On the end, a man in a heavy green coat was leaning against a white van unwrapping a KitKat. She vaguely recognised his face from various media briefings and open days:

youngish, designer stubble, earring, no hair in his nose or ears – which was more than could be said for half the people they had turning up.

'Busy?' she asked.

He bit into the first chocolate finger. 'We're going live on Radio Manchester in ten minutes.' He nodded towards a hedge behind her. 'That clown's busy rehearsing what he's going to say. They bring in all these new guys because none of the proper reporters want to do weekends, but they're all straight out of college and can barely get a sentence out without chucking a "y'know" at the end of it.' He gave her a wink. 'Y'know.'

'How long have you been here?'

He checked his watch. 'Half-hour? Perhaps longer. I've got to set up the technical stuff – he's just got to talk but he's acting like he's about to give the Sermon on the Mount.' He paused for a second and then shouted over Jessica's shoulder while tapping his watch: 'Oi, Gibbo – sort it out, mate. We're on air in a few minutes.'

Jessica nodded towards the line. 'Who are this lot?'

Finger two of the KitKat was devoured in one go: 'Everyone's in – BBC TV, ITV, the *Herald*, *Evening News*, that local TV channel. Have you ever watched that shite? They've got this woman who can barely say her own name.'

'How did you get here so quickly? We only found out a little over an hour ago – so you must have got your skates on.'

He shrugged. 'No idea, love – I just go where I'm told.' He stopped to shout over her shoulder again. 'Oi, Gibbo –

stop fannying about, they're coming to us early now. Pull your finger out your arse and get over here.' He uttered a final 'amateurs' in Jessica's direction as she headed past the constipated officer towards the house where another man in uniform stood next to the front door.

'Sodding freezing out here,' he muttered, opening the door for her.

Jessica muttered something about thermal underwear as she went inside. What did they tell people in training nowadays? Wasn't that day two? Forget anything fancy; get a vest and tights – something that didn't chafe.

Edward and Frances Shearer were exactly who Jessica would have expected: well-dressed, well-manicured, well-spoken and bit annoying. Edward was wearing something that Jessica assumed he thought was 'dressed down' – suit trousers and a shirt without a tie or jacket. He was in his fifties with big hair swept away from his face and clipped salt and pepper eyebrows that looked as if they were glued on. He took Jessica on a tour of the house, beginning in the kitchen where the back door was.

For her, it was like walking into a science-fiction movie: everything was white and the thin shards of afternoon sunlight eking through the back window made her squint as if she needed sunglasses. Getting everything to look like this must have taken some scrubbing.

Edward pointed towards the back door, where a Scene of Crime officer was carefully picking pieces of glass up from the floor. 'We were both upstairs but I heard what I thought was a crash and by the time I got downstairs, they were already in.'

Jessica narrowed her eyes against the light to take in the scene. Her question seemed obvious but she wondered if she had missed something. 'How did they get in?'

Edward blew a raspberry with his bottom lip. 'I suppose they smashed the glass of the door and reached in to unlock it and turn the handle. By the time I got down they were inside. We always leave the key in the lock on the inside because Frances – bless her – is always losing keys.'

'How would they know the key was in the lock?'

'I don't know – don't most people do that? Perhaps they looked in and saw it?'

Jessica glanced around the kitchen, where the window over the spotless sink would have offered a clear view of the back door. Anyone who had come through the gate and around the side of the house would have been able to see it. Now she had adjusted to the light, Jessica took a few moments to look at the rest of the area. Aside from a pair of muddy boots sitting on newspaper close to the back door, everything else was flawlessly sparkling.

Edward led Jessica through the ground floor to a study, where there were more Scene of Crime officers working. Jessica poked her head around the door – lots of cream, antique wood computer desk, bookshelves, wide-open safe under a table – and then returned to the living room. Edward's wife Frances was already being interviewed by another officer, so Jessica took a seat at the dining table in an adjacent room with Edward slotting in next to her.

Jessica made sure Edward was comfortable and then asked him to talk her through what had happened. He made a point of making eye contact as he spoke. 'As I said, we were upstairs putting a few clothes away when we heard the bang. At first I thought something had fallen over but then it felt like the house was shaking.'

'How do you mean?'

'It's difficult to describe. There was this pounding sound – I suppose from their feet.'

'And were you still upstairs when you heard that?'

He stared up to the ceiling, biting his bottom lip. 'I suppose I was halfway down the stairs.'

'And what did you see?'

'When I got to the bottom, I turned towards the kitchen – where the noise was coming from – and there were these men there.'

'What were they wearing?'

'Black – they had these padded top things and plastic bags over their shoes, plus balaclavas.'

'How do you know they were men?'

'Sorry?'

'You said they were all in black plus they had balaclavas on, so how do you know they were men?'

Edward paused again: 'Um . . . I suppose I don't – they *looked* like men and the one that spoke had a man's voice.'

'Did he have any sort of accent?'

'Oh . . . I wasn't really paying attention. He asked who was in the house and then wanted our phones. He got Fran and myself sitting in the living room and then smashed them. He said they'd cut the phone line too.'

'What did they do to make you go along with them?'

'Well, there were five of them.'

'Is that all?'

'One of them had a gun.'

'Did he point it at you?'

Edward shrugged. 'I don't know . . . I suppose he waved it around a bit. It all happened really quickly. I wasn't thinking.'

'Was there anyone else in the house?'

'Mercifully not – our children were at their grand-parents' house.' He made another point of catching Jessica's eye. 'Small mercies, eh?'

Jessica nodded in agreement. 'What time did every-thing happen?'

'We'd gone upstairs a little after midday, so I suppose shortly after that.'

'You called 999 at 12.34 – so that would indicate they were here for half an hour, perhaps a little less?'

'I suppose.'

'That's quite a long time – aside from smashing your phones, what else did they do?'

'They cleared out the safe.'

'Anything else? Did they check the other rooms? Touch anything? Have a wee?'

Edward was struggling to maintain the eye contact he'd initiated, not exactly stumbling for words but certainly having problems remembering. 'It's hard to recall. You say it was half an hour but it felt a lot quicker. I don't know.'

'Was it you who opened the safe?'

'Yes.'

'Tell me about it.'

'I've been doing a lot of business from home, so we moved a few things here that used to be in the office;

documents and the like but cash too. They asked where the safe was and there wasn't much I could do. He had that gun and—'

'Who was he pointing it at?'

Jessica's interruption threw him off his story and he started waving his hand in a circle to find the next word. 'The gun?'

'Yes – who was he pointing it at?'

'Well, me, I suppose.'

'Okay, he was pointing the gun at you, so you showed him where the safe was. Is it easy to open?'

'It's just a keycode.'

Jessica scanned through the handwritten note in her hand. 'It looks like they got away with an awful lot – twenty thousand in cash?'

'I said – it's because of the business.'

'One hundred and fifty thousand in jewels?'

'They've been bought over many years. They're in a fireproof box within the safe.'

'Most people's insurance wouldn't cover those sorts of figures.'

'We had to switch the business insurance to the house because of the office move.'

Jessica checked a few more things but it didn't change her opinion of him. As well as the work Archie was hopefully doing, she now had a job for Izzy too.

Back into the living room, Jessica spoke to Frances Shearer. She was dressed immaculately – matching dark pink skirt and jacket, silky shirt, shiny bracelet, painted nails, matching bag on the sofa. She confirmed everything her husband had said, only elaborating when it came to the children – they were at her parents' house.

When she was done, Jessica had two phone calls to make: one to Garry Ashford at the *Manchester Morning Herald*, one to Izzy at the station.

For a Saturday she wasn't supposed to be at work, she really had spent a significant amount of time being lied to.

25

After visiting the robbery scene, Jessica stopped at Long-sight to pick Archie up and then they were back on the roads again. Archie was thinking along the same lines as her and had switched into enthusiastic puppy-dog mode. Any awkwardness from earlier was gone as he chatted about the names he'd stumbled across going back almost two years. A few phone calls later and he had a shortlist of eight couples who had been married at the same church as Pavel and Rosemary.

As he spoke, Jessica tuned out, instead remembering what DCI Topper had accused her of: profiling.

This time, there was no doubt that was what she had done, asking Archie to find certain types of couple based entirely on their names. John and Jane Smith – ignore. Anyone a bit foreign-sounding, make the call. Topper was right – this wasn't supposed to be how they worked and yet sometimes short cuts were the only way.

Their first stop was a flat above a Chinese takeaway in Rusholme. The whole vicinity smelled of fried . . . something-not-too-nice. After weaving in and out of overflowing wheelie bins and heading up a set of echoing stone steps, Jessica knocked on the rickety wooden door.

It opened a sliver; a blue eye and blonde flash of hair

peeping through. 'Who is it?' asked a woman's voice with a local accent.

Jessica held out her ID, even though there was no way it would be seen through the tiny gap. 'I'm looking for Anton.'

'Why?'

'Because I am – where is he?'

There was a scratching sound and then the door closed even further until Jessica could barely see the woman's eye. 'Out.'

'When will he be back?'

'I don't know.'

'Aren't you married to him?'

'Yes but I'm not his keeper.'

Jessica turned to Archie, giving him a knowing look, only to feel a lot less confident as the outline of a man appeared at the bottom of the stairs. As he came closer, the dim light overhead revealed the heavy work boots, muddy jeans, thick jumper and rough hands of someone who knew their way around a building site.

The passageway was only wide enough for one person so the man had to stop behind Archie and peer up at the two officers. His accent wasn't thick but there was a definite Eastern European edge: 'Hello . . . ?'

The door in front of Jessica swung open, revealing the blonde woman, who was holding a baby. 'Anton, hon?'

'What's going on?'

Jessica looked from Anton to his wife and back again. She could feel Archie staring at her, his cockiness from the journey evaporating in front of her.

Shite, shite, shite.

She had been so confident that the priest was a fraud, selling sham weddings for a premium in order to do up his crumbling church, that she hadn't even thought of what to say if it turned out to be a genuine marriage.

As she began to stumble, Archie saved her: 'We've had a few reports of rowdy behaviour around the front of the Chinese, so we were wondering if you'd heard anything?'

Jessica glanced sideways at the woman in the doorway. Her shoulders had relaxed and she wasn't gripping the baby quite so tightly.

Archie pressed himself to the wall and Jessica wedged herself into the corner, allowing Anton to join his wife in the doorway. 'There's always a bit of noise at night,' he said. 'Sometimes it's hard to keep our baby asleep but it's not been too bad recently.'

'That's all we were checking,' Archie said, peering towards Jessica as she gave him a faint nod. 'Obviously if you've got any future problems then you should call 101 or 999. Thanks for your time.'

Before anyone could query why Jessica had specifically asked for Anton, both officers had hurried down the stairs and were back in the car heading to the second address on the list.

For a few minutes, Archie said nothing but then, as they waited at a set of traffic lights, he finally opened his mouth: 'Do you think . . . ?'

'Of course I do; I'm a sentient human being. Thinking is what sets us apart from the animals.'

Archie didn't laugh. 'You know what I mean.'

'So say it then.'

'Are you going to shout at me?'

'I'm not your mum.'

This time there was a smile and a small laugh. 'Could you be wrong?'

'I bloody hope not.'

'If it's any consolation, I thought it made sense too – the church is falling apart so the priest thought he'd make a few quid on the side by marrying off English girls to blokes who wanted to stay in the country. He wouldn't be the first.'

'Let's wait and see what happens at the next place.'

A few streets over into Moss Side and Jessica got her answer when Aleksey Pashkievich opened his front door to confirm he hadn't witnessed any anti-social behaviour recently but that his wife was at work and their child was sleeping, so if they could keep it down and not go banging on his door for a reason he didn't understand, then it would be much appreciated.

Pavlo Dolinski was visiting his family at home in Belarus; Ivan Maruska was at work in the Trafford Centre but his wife said he was available on his mobile if they really needed to talk to him; Marko Novosel was cooking tea for his wife; Fedir Petrik's wife said he was in the pub around the corner if they wanted him; nobody answered the door at Vasyl and Carol Rybak's house.

Jessica didn't bother checking the final two names on her list: she'd tried to be too clever for her own good. Her only consolation was that because she wasn't actually at work, she'd had no reason to tell DCI Topper how she was spending her afternoon.

Archie said nothing, which spoke volumes in its own way: an accusing, intimidating silence. This was exactly what Topper had told her about – she'd even been called into professional standards and yet here she was jumping to conclusions again. There were other ways she could have checked that didn't involve going to the house of everyone who sounded a bit foreign.

Jessica drove Archie back to the station so he could finish his shift but he waited in the passenger seat before getting out. 'You a'ight?' he asked.

'Fine.'

'Everyone ballses stuff up.'

'How wonderfully eloquent.'

'What you up to later?'

Jessica kept her eyes level through the windscreen, not turning to face him. 'Can you do something for me, Arch?'

'What?'

'Not ask me that in future. Now sod off – I'll see you next week.'

Jessica walked into her house to be met by the smell of something sugary and sweet. Bex's voice called 'in here' from the living room, so Jessica entered to find her and Sam at the dining-room table, textbooks and A4 pads open in front of them. Each was dressed in cotton pyjama-style trousers and tops.

'You do know it's a Saturday?' Jessica said. 'You could

be out doing . . . whatever it is teenage girls do nowadays. I'm sure it's not revising.'

Bex grinned, tucking a long strand of black hair behind her ear: 'I hope you don't mind – we did some baking too.'

'What did you make?'

'Bread and cookies.'

'Why would I complain about that? Well, as long as there's some left.'

'There's loads! It's all in the bread bin.'

'I hope you've done something other than bake and revise? It's a weekend – you're young.'

The two girls exchanged a short, knowing glance. 'What have *you* been up to this weekend?' Bex asked.

'Working.'

'All night?'

Jessica couldn't stop herself from grinning. If there was one person she was happy to have tease her, then it was Bex. 'In a manner of speaking.'

'Are you *staying out* tonight?'

'No.'

'We were thinking about streaming a movie, if you don't mind.'

'I don't mind – but I've got to be up early,' Jessica said. 'I'm going to church.'

Both girls stared at her.

Sam eventually broke the silence: 'My parents are both really religious. I used to go every week as a kid.'

'Are you Catholic?' Jessica asked.

'I'm nothing now. My mum and dad are Anglicans.'

Bex was staring at Jessica in a way she hadn't before,

her head at an angle, eyes slightly narrow. 'Do you usually go to church?'

They'd been living together for a few months but Jessica had never been in that time. 'No – I've got someone I need to talk to.'

'For work?'

'How did you guess?'

Bex bit her bottom lip, suppressing a smile. 'Can I come?'

'If you want—'

'If I'm going to get in the way, then don't worry – but I've never been inside a church before.'

Sam replied before Jessica could: 'Really?'

'My mum would've never taken me and then it wasn't the type of place you go to when you're on the street. There was this church hall that used to give out food but that was it.'

'What are you hoping it'll be?' Jessica asked.

Bex shrugged: 'I don't know – something different.'

26

Jessica sat near the back of the church taking in the largely empty pews and not really listening to much of what was going on. When the congregation stood, she stood. When they sat, she sat. When they sang, she opened and closed her mouth silently, like a fish bobbing around a tank. Bex seemed fascinated, whispering questions about everything from the coloured windows, to the incense, to why people were kneeling. Jessica knew some of the answers but was more aware of the glances they were getting. People would quickly peep over their shoulders as if looking at one of the windows, scan across Jessica and Bex, and then turn back to the front again. Some of the younger children in particular seemed fascinated by Bex – skinny, striking straight black hair, multiple piercings through her ears and nose, casually dressed in jeans and a top sporting the logo of some band – there was certainly no one else present who looked like her. At least there was honesty to the children's interest; the adults pretended to look at something else, acting as if they weren't interested in the two women sitting together near the back.

The priest had spotted Jessica relatively early on and she could feel his eyes wandering towards her throughout the service.

When it was time to receive communion, Jessica stayed

in her seat but Bex joined the line and mimicked everyone else by crossing herself and taking the wafer. Jessica didn't know enough to tell whether she had broken some sort of religious law by doing so when she wasn't strictly a Catholic but she said nothing.

Afterwards, Jessica waited in her seat as people began to file out. A few stopped to talk to the priest, with a handful of others leaning across and telling Jessica how wonderful it was to see a new face. Suddenly she felt silly for being suspicious of their earlier glances: they were simply interested in someone different and perhaps making sure that she and Bex were okay and hadn't run away. Why was she always so suspicious of people?

Jessica told Bex she needed to wait but the teenager didn't mind, skim-reading parts of the Bible as the church emptied. Eventually, it was only the pair of them remaining. The priest made his way towards the back of the church, looking slightly weary and rubbing his forehead. He smiled thinly at Jessica but didn't seem to know what to say about the younger woman engrossed in the Bible.

'I take it this isn't a social visit,' he said.

'Shall we go to your side room?'

The priest shook his head slightly. 'It's a gloriously sunny day and it's so dark back there. Don't you think it'd be nicer to talk here?'

Jessica only needed a moment to glance at the dancing multi-coloured beams of light streaming in through the stained glass before she shuffled along the pew, nudging Bex along too.

'Is there something I should call you?' Jessica asked as

the priest sat alongside her. 'I know you said James before but it doesn't feel right now we're in the main church.'

'You can call me "Father" or "Father James" if that makes you more comfortable. Do you mind if I ask you something first?'

'Go for it.'

'Are either of you Catholic?'

Bex looked up from the Bible: 'This is the first time I've ever been in a church.'

The priest turned to Jessica: 'And you?'

'No.'

'Then why would you want to sit in one of my services? If you want to talk to me, you could come at any point.'

Jessica felt uncomfortable, knowing Bex was at her side. 'Can I be honest?'

'If ever there's a place for it, then that's here.'

'I thought you were a fraud, Father. When we were here yesterday asking about marriages, I saw the state of the church and you didn't seem to know very much about the wedding I wanted to hear about. I thought you were marrying people for money, so we started looking into things . . .'

Jessica stopped because the priest was looking at her so intensely that it was as if he had halted the words in her throat. A shiver slid along her spine and it felt like he could see the real her – the self-doubt that was constantly there under the aggressive air of confidence. The guilt at what had happened to Adam and that unrelenting feeling that if she had done things slightly differently then he might still be there.

Even though she was facing the priest, Jessica knew Bex was watching her, perhaps for the first time understanding what it was she did.

She doubted people.

Father James flattened what was left of his hair and replied slowly and deliberately: 'Did you find anything?'

'Is there something to find?'

He smiled slightly and Jessica could feel his searching eyes again. She had answered as if she was at work, not as someone who had come along to a church service to talk cordially. Jessica could sense him wondering what had made her so cynical and distrusting.

'My dear, my faith is too important to me for that. Money comes and goes, buildings come and go, people come and go – but the love of Our Father is enduring. Why would I sacrifice that?'

'I'm sorry, I—'

He reached out and touched her on the arm. 'You have no need to apologise to me.'

'We can't find either Pavel or Rosemary. We're wondering if something's happened to her.'

'Do you have good reason to think that?'

'I don't know.'

'All I can tell you is of my experience of them. To me, they seemed a couple who wanted to marry and who were willing to undergo what was required of them by the church. If there was anything else going on, that is something for them to reconcile with God.'

'How did they come to you?'

'Much like you have now – they attended on a Sunday

and approached me at the end, asking if I would marry them. I talked to them about what God expects and what the rules of this church are but they were happy with everything. I saw no reason why we couldn't go ahead.'

'It was just . . . you were so . . . I thought you were being deliberately obstructive.'

The priest continued to smile: fatherly in more ways than one. 'Oh, my dear, the perils of age. It'll come to you both at some point. When I was your age, I'd remember every face, every name – now it's not quite so easy.'

'You said last time that Pavel was the more committed of the two . . .'

'Indeed – I believe he was a practising Catholic in his home country. Rosemary was somewhat lapsed. Not that God ever gives up on us, of course.'

'Did he ever confess to you?'

The smile cracked slightly. 'You must know that anything said in such a holy circumstance is uttered with confidence.'

'Even if it was something serious?'

'We have procedures for if we are told something potentially damaging. Rest assured, if I felt I had something to tell you then I would do.'

Bex returned the Bible to the pocket hanging from the chair in front. 'What's confession?' she asked.

Father James explained what it was but said that, as she was a non-Catholic, he was unable to hear anything Bex might want to say. That seemed fine by her.

Jessica felt she was getting nowhere but continued anyway: 'Is there anything else you can remember about

Pavel or Rosemary. Did they tell you how long they'd been together? Or where they met?'

He tapped his forehead. 'If they did, then I'm afraid it's lost to the annals of time.'

'Is there anything else you can remember at all? Did they come here because they knew someone? Did Pavel ever talk about his home country? Or why he was here?'

The priest shook his head sadly. 'I'm sorry – I'm really not trying to be obstructive. I suppose . . .'

Jessica could see in his eyes that he'd remembered something and couldn't stop herself from interrupting. 'Yes . . .'

'There was a name he called her: something, I don't know – flowery.'

In a panic, Jessica said 'Rose', even though that was the woman's name anyway. The priest shook his head when she mentioned 'Primrose' too.

'It wasn't her name, it was something else.'

'Lily?'

'No.'

Jessica, uselessly, couldn't think of any other flower names but Bex jumped in: 'Holly?' 'Jasmine?' 'Daisy?' 'Iris?' 'Violet?'

Each suggestion was met with a shake of the head but Father James had his mouth open as if the name was on the edge of his tongue.

Jessica was struggling until a single word popped out: 'Chrysanthemum?'

Both the priest and Bex stared at her but it was the

teenager who spoke: '"*Chrysanthemum?*" Have you ever known anyone named that?'

'No . . . I thought it could be shortened down to . . .'

'"Chris"?'

Jessica went quiet, chastened by her own stupidity. The priest was still whirling his hand around. 'No, you're nearly there. I keep thinking of the colour red . . .'

Jessica thought 'Poppy' but said nothing, just in case.

'Poppy?' Bex said.

Father James clicked his fingers. 'Poppy, that's it. He called her Poppy.'

Jessica bristled but kept her cool. 'Do you have any idea why?'

He shook his head. 'I can't imagine how I forgot. I kept calling her Rosemary and she never corrected me. I suppose I thought it was a pet name – Poppy. It's quite nice, really.'

27

Jessica called the station to leave the names 'Poppy Dean' and 'Poppy Adamek' but then took the rest of Sunday off – not that she was supposed to be working anyway. On the journey back to the house, Bex seemed fascinated by the idea of church, if not the beliefs themselves. She and Sam spent part of the afternoon discussing religion, then politics, and then getting angry. That was at least some relief to Jessica – they were teenagers after all. She could remember when she was idealistic before the crushing reality of having bills to pay eventually weighed her down.

After a lazyish day, Jessica was up early on the Monday. Her apparently unfounded suspicions of Father James didn't mean there weren't other things of which she should be wary.

At the station, there was the usual weekend fallout as the drunks and shouty abusive types arrested in the city centre over the course of Friday night and Saturday were carted off to court, largely feeling a bit silly after spending a night or two in the cells.

The Sunday crew had at least been busy, even if they hadn't come up with much.

Poppy Dean: no trace of anyone with that name;

Poppy Adamek: ditto;

C&A: no idea. A few faint leads on potential Slavic

words that could fit but nothing that could be related back to Manchester. No trace for the pre-paid mobile phone from which the message had been sent either.

Surveillance of Ana: she'd watched a lot of television and only left the house to go to the local Spar for a microwave meal. No sign of Pavel.

Jessica couldn't help but feel that she knew the name 'Poppy' from somewhere, although she couldn't place it. All in all, it had been utterly fruitless – although the early forensic results were back from the robbery at Edward and Frances Shearer's house. Much of them seemed to be the same as in the previous robberies but, as Jessica had noticed at the time, the method of entry was different. For the first three, the door had been hammered open by something large. With this one the window had been broken and someone had reached through to unlock the door. Whatever had been used to break the glass was different to the implement in the first three robberies.

'Everyone ballses stuff up.'

Archie might have put his own Mancunian spin on the statement but he wasn't wrong. Jessica had been incorrect about Father James but she'd got things wrong in the past. It was getting the big things right that counted.

Wanting to be by herself, Jessica asked Izzy to oversee some background research into the Shearers while she went for a drive north of the city onto the country roads that linked Manchester to Bolton.

Neil and Bea Wilkie lived in a cottage on the edge of a hamlet fifteen minutes but a world away from the motorway. They were both retired but still fit and active, faint traces of the dark hair they'd once had replaced by grey, eyes still alert. When Jessica arrived, Bea was in the front garden, on her knees with a trowel and bucket as her husband buzzed his way up and down with a lawnmower.

The Greater Manchester spring was providing a summer-worthy morning, gentle sunshine beaming and warm. Bea asked if Jessica wanted to sit on the porch to chat, popping inside and returning a few minutes later with a pot of tea, three cups, three custard creams and a single cupcake with a strawberry on top. 'I made them freshly yesterday,' Bea said, insisting the cake was Jessica's and that she and her husband had eaten quite enough.

Neil came to join them, forehead dripping with sweat, shreds of grass clinging to the hairs of his arms. He leant against a wooden railing that separated the porch from the garden. 'Nothing beats a cuppa after a morning of work.'

His wife scolded him for dripping sweat on the decking and gave Jessica a wink. 'When you phoned, you said it was because you wanted to check a few details about the robbery at our Fran and Edward's – but I'm not sure there's much we can add. It sounds so awful. Can you imagine? It's a good job the children were here.'

Jessica took a bite of the cake, figuring it was rude not to. Well, that and it looked amazing. 'It was more for a little background. I was wondering how often you have your grandchildren over.'

The couple looked at each other but Bea answered: 'Usually the last weekend of the month. We'll take them overnight to give Fran and Edward a night away from it all.'

'And do you get on well with your grandchildren?'

'As well as you can with a six- and eight-year-old. We'll take them walking in the hills around here, or sometimes to the cinema or bowling. It depends what they want to do. You know what kids are like – most of the time they want to watch TV or play games.'

'This wasn't the last weekend of the month . . .'

Bea took a sip of her tea and Neil answered while trying to pick the blades of grass from his arms. 'No – it put us out a little to be honest. We were going to scoot up to Southport for the weekend but had to cancel the Friday night, in favour of the Saturday. You don't want to say "no" because you don't get to see them enough anyway. Do you have kids?'

Jessica was now used to answering automatically, emotionlessly. 'No.' She took another bite of the cake to ensure she didn't have to follow it up.

'It's hard to describe then – especially when it comes to grandchildren. You don't want to go behind their parents' backs discipline-wise but then sometimes it's you they want to talk to about things. If you immediately went to their parents, you'd lose the trust. It's a difficult relation-ship sometimes: not one you'd want to change, though.'

'Are you saying they've confided something in you?'

'No, sorry,' Neil added. 'I was speaking generally. Honestly, I'm not sure what you want . . .'

He wasn't speaking harshly, simply stating a fact. Jessica knew she'd come this way to ask a single question, one that could have been put to either of them over the phone. She knew she was constantly searching for reasons to be out of the station, feeling active. This was another such example – though it was good to stare into someone's eyes when they told you the truth.

'When did your daughter call you to ask if you could take the children?'

Bea answered: 'Friday evening. We were sitting down for tea.'

'Has it ever happened before that you've only had a few hours' notice?'

The couple turned to each other again, shaking their heads, wondering why she was asking. Bea replied again: 'There was once when Edward had a late trip to Germany and Fran wanted to go with him but we had a couple of days then. I suppose this is the only time with really short notice.'

She shifted her attention back to her husband, but Neil was focused on Jessica. There was a slight change in the way he was standing. Rather than leaning, he'd pushed himself up straighter and was watching her carefully. His lips were pressed tightly together, eyebrows drawn downwards. Jessica could see in his face that he'd had the same thoughts as her. He spoke slowly, words chosen purposefully: 'I just hope the children aren't affected by all of this. They're too young to be involved in everything.'

Bea missed the meaning in her husband's statement, even though Jessica heard it clearly.

'I spoke to Fran last night and she said they're perfectly fine,' Bea said. 'By the time we returned them, everything had been cleaned up. They don't even know someone broke in.'

Neil nodded towards Jessica as she took the final bite of the cake. He stretched his hand out for her to shake, not gripping too hard but making a point of looking into her eyes. 'Thanks for coming, Inspector. It sounds like we'll be hearing from you again soon.'

Edward Shearer was at the desk in his study when Frances showed Jessica into the house. The safe was closed underneath him and everything looked the way it had likely been before Saturday.

Edward seemed surprised to see her, spinning in his chair away from the computer. 'Oh, you're back . . . do you have news?'

Jessica shook her head. 'You seem to have cleaned everything up well enough.'

'That fingerprint powder stuff was a nightmare to get rid of in here but Frances did a fine job.'

'Can you come with me into the living room? There's something I'd like to ask you about.'

For a moment, Jessica didn't think he was going to move but then Edward clambered to his feet and strode past her through the house. He took a seat on the sofa next to his wife, leaning forward irritably as Jessica perched on the armchair.

'Where's the kitchen from here?' Jessica asked.

'You already know – you were here on Saturday.'

'I know but point me in the right direction anyway.' Edward stretched out an arm but Jessica grabbed it, pointing to his watch. 'Is this genuine?'

He pulled himself away. 'What?'

'It looks expensive – is this real or a fake?'

For a moment, Edward hesitated. She knew that he wanted to lie but, if need be, the watch could easily be examined by their own people. 'It's real,' he said.

'Where was it during the robbery?'

'I don't know – I don't see how this matters.'

'It matters to me. Think about it. Clearly it wasn't in your safe, else it would have been stolen – so where was it?'

'Upstairs, I suppose.'

'*Where* upstairs?'

'I suppose on the nightstand.'

Jessica nodded at Frances, who had shrunk into the sofa as if she wanted it to swallow her. 'On Saturday, you were wearing a bracelet. Pardon me for talking out of turn but you don't seem the type of couple to keep cheap jewellery, so what was it made from?'

Edward tried to butt in – 'I don't see how—' – but Jessica stretched a hand out towards him to stop him talking, still watching his wife.

Frances glanced at her husband but was cowering under Jessica's stare. 'It was gold.'

'And where was that when the robbers broke in? I saw you a couple of hours after they left and you were wearing it – so did you have it on while they were here, or did you put it on after they left?'

'I'm not sure . . .'

'You must know if you put it on afterwards – it would be a very deliberate thing to do.'

'I didn't—'

'So you were wearing a gold bracelet but robbers – who took one hundred and fifty thousand in jewellery – didn't take that?'

Frances glanced at her husband again: 'I suppose—'

Edward finally took charge, leaning in and jabbing an accusing finger at Jessica. 'Look, I'm not sure what you think this has to do with anything. We told you everything on Saturday.'

'It's your statements from Saturday that I'm following up. I was wondering how the media got here so quickly?'

'I don't know, I—'

'You called them. While your wife was calling us, you were talking to the papers. I spoke to the receptionist at the *Manchester Morning Herald* and the one at the BBC. If you want to say you didn't, we can check your phone records.'

'No, I did. I thought they'd want to know. It's not a crime, is it?'

'Not at all but it's not what most people would do. Most people wouldn't want cameras at the end of their driveway – especially after a robbery. They'd want privacy. I suppose the only reason you'd call the media at the same time as the police was if you wanted to ensure the story was covered.'

Edward had no reply because she was right. As his wife shuffled away from him to the far corner of the sofa, he turned to Jessica. 'What exactly do you want?'

'I think you know.'

'Know what?' He poked a thumb at his chest. 'We're the victims here. Is this how you work? I've read about how you fit people up – it was in that report. "Institution-ally corrupt", wasn't it? Is that what's going on here?'

Jessica remembered the feeling in her stomach when Anton had walked up the stairs, disproving her theory about Father James. She'd been wrong then – but not this time. She reached into her pocket and unfolded a sheet of paper.

'I printed this off from a news report on the Internet,' Jessica said. 'It's about the third robbery, where Ian and Harriet Blackledge's house was broken into. It says that the back door was broken open, that cash and jewellery was taken and that the robbers wore black.' She unfolded a second sheet. 'In this report of the second robbery, it says they wore bags over their feet. In two others, it mentions the gun. By reading all of the reports together, funnily enough, you'd have the exact details you gave us.'

'What do you mean?'

'Nowhere in any information we've released, or in any of the news articles, does it say *how* the robbers broke in through the back. They got into your house differently to the others.'

Edward was struggling to get his words out. 'I suppose they altered their tactics.'

'Also in the articles, it never mentions a time of day – but yours worked out relatively well for you because your children were at their grandparents'. If it had happened in the evening, like the other three, the kids would have been back in the house because you only had babysitters for Saturday daytime.' She nodded at Frances. 'Your parents were going away for the Saturday night.'

Edward was still resistant. 'If you're saying that it's lucky our children weren't here, then of course it was.'

'None of your neighbours saw or heard anything, despite it being daytime. The only fingerprints we found were from you. Then we've been looking into your accounts this morning and we know your business lost a key client at the start of the year. That insurance money could turn out to be a blessing . . .'

'If you're accusing me of something then I hope you have proof – I've got lawyers who'd love a battle with an "institutionally corrupt" police force.'

Jessica didn't flinch. 'How many guns have you ever had pointed at you, Mr Shearer?'

He rocked back slightly in his seat. 'Just that one.'

'I was in a nightclub a couple of years ago where a man pulled a shotgun from under the counter and pointed it towards me and my colleague. I still remember it. Every now and then, I'll wake up in the middle of the night and I'll be looking down the barrel, seeing his finger on the trigger, wondering if he's going to flinch. It doesn't matter what type of training you've had, it's terrifying. If you want to know where your story went wrong, it wasn't in keeping your watch or bracelet, it wasn't in calling the media, it wasn't even in dropping your children off with their grandparents at such short notice – it was in not mentioning the gun first.'

Edward stared at Jessica open-mouthed but didn't interrupt.

'If someone breaks into your home and you're asked about it, you don't say, "they were all in black"; "they had balaclavas", "there were five of them" – you say, "one of them pointed a gun in my face – in my wife's face". It's horrifying. When I talked to you, it was almost an afterthought. When I asked about why you'd gone along with them, it wasn't "because they had a gun", it was: "because there were five of them". You can rehearse the details of your stories over and over – but if you've *ever* had a gun pointed at you, then you don't speak so mechanically about it.'

Frances was gaping sideways at her husband in as clear an 'I-told-you-so' look as Jessica had ever seen.

Edward stumbled over a reply. 'I-I-I-don't know what you mean.'

'The muddy boots by the back door didn't help either. You've got a spotless house and yet you left something completely filthy by the back door and they weren't knocked over by any of the five robbers on the way out. We can do this as easily as you want: you can either tell us where you buried the rest of your jewellery in your back garden, or we'll dig the entire thing up. You're already facing charges of insurance fraud and wasting police time. If you want to add something else to that by not cooperating then be my guest.'

Jessica had actually guessed the final part of her theory but she could see the defeat in Edward's eyes. 'Am I allowed to call my lawyer?' he asked.

'I'll even lend you my mobile.'

28

Back at the station and Jessica wasn't exactly being treated like the conquering hero as she might have expected. Pat was halfway through an eclair as she entered through the main door and he simply pointed upstairs.

DCI Topper was on the phone as he waved Jessica into his office, not stopping as she took a seat: '. . . well, I'll keep an eye on things . . . I understand what you're saying but things are awkward here too.' His eyes flickered towards Jessica, making her feel self-conscious as if he was talking about her. He finished with a terse 'goodbye' and then hung up, addressing her without looking up. 'What's happening with Shearer?'

'He and his wife are talking to solicitors. I think they'll cooperate. He knows we've got them.'

'What about the *actual* burglaries?'

That was it – no 'well done', not a hint of 'excellent work, you've saved us a lot of hassle from assuming there were four burglaries, not three'. Nothing.

Jessica wanted to say something but didn't need reminding she was still on thin ice from the run-in with professional standards. 'We're doing all we can.'

'But Pavel Adamek is still missing?'

'Yes.'

'And the expensive, time-consuming surveillance of some prostitute's flat is still ongoing with no results?'

Jessica felt stung to hear Ana referred to in such a way, even though it wasn't untrue. 'We don't know if and when he could return, Sir . . .'

'What about his wife?'

'We've got a new lead on a nickname she might be known by, but it's not easy.'

'C&A?'

The exasperation finally crept out through Jessica's tone: 'We're trying!'

'Whatever it is is supposed to happen in two days' time. You've got to try harder.' Topper turned and pointed at his board. 'What about this woman who's skipped bail on assault charges?'

'I have someone on it.'

'That hit and run from last week?'

'Bradford Park are clearing up CCTV footage so we can ID the number plate.'

'Half-a-dozen street muggings just off Oxford Road?'

'We've got posters going up around the universities. We think it's a student.'

Jessica had answers for everything he threw at her but he still wasn't happy, quoting statistics and 'pressure from above' as she sat silently wondering why it was worth it.

'. . . are you listening?' he added.

'Yes, Sir.'

'Good, then let's get this sorted and hope to God nothing else happens this week – there's not been a murder in a month, so we're overdue.'

Jessica stood and left, biting her tongue and not sighing. How the job had come down to counting the number of days since they'd had a murder, she really didn't know.

Archie unscrewed the bottle of wine and poured a small amount into the bottom of a pint glass. He looked up at Jessica. 'It's pink.'

'What colour did you think rosé wine was?'

'I don't know – I've never had it.'

'But you've been in pubs and restaurants. You don't live in isolation from the rest of the world.'

He took a sip and smacked his lips together. 'It's sort of fruity.'

'It's made from grapes!'

'I don't see what's wrong with drinking what's already here.'

Jessica leant back onto his sofa. 'Because you've got a shite taste in booze and an even worse taste in decor.'

Archie passed her the bottle and reached for a bottle of ale that had a picture of a rabbit on the front, popping the top off and taking a large mouthful. Jessica poured more of the wine into her pint glass – he'd still not bought new ones – and sniffed it before having a large gulp.

'So, Topper's a twat then,' Archie said.

He's even got a stupid first name.

Jessica drank more of the wine. It was cold and smooth: a little sharp but not too over the top – perfect. Archie joined her on the sofa, bottle in hand. His living room was exactly the same as it was the last time Jessica had been there, messy and adolescent.

She pointed to the poster of the woman bending over the car. 'Is that your type then? Big boobs, round arse.'

Archie failed to suppress his smile. 'There's a woman on that poster? I'd put it up for the car.'

'What about the one next to it?'

'If you look behind the woman, there's some foliage and a fountain. I'm a big fan of greenery – that's why that one's there.'

'Yeah, sure it is.'

Jessica drank again, enjoying how cool it was, then poured herself another glass.

Archie was drinking much more slowly than she was, sipping from his bottle. 'So what's your type then?'

Jessica hid behind her glass. She replied quietly. 'Don't spoil it.'

'Sorry . . .'

'This place reminds me of being a student,' Jessica said. 'I lived with my mate, Caroline. She'd pick up after me and keep everything tidy but I'd always be leaving things around.'

'You still friends?'

'Sort of. We didn't fall out, she's just busy a lot and I've always got stuff on. She called me after . . . Adam . . . but there wasn't much I could say. She's in Albania at the moment.'

'Why?'

Another drink – a little over a third of the bottle gone already. Good job she bought two and Archie's fridge worked. 'Her boyfriend, Hugo, is a magician. He's really popular in Europe.'

'I think I've seen him – he does this thing with puppets. Do you know him?'

'Too well. He was at university with Dave. One of them ended up touring Europe, the other spends his time running errands for Wanky Frankie. He came to a wedding with me once.'

'Whose?'

Jessica giggled as she remembered. 'Caroline's . . . the girl he's now going out with. Sorry, it's complicated.' More wine. Yum yum. 'She wants to settle down and have babies but Hugo's Hugo. I don't think that's really his thing. He has a publicist-agent woman that travels with him – Caroline hates her but if it wasn't for her getting him places, Hugo would probably be sat on a bench in Heaton Park doing magic tricks for the kids.'

They sat in silence for a few moments before Archie flicked on the television. There was a dating show with a bunch of fake-tanned, big-haired, push-up-bra-enabled women cackling manically at some dancing prick in a shirt way too tight who told jokes and generally acted unlike anyone Jessica would want to spend time with. In the unlikely event of her becoming Prime Minister, anyone ever associated with this show would be the first to be exiled to somewhere where they had to watch the show on an endless loop until the end of time. Even that didn't seem a fitting punishment.

Then she realised Archie was laughing at it.

He was exactly the type of bloke who'd squeeze himself into a pair of too-tight jeans, puff his chest up and strut onto a TV dating show trying to impress someone whose name he wouldn't remember five minutes later.

As an advert break came on, Archie started humming along to the theme tune and it was then that Jessica realised that, work aside, she really didn't like him. Izzy and Dave acted the same out of the station as they did in it – and unfortunately so did Archie. He was a Jack-the-lad Manc who'd try it on if he thought he could get away with it – and she'd let him get away with it.

Jessica drank the rest of her wine quickly and then picked up the remote control from the table and switched the television off. Archie spun quickly: 'What—' but Jessica shut him up by grabbing his hand and leading him towards the bedroom. The last thing she wanted to do was actually talk to him.

The green blocks of square lights on the alarm clock beamed through the darkness of Archie's bedroom: 02.41. Jessica had been asleep for less than three hours. She'd got through both bottles of wine and one of Archie's Hair of the Rabbit ales, or whatever it was called. She expected to feel sick, or dizzy at the absolute least, but instead felt nothing other than a slight pain in her stomach which she didn't think was down to the booze.

Her eyes focused on the clock digits and then zoned out again, peering through the darkness towards the ceiling above. Next to her, Archie was lying on his front, his body rising and falling every few seconds in the grip of a deep sleep. She'd never known anyone who slept on their front before but here he was, face buried in the pillow, slightly curly hair catching the scraps of moonlight seeping through a gap in the curtains as his body rose. One of his legs was underneath the covers but the rest of his naked body was on top.

Realising that he had no clothes on, Jessica suddenly felt conscious that neither did she. She scrambled on the floor for the work shirt she'd had on all day, knowing she couldn't wear the same clothes the next day – not again. She should be at home making sure that everything was all right with Bex and Sam, not here doing whatever it was she was doing. They were teenagers for whom she was ultimately responsible, yet here she was acting far more like an irresponsible child than either of them.

Delicately, she slid out of the covers, picking up her underwear, trousers and shoes, and opening the door as quietly as she could . . .

'Jess . . .'

'Go back to sleep, Arch.'

'You don't have to leave.'

'I know.'

In the gloom, Jessica saw Archie shift into a sitting position. She heard him yawning through the dark. He sounded groggy. 'Is it me?' he asked.

'Is what you?'

'You left last time – am I doing something wrong?'

'It's not you.' Jessica started to move away again but Archie called her name. 'What?' she hissed, too loudly.

Archie was on his feet, stretching, still naked. 'Will you come back?'

'Why?'

'I'd like to talk.'

'I'm not your girlfriend – we have nothing to talk about.' He took a step towards her but Jessica moved backwards through the door. 'For God's sake, put some pants on. It looks like something left over in a butcher's shop.'

'Sorry.'

'Just put some clothes on and I'll be on your sofa.'

Using the light from her phone, Jessica got dressed in the living room, scrambling to find a sock that she'd dropped somewhere on her short route and then picking up her suit jacket from the back of the front door.

Archie soon joined her, thankfully wrapped in a dressing gown. 'Do you want a brew?' he asked.

'No, I want to go.'

'Why?'

'Because we're not going out. I've got to go home and change – I'm on shift tomorrow.'

'If we're not going out then why did you come over again tonight?'

'You know why. I'm not paying you compliments if that's what you're fishing for.'

'I'm not.'

'So what do you want?'

Archie yawned, which set Jessica off. Suddenly she wished she'd accepted the tea.

'I don't know,' he replied.

The lights were still off, with the only illumination coming from the moonlight into his bedroom where he must have opened the curtains. Jessica could just about see him lift his knees up to his chest. 'I was thinking about you over the weekend – after you told me to sod off home.'

'Shut up, Arch.'

'I don't know what it is. I mean I've been with girls before, obviously—'

'Arch.'

'. . . but I suppose I usually forget them straight away. On Sunday, I was wondering what you were up to and not in a work way. I was off to the football and—'

'Arch.'

'. . . even when we were one-nil up, I was wondering if you've ever been to the football. I know you say you don't like it but it's different live than watching on TV, so perhaps we—'

Jessica leant forward and slapped him hard across the legs, the clash of flesh on flesh echoing around the small flat.

'Ow! What was that for?'

'Because I was trying to shut you up but you weren't taking the hint.'

'Christ, it bloody stings.'

'So stop talking about it then.'

Archie went quiet for a moment and Jessica thought he was ready to let her go. Then his voice broke her with a single question: 'Is this because of Adam?'

There was no reason why he shouldn't have asked but, as Archie said his name, Jessica felt the lump in the back of her throat. She tried to swallow but it was too late and a soft blub erupted. In a second, she was crying as hard as she had in those days after her car had exploded. Archie reached out to comfort her but she batted him away. He stood and left the room, returning moments later and handing her a toilet roll with a glass of water.

She took it and curled herself up into the corner of his sofa, wanting Archie to comfort her but not wanting him anywhere near her. He sat at the other end, saying nothing.

Eventually she managed to swallow the water and bite the lump back. 'Of course it's Adam,' she croaked. 'What did you think? It was only four months ago.'

'I don't know . . . I didn't take advantage, did I? I didn't mean to, I—'

'I know what I'm doing.'

She didn't.

'Do you want a lift home?' he asked.

'I'm going to go for a walk to the main road and get a taxi.'

'Okay . . . are we all right – still mates?'

'Something like that.'

'I'm sorry if I—'

'It's me, not you. I know that's what people say but it really *is* me. Just please don't say his name.'

Archie didn't move as Jessica let herself out. She was halfway down the hard, cold staircase when she realised she still had half a toilet roll in her hand. Jessica slipped back up the stairs, placed it by Archie's front door and then bolted back down, through the heavy main door and into the cool night air.

Somewhere, she'd lost her hair tie but if that was all then she'd done well. The days might have started to take a turn towards spring but the nights were still firmly rooted in winter as a sharp breeze fizzed across her. Jessica pulled her suit jacket tighter, knowing exactly where her coat was: on the back of her chair at the station with her car keys in the pocket. She was pretty sure no one had seen Archie pick her up around the corner from the station but it was more worrying that this was what her life had come to – sneaking around hoping not to be seen by her colleagues and then creeping out in the early hours like a hungover student making the barefoot Sunday morning walk of shame. Except this was worse because it was the early hours of Tuesday and she had to be at work soon.

Jessica hurried back down the stairs, only pausing when she thought she saw a shadow hovering close to the front door of the flat below. She stood still for a moment, wondering if there was someone there or if it was a trick of the light, before deciding that she didn't care.

After leaving in the early morning the previous time, Jessica knew roughly where she was heading. She passed a garage, crossed the road, kept going for a few hundred metres and then moved into the centre of the deserted road, walking across a roundabout towards a pub with its lights off. In former days, the inn would have been impressive, heavy beams jutting down from the roof and wide thick-rimmed windows that could easily be painted stylishly. Instead, everything had a peeling brown feeling to it: abandoned and unloved.

On the other side of the road there was an alley that led behind a row of shops towards the main road. Jessica stood in the middle of the street staring at it, exhilarated by the darkness. She felt slightly scared of what the alley might hold. There were no lights, no one to protect her, no stupid Archie wanting to fucking cuddle. In her pocket was another pepper spray, a replacement for what she'd emptied into Ana's eyes.

Somewhere in the murk, she heard a squeak. Given the area and the amount of rubbish most likely overflowing in the alley behind the shops, it was probably a rat. Jessica took a step away, ready to stick to the pavement where the street lights were, when she heard another noise – definitely a female voice. At first it drifted on the breeze but then there was a sharp squeal and a bang. Jessica crept towards the alley, trying not to make any sound. Now she could hear two voices: one female, one male. The woman's was high and had an edge of terror to it.

Jessica slipped into the gap between two houses, an overhang blocking out the light from behind as she edged into the shadows. Holding her breath, she moved around a large metal wheelie bin. She could hear the voices more clearly now.

There was a definite sense of . . . something . . . in the woman's voice. At first Jessica thought it was fright but now she wasn't entirely sure.

'I don't have any money on me, honestly,' the woman said.

The man's reply was low, almost a growl. 'I don't believe you – empty your bag.'

'Please . . .'

Jessica kept her back to the wall, staying in the shadows as she approached the end.

'That's all I've got . . .'

She glanced quickly around the corner into a short connecting walkthrough between two shops on the main street. In the fraction of a second she had to peep around the corner, Jessica saw two figures: a woman kneeling on the floor, the contents of her bag on the pavement; and a man largely in shadow standing over her.

'If that's all you've got then I'll have to find another way to get what I want.'

The woman squealed slightly: 'No, you can't . . .'

Jessica risked another look around the wall. The woman was now closer to the shadows, on her front, bottom in the air as the man yanked at her underwear.

'Please . . .'

29

Without thinking, Jessica barrelled forward, largely staying in the shadows before launching herself at the man just as he got onto his knees. She caught him across the cheek with her knee, sending him spinning sideways, and her leg crunching off at an angle. Behind, the woman screamed loudly but Jessica ignored her, scrambling after the man who had landed next to a bin in an alcove of the wall. He was still on his front, struggling to roll over with his dark trousers around his ankles. When Jessica reached him, she arched her knee up a second time, feeling the crunch between his legs. He slumped to the floor with a groan as Jessica drew back and elbowed him under the ribs for good measure, not wanting to risk him swinging around and catching her.

Jessica unclipped the handcuffs from her pocket, wrenching his left wrist backwards and snapping them on, before twisting and pulling his right one too, clicking the cuff into place. The moon was illuminating his naked hairy arse, leaving her wondering whether to give him a kick for good measure. She doubted that 'police brutality' would go down too well with the 'institutionally corrupt' crowd, so controlled herself. Apart from a slight pain in her knee, she'd done surprisingly well, not even having to bring out her pepper spray.

Using the wall to pull herself up, Jessica turned to where the woman was still on the floor, wide-eyed in the light, staring towards her.

'Everything's going to be fine now,' Jessica said, trying to sound reassuring.

The woman slid her knickers up, still staring. Her slim bare legs were like sticks, her top crumpled and possibly ripped. Behind Jessica there was a low groan as the man rolled onto his back.

'Are you okay?' the woman asked softly.

'I'm fine,' Jessica replied. 'I think I twisted my knee a bit but I caught him good. Don't worry – he can't harm you now.'

Jessica suddenly realised the fright in the woman's face wasn't because she was worried about the man, it was because of her. She held her hands up to show she was no threat.

'It's not you I'm asking,' the woman said, her eyes flicking to the man crawling on his knees. 'It's my boyfriend – what the hell did you do that for?'

Jessica spun around to see the man struggling to get to his feet, black PVC cowl over his head, small triangle ears pointing into the air.

Oh no.

30

Jessica sat in her office, pint glass full of water in front of her.

'It really could have happened to anyone,' Izzy said. The sergeant was sitting in the spare office chair, spinning herself back and forth, which was only making Jessica dizzier.

Jessica took a sip of her drink and then closed her eyes. 'Topper threw a fit. There's this vein above his eyebrow that looked as if it was going to burst.'

'Talk me through it.'

'Why?'

'Because . . . er . . . all right, I'm not even going to try to dress it up. Sorry, er, wrong choice of words. Basically, because it sounds bloody hilarious.'

'As long as someone's finding my tatters of a career funny.'

'In fairness, it's not just me. Franks practically skipped into his office this morning and Pat couldn't get his words out quickly enough. I thought he was going to have a coronary.'

'How was I supposed to know it was some kinky sex game?'

'Wasn't he dressed up as Batman?'

'He was in the shadows! I could only see his bottom

half. I thought he was attacking her. Anyway, why would Batman be attacking someone – isn't he a good guy?'

'I'm guessing that wasn't at the front of their minds.'

'It was after three in the sodding morning – who's horny at that time?'

'Superheroes?'

'Har-dee-bastarding-har.'

'What's going to happen now?'

Jessica took a drink of her water and leant back into her seat, reclosing her eyes. The office lights were hurting. 'Topper says nothing. Apart a bruise on his face and a pair of firmly kneed bollocks, the bloke's absolutely fine. His girlfriend's all right too. Topper says they're a bit embarrassed by it all and don't want to make any other complaints in case it ends up in the paper.'

Izzy giggled girlishly. 'Sorry, it's just hilarious. I've got this picture in my mind of this bloke, dark trousers around his ankles, Batman mask on, about to, ahem, *save* his damsel in distress – and then you come steaming in and knee him in the balls. I hope there's CCTV.'

'There'd better not be.'

'The poor sod.'

'What about me?! Just because they're a pair of perverts, now I've got Topper talking about disciplinary action again. He should be giving me a medal.'

'What for? Best knees in the business?'

'I'd take that.'

Izzy was still laughing: 'Do you want to know what they're calling you around the station?'

'For God's sake . . .'

'Ball-breaker. Someone started the rumour that you perforated one of Batman's bollocks and now Franks has got someone Photoshopping a picture of you. It looked quite good actually.'

'If I knew how, I'd Photoshop a picture of him skulking around public toilets – except I could probably just follow him and take a real one.'

'Look on the bright side – no one's taking action and now all of the constables are terrified of you. They'll do whatever you tell them just in case you put those knees to work again.'

'Thanks a lot – what a legacy to have.'

'Why were you out in Stretford at that time of the morning anyway?'

Izzy was fishing for an answer she already knew but Jessica wasn't ready to tell her. 'I'd been at a mate's house.'

'Archie lives close to there.'

'Does he?'

'Less than five minutes' walk . . .'

Jessica opened her eyes as her desk phone began to ring. In her hurry to answer it, she sent the glass of water hurtling to the floor. Izzy jumped out of the way as the liquid drenched a stack of folders.

With an irritated sigh, Jessica listened to the voice on the other end of the phone and then reached for her jacket.

'What's going on?' Izzy asked.

'Something's finally happening at Ana's.'

31

Jessica let one of the uniformed officers drive as they zipped across the city to Sam's apartment, blue lights flashing but with the sirens turned off long before they got within hearing distance. He parked around the corner, following Jessica through a side alley and then quickly around the front of the converted house. Through the slightly open door, Andy Whatshisface and Joy Bag Jane were waiting for them. They'd been on the main street for under ten seconds and hopefully hadn't been spotted.

'What's going on?' Jessica asked.

Jane nodded at the monitor. 'Ana's phone started going off first thing this morning. It sounded like she was organising meetings but we didn't want to call the station in case it was nothing. We heard you had a *busy* night too.'

'Yeah, sod off. What's going on now?'

Andy answered, handing Jessica the remote. 'We didn't feel comfortable watching but it's on channel six. He paid her as soon as he arrived and then she took him into the bedroom.'

'Didn't you stop it?'

'We were told not to intervene unless Pavel arrived or we were told specifically to act.'

'Do you always do what you're told?'

Jessica gave Andy an accusing stare, wishing she could

remember his last name. As the room went silent, she didn't have to change channels because she could hear the 'Eh-eh-eh-eh' and a faint sound of probably fake moaning. She turned to the biggest of the uniformed officers. 'Fancy coming upstairs with me?'

'You're not going to knee anyone, are you?'

'Of course I'm not. Just stop the bloke before he runs and don't hit anyone unless you get a thumbs-up from me.'

'An actual thumbs-up?'

'Or a nod – any sort of positive gesture means you can wallop someone.'

Jessica led the way out of the house, ringing Ana's doorbell over and over as she had done previously. A minute or so later and there was a rush of feet followed by a bang. Jessica stood to one side as a large man bustled out of the door. His jeans were undone and his shoes untied. As he looked both ways, the uniformed officer clamped a hand on his shoulder.

Jessica headed past the pair of them, up the stairs and through Ana's recently opened flat door.

Ana was halfway across the living-room floor, naked from the waist down, when she spotted Jessica, eyes widening. 'You?'

'Yes.'

She struggled with her English, eventually settling for the word 'why?'

'Because I know that you know something about Pavel and unless you help us, we'll keep coming here every day until you tell us what it is.'

Ana scowled at Jessica, picking up a thong from the floor and putting it on. She sat on her sofa and lit a cigarette. Jessica sat at the far end of the sofa, trying not to breathe in the smoke.

'You don't know Pavel,' Ana said.

'I thought you said you didn't know him . . .'

Ana shrugged, her English a lot better than she had previously let on. 'You must go.'

'Why?'

'People watch. They go past and report back.'

In all of their discussions about surveillance, it hadn't occurred to Jessica or anyone else that Ana could be watched so surreptitiously. They had jumped to the conclusion that if Pavel or one of his men wanted to contact Ana then they would do so directly.

'The Spar?' Jessica asked. The reason for Ana's frequent trips to the shops had finally dawned on her.

'What?'

'The shop around the corner – that's where you drop your money off.'

Ana shrugged a blasé acknowledgement.

Jessica dashed down the stairs and told the officer to get Mr Pants-Round-His-Ankles firmly out of sight. She closed the door and then ran back up the stairs. Ana was stubbing out her cigarette onto a saucer, having apparently smoked it in record time. She was spraying the room with lemon air freshener which, if anything, smelled far worse.

'If you stop me going out, or having men around, he will take it out on me or someone else.'

'Who's "he"?'

Ana shook her head, unwilling to give a name. Jessica assumed Pavel. She dug into her pocket and pulled out a scrap of paper with the letters 'C&A' written on. The meeting time was at eleven the following day – if that meant the morning, they had barely twenty-four hours to figure out what the text message to Pavel referred to. If it was the evening, they still had only thirty-six.

'Do you have any idea what those letters mean?' Jessica asked.

Ana turned the paper around in a full circle and then turned it over before returning it to the original position. 'C and A,' she said slowly, as if the letters were foreign which, of course, they were.

'We think it's somewhere in Manchester,' Jessica added. 'Have you ever heard Pavel or anyone else talking about a place like that?'

Ana's eyes darted towards the door. 'You must go.'

'You know, don't you?'

'You go.'

Jessica shook her head, gripping Ana's wrist firmly but trying not to hurt her. 'You have to tell us if you know.'

Ana snatched her arm back, eyes still peering over Jessica's shoulder towards the exit. 'My sister . . .'

'Is she over here?'

Ana shook her head. 'At home. There are men.'

'They're threatening your family at home?'

A reluctant nod.

'We can protect you from Pavel and anyone else while you're here, plus arrange with police in Ukraine to look after your family.'

'No passport.'

'We can take you to your embassy to sort that and then arrange for you to go home. We have agencies to organise everything. We'll put you in a flat somewhere and you'll be safe.'

She shook her head.

'Ana . . .'

'No. You go.'

It was Jessica's turn to shake her head. 'We're not going to leave you alone if we think you know where Pavel is. We'll put someone in a uniform outside your door if that's what it takes.'

'No!'

'So tell me what C and A means.'

Ana was flailing her arm around, scowling at Jessica but knowing she wasn't going to get her own way. 'It's a, how you say . . . a bar.'

'A pub?'

'Crown and Anchor.'

How a group of police officers had managed to miss the name of a pub, no one seemed quite sure. It was like someone being knocked over in front of a solicitors' office and none of them realising, or a celebrity being shagged in the reception area of a newspaper and journalists walking past. Frankly, it was embarrassing. No wonder Topper thought they were all useless. Still, with a day to spare, they had a time and a place for where Pavel was supposed to be.

The Crown and Anchor was in Cheetham Hill, north

of the city centre, close to a community of Eastern European immigrants, who lived in houses that – according to Katerina – few Brits wanted to go anywhere near. After checking the call-out records, it became clear that the pub was something of a battleground. In the past fifteen months, they'd had seven separate reports of violent incidents close by and the council had even applied for a closing order that had been denied after the brewery brought in a new manager.

The assaults seemed to be part of an ongoing battle between immigrants who were living there and locals who didn't seem too pleased about it. It was always the way as the demographic of an area began to change – the newcomers would fight, sometimes literally, to protect their wives and children from the daily abuse they took, while the people who'd lived there for years objected to those they saw as not knowing the language coming in, taking their jobs and claiming their benefits. Of course, the majority simply wanted a quiet life: to go to work and come home again in peace, but if a minority wanted to have a ruck then everyone was drawn into it.

Which side was right? Perhaps both, perhaps neither – but it wasn't a new problem and it was something that affected all of the bigger towns and cities around the country.

After checking their facts ready for the next day, Jessica turned her attention to the man who had been arrested at Ana's house.

Mr Pants-Round-His-Ankles turned out to be called Leon Middlebrook. He sat in the interview room squirming, eyes darting from the camera, to Jessica, to the door, to the floor and then the duty solicitor. He looked bigger under the bright white lights than he had in daylight. He tugged his T-shirt down until it was covering all but the lowest part of his stomach. He had slightly Mediterranean looks, olive skin, black short hair and sideburns around his sticky-out ears. Quite the catch . . . if you had a thing about ears.

'I've got to get to work,' he said.

'Where do you work?'

He shuffled in the seat. 'I, er . . .'

'You're not going to be leaving here any time soon, so you may as well say.'

'I don't understand what I've done wrong.'

Jessica glanced across to the duty solicitor, who leant in and whispered in his client's ear. Leon shrugged him away, raising his voice: 'I know but . . .' He lowered it again, speaking through unmoving lips, even though Jessica could hear him clearly. '. . . it's not illegal, is it?'

Jessica interjected: 'This is the problem when you want to do something as simple as pay for a quick you-know-what. In some countries, it's either illegal or it's not – over here, some things are fine, others are going to leave you wound up in here. Your biggest problem is that it's unclear if the girl you gave forty quid to – Ana – is doing that job by choice, or if she has someone controlling her and taking her money. At this exact time, it's not easy getting that information but if it turns out she's being forced to do that job, then you, my friend, are in some serious shite.'

Leon slumped forward, cradling his head in his hands. 'I didn't know.'

'Unfortunately for you, that no longer matters. You're supposed to do the asking: "All right, love – here's forty quid. Oh and by the way, you are doing this by choice, aren't you?"'

He started to sob. 'What's going to happen to me?'

'For a start, you tell me everything about how you found out about Ana, then you'll be bailed awaiting further statements from Ana and anyone else we can get our hands on. At some point we'll be back in contact.'

'Do I have to tell people?'

'That's up to you.'

He wasn't wearing a wedding ring but then he could have taken it off.

'I'm sure you want to get out of here, so let's start with Ana – how did you know she was there?'

Leon spoke between coughed sobs. 'There's this Internet site – you need a password.'

Jessica slid a pad and pen across the desk for him to write it down. When he was finished, she took it away again. 'What's on the site?'

'It's a list of everywhere in Manchester where you can find girls. Prices, services and then ratings.'

'Who runs it?'

'I don't know. Some bloke at the football mentioned it once – I don't know his name – you need to have your registration approved and then it's all there.'

'And Ana was listed on there?'

'Yeah, she seemed all right.'

'How do you mean?' Leon looked up from his hands to the solicitor, clearly not wanting to answer. 'Cooperation will get you everywhere here, Leon.'

'She had a few good reports, y'know – from other lads. Plus she wasn't too expensive, so I called her . . .'

Jessica listened to the rest but it was more or less as she'd expected. In some ways, she felt sorry for Leon but there was little his solicitor – or anyone – could do for him. There was no doubt what he was paying for, the only issue was whether Ana was under the control of someone else. Arguing he didn't know would do him no good because of the way the law was worded. It was one of the few areas where Jessica didn't know where she stood. For Ana, being thrown into a flat, being monitored from the outside and having to give away the money was awful. For Leon, he had simply chosen the wrong girl and not asked the question that no one, realistically, was going to ask. From his point of view, he'd given money to a woman in a flat where there were no obvious signs she was under anyone else's orders. There were no winners.

When Jessica was done, she sent him back to the cells while bail was sorted out and then went to make a phone call she always hated. Serious Crime Division were in charge of investigating vice issues around Greater Manchester – and if she was going to do anything further, she would have to talk to them first.

32

The Crown and Anchor pub sat on the edge of a patch of wasteland that had once been a block of flats. Abandoned by the council, the flats had been imploded a few years ago, much to the delight of everyone who had lived in their shadow for so long. The remains were cleared and then the site was promptly ignored. Aside from flimsy wire fences that wouldn't stop a child climbing over, there was little else other than a vast area of mud and random piles of rubble.

The fact its surroundings were so open made surveillance of the Crown and Anchor and its adjacent disintegrating car park increasingly awkward. In case the text message Pavel had received did mean eleven in the morning, they'd had people holed up since first thing that day. Jessica had opted for the late shift, knowing that whoever had been planning things was unlikely to work under the non-existent cover of daylight.

By nightfall, Jessica was sitting in the back of an unmarked police van around the corner from the pub. A hidden camera on the top of the vehicle gave them a view of half the car park, while two other vans on the side roads allowed them to see approaching vehicles. It wasn't the best set-up but given the lack of time they'd had to put everything together, it wasn't too bad.

Ana had been moved into protective custody, her flat cleared of surveillance devices and Sam – slightly to Jessica's disappointment – had moved back into her own flat.

Given the choice of switching shifts to enjoy the action, Archie had jumped at the chance and was sitting next to the monitors as they watched nothing happen outside the pub.

'How do we know your man's not already inside?' he asked.

'If Pavel's hiding in a room upstairs and has been for the past week then we don't know. If nothing happens tonight, we might look for a warrant anyway based upon Ana saying it was this place and Katerina's expertise in the area. If he shows up in the main part of the pub, we've got a pair inside. They're apparently keeping their heads down and simply watching, which means they're almost certainly sticking out like a pair of nuns in there. Hopefully it won't get that far – the moment anyone sees Pavel, we've got those other two vans full of blokes with MP4s ready to cart him off.'

'What if he brings a gun and starts a shootout?'

Jessica frowned at him. 'Don't be a dick, Arch. Stop tempting fate.'

'I was just saying.'

'Well, don't. Say nice things – "What if he turns up with a super soaker? Have we got enough towels?"'

One of the other officers who definitely wasn't listening in to their conversation sniggered.

'Anyway,' Jessica continued, 'how have my friends at the SCD been treating you?'

'Like they've just shat me out.'

'That's how they treat everyone. Are they at least co-operating?'

'Only in the sense they've sent all the paperwork our way. We've been working our balls off today to go through everything.'

'You didn't have to hang around this evening.'

'Aye, well, didn't want to miss a good ruck, did I?'

Jessica had spent most of the day liaising between the Serious Crime Division's vice team, the superintendent and DCI Topper. When she wasn't doing that, she'd been talking to the Tactical Operations team about how their day-long surveillance of the pub had gone.

'The guy at the SCD said they've been looking into closing a few of the flats and small brothels down for a while,' Jessica said. 'Now we're interested too, they probably see it as a way of halving the costs on their budgets. If everything goes well, they get the credit; if it goes arse-up, we get the blame.'

'I didn't realise what a bunch of dirty bastards those SCD lot are. They literally know every knocking shop with an M at the beginning of the postcode.'

'I phoned up to give them that website address Leon gave me but the guy practically laughed, saying of course they knew about it. They have a back door into the site and about a dozen others.'

'Why haven't they raided before then?'

'That's part of the problem – it's not easy to know which girls are doing it voluntarily and who might be trafficked. They act on anything obvious but some of the women see it as easy money and don't mind. Trying to police this stuff is a bloody nightmare.'

'What's going to happen?'

'Using a mixture of their intelligence – a loose term, I know – and anything else we know via Ana and Katerina, we're going to raid a few brothels at the same time. I don't know when yet. I think the super wants to make sure the papers know about it so we can have a few cameramen taking pictures and making it look like we know what we're doing. I'm a bit out of the loop – I'm just waiting to be told where and when to go.'

They were interrupted by a man's voice on the radio: 'Vehicle on one.'

Jessica checked the clock – 22.45 – and then turned her attention back to the screen where a white estate car was surging past one of the monitoring vans. A wheel screeched somewhere nearby and then the vehicle appeared on their camera. After doughnutting around the largely empty car park, the driver skidded to a halt across two spaces and then he emerged, baseball cap at an angle, arse hanging out of his jeans, basketball shirt five sizes too big, shiny thick fake gold chain hanging limply around his neck. The man who slumped out of the passenger seat looked equally stupid, slouching his way towards the pub's entrance with one hand on his crotch, the other holding his mobile phone to his ear.

'They're going to get bloody lynched in that pub,' Archie said.

'Compared to our lot, they'll probably blend right in.'

Time ticked away until it was five minutes to eleven

when the radio sparked into life again. 'Grey van on two.'

On the monitor, a van similar to the one housing Jessica eased between two parked cars. It edged past their van and then accelerated gently towards the pub. The headlights dimmed and then went off as it pulled front-first into the shadows, leaving only the back window in view of their camera.

The officer who had driven them there leant across from where he'd positioned himself behind the driver's seat. 'Should I try to move?' he asked.

'No,' Jessica replied, 'we don't want them to think anything's up.'

As well as Jessica, Archie, the driver and the banks of equipment, there was one more officer, two empty pizza boxes, and wires running in all directions. Jessica stood as tall as she could, slipped around Archie without touching him, slid across the other officer's lap and then do-si-doed with the driver until she was behind the passenger seat. As elegantly as she could, she pressed herself in between the gap between the two front seats, ending up lying on her belly with the handbrake pressing into her stomach.

Slowly, she pushed herself up onto her elbows until she could see the car park through the passenger-side window. As gymnastic manoeuvres went, it wasn't quite Olympic standard but she hadn't stuck her arse in anyone's face, which was always a bonus for them and her.

Because of the shadows, she still couldn't see the entire van but there was movement in the front seat where something head-like was bobbing back and forward with the faint glimmer of light that was most likely a phone.

Archie's voice hissed through the van: 'What can you see?'

'Not much.'

Jessica wriggled, trying to get the pointiest part of the handbrake away from her belly button, when the radio reported there was another van on its way. Moments later, a grimy-coloured piece of rust on wheels pulled in next to the first van.

'It's eleven,' Archie whispered loudly.

Jessica could see the back of a man's head in the driver's seat leaning towards the first van. Gentle plumes of steam were drifting upwards from where the drivers were talking to each other through open windows.

A man's voice hissed across the radio. 'Do we go?'

Jessica didn't move, in case someone was looking towards their position. 'No, wait.'

One of the officers repeated her instructions via the radio as a calm silence fell across everyone, as if they were all holding their breaths. Jessica was beginning to feel an ache in her forearms from propping up the rest of her body but gritted her teeth and tried to ignore it. In the car park, nothing was happening.

'It's five past,' Archie whispered.

'Shh!'

'It's not like they can hear me.'

'*I* can hear you.'

The spirals of air continued to drift, joined by the orange spark of a cigarette being lit. The radios were disconcertingly silent – no vehicles on their way. Were these the only two vans coming? Was Pavel in one of them? Why wasn't anyone getting out?

Suddenly, as if there had been a cue no one else had heard, the drivers' doors clanged open and two men climbed out, walking to the back of the vans and leaning against the second one. Jessica watched one of them light a cigarette for the other but the men were too small to be Pavel. A laugh echoed across the deserted street as one of them bent over double, using his cigarette to point at the first man, whose grin was illuminated by the moon. Both of them were white, both dressed unassumingly in jeans and dark tops. If they hadn't been hanging around after dark in a pub car park next to a pair of vans then no one would have looked at them twice.

Someone behind her started shuffling, making Jessica shush them again. She heard Archie mumble a swear word in her direction.

Just as she was beginning to think they were going to have to raid the vans regardless, a single word hissed across the radio: 'Cars.'

Jessica tried to wriggle to peer between the gap in the seats but she could hear the engines anyway. 'How many?'

'Four . . . five . . . six,' Archie said.

Jessica dropped down flat as the noise from the car engines became louder and then gradually propped herself up again until she had a clearish view of the car park. The half-a-dozen cars turned their headlights off and pulled up front-first in a line, boots facing the vans.

The voice sounded across the radio again: 'Now?'

'Hold on.'

Six more white men got out of the drivers' seats and assembled at the back of the vans, exchanging back-slaps and jokes. From what Jessica could tell, their cars were empty – all with number plates at least eight years old, all not worth very much.

One of the drivers tossed his cigarette to the floor and stamped it out, pointing at one of the other men and smiling. He reached up to the van door and heaved it open.

Jessica could feel her heart pounding: doof-doof-doof-doof.

Under the bottom of the van door, she saw a pasty, thin white leg stepping down and then a woman with long blonde hair and nowhere near enough clothes for the conditions stepped into the centre of the circle the men had formed. Even from a distance, Jessica could see she was confused. One of the men reached out and squeezed her breast, nodding approvingly.

Suddenly the realisation of what was going on dawned on Jessica: the men were here to bid on the woman.

She turned towards the back of the van: 'Go.'

The officer repeated her message and then, as he, Archie and the other officer piled out of the back of the van, Jessica slipped between the two seats and set herself to watch the action on the monitor.

The other police vehicles screamed around the bend, blocking the exits from the estate, as the men began to panic. The woman was ignored as they all raced for their cars and vans but it was too late – black-clad officers with the semi-automatics and body armour raced towards the scene demanding everyone get on the ground. The poor woman – mini-skirt, low-cut top, large hooped earrings – turned in a full circle, unsure what was happening as everyone around her either shouted or dropped face-first to the tarmac.

Moments later and the scene was secure. Jessica climbed down and dashed across to the car park. The handcuffed men were being ordered back to their feet and lined up against the wall of the pub. One of the officers from the back of Jessica's van was draping a blanket around the frightened blonde woman and trying to explain that they were the good guys. Moments later and the final car arrived, with Esther and Katerina climbing out and hurrying across. Katerina batted the officer away and said something to the woman in a language Jessica didn't know.

'Got him?' Esther asked.

Jessica scanned the backs of the men being lined up. None of them was big enough to be Pavel. 'No.'

'You could give me a bit more notice in future – I was lucky to find Katerina at home.'

'Sorry.'

Katerina had a hand on the woman's shoulder, speaking quickly. She turned to Jessica, eyes wide: 'Did anyone check inside the vans?'

Jessica turned to look at the still-closed vehicle doors. 'No.'

'She says there are others.'

The armed officers were on the far side of the car park, so Jessica did what she definitely shouldn't have, reaching up to the first van's door and wrenching the handle down.

With a groan, the heavy metal door swung open and Jessica heard the female gasps. Through the gloom and the dust, she peered into the hot metal box to see seven more women, all wearing short skirts and barely there tops. They cowered at the back, pressed against the rear of the driver's seat, chattering in a foreign language, all utterly terrified. She could see the bruises on their arms, black marks across their legs. They stared at her, wondering what was going on, if this was part of some new type of torment.

Jessica opened the back of the second van where there were six more girls, all cowering, all hugging themselves.

She exchanged a look with Esther. Until now this had been about the hunt for someone who could be connected to a burglary. Ana had been so uncooperative – not to mention that she'd attacked her – that Jessica found it hard to empathise with her. Now it felt real. Fourteen young women, all brought here to be sold to the highest bidder and stuffed into the back of an estate car before being driven to various parts of the north to make money for their new owners.

Owners.

Jessica felt sick.

Archie was on the radio saying they needed far more cars than they'd first thought plus support officers, blankets, translators – basically anyone remotely associated with the force who was still awake at this time of night.

Jessica stepped away from the others, wishing she knew what to say to let the women know they were safe. She didn't even know what language they spoke, let alone have the capacity to reassure them. Her stomach creaked.

Owners.

She couldn't think past the word.

In the thick of it all, somewhere, was Pavel. He'd been texted the details of this meet because he was central to it. Jessica could feel it – the six drivers who had turned up might be working on his behalf in some way, deciding which girl went to which area and trying to haggle down the men with the vans. Perhaps he was the middle-man between whoever had smuggled the women in and the men in the cars who were buying, keeping a cut for himself? Perhaps he took a cut of everything?

She stared across the wasteland. Bricks, scraps of wood, crisp packets and chocolate wrappers fluttering in the breeze – and the outline of a figure. She squinted: it was a man, a big man, perhaps a hundred metres away, watching, almost entirely swallowed by the shadows but the moonlight caught the lens of the binoculars he was using and, for a fraction of a second, Jessica could see the outline of his squat head. She took a step towards him: two, three, four.

And then he noticed her.

Through the impossible light, Jessica knew he was staring straight at her.

With a skid across the tarmac, Jessica started running. She hurdled the waste of a fence in one and sprinted for all she was worth. Behind she could hear someone shouting her name but if they couldn't figure out why she was running then they should probably get a different job.

The rough wasteland dipped up and down across mounds of sand, dust, dirt and rubble. Jessica felt her legs buckle, her knees bend, but she kept going. Pavel had turned and was rushing towards a similar fence on the far side but his size made him slow and Jessica had got off to such a flying start that she had already wiped thirty metres from the gap between them.

He lumbered over a ridge and slid down the other side but Jessica dug in, ignoring her stomach, ignoring the shouting, and running like she couldn't remember running before.

Owners.

Her foot clipped a loose brick, making her stumble, but Jessica reached down and used her palm to propel herself onwards. Ahead, Pavel was at the fence but didn't have the physique to hurdle it and was climbing over one leg at a time.

The gap was fifty metres at most now. Jessica could see his breath trailing into the air; his heavy coat, thick boots, enormous hands. In the short period she'd seen him in Ana's flat, he'd appeared huge; from a distance he seemed even bigger.

Clear of the rocky ground he picked up pace just as Jessica was losing it, the burn in her chest, ache in her legs and the crumbling, sorry nature of the ground taking its toll.

By the time she reached the fence, Jessica didn't have the strength to hurdle it, stepping over one leg at a time and jogging towards the main road, trying to catch her breath. She leant against the corner of a house, breathing heavily, peering from side to side for any hint of movement, knowing that she'd let Pavel go for a second time.

33

Katerina's battered Fiat reminded Jessica of her old car, except that the other woman was a far more reckless driver than Jessica had ever been. Jessica ran her finger along the clasp of the seatbelt, hoping it would hold as Katerina accelerated along a street with parked cars packing either side. She swerved around a blind bend, jumping over the speed humps, and then skidded to a halt close to a row of shops. As the car came to a stop, a towel leapt off the back seat, landing on the back of Jessica's head with a sweaty-feeling splat. She peeled it away from the back of her neck, glancing at it quickly, before throwing it onto the seat behind on top of a pair of trainers and some hand weights.

Ugh.

Katerina's accent sounded more pronounced than when Jessica had last spoken to her. 'You all right?'

'Fine.'

'Aah, don't worry – they say I drive like a Hungarian.'

'What does a Hungarian drive like?'

Katerina turned to face Jessica, a twinkle in her eye: 'Like there are only twenty-three hours in a day. Us Monte-negrins aren't much better.'

The two women got out of the car and Katerina waved Jessica around to the driver's side, offering her a cigarette.

Jessica batted it away but Katerina lit one herself. 'You know about Cheetham Hill, yes?'

'Only what I read up on for the pub raid last night. It's not somewhere I usually end up.'

'There's a wide immigrant community here – Ukrainians, Kosovans, Poles and all sorts of others. I know you're on the right side but that's not how some of them will see it. Some will have had bad experiences with the law at home; some will have seen some of your, how you say, "boys in blue" side with the English if there's ever a problem here.'

'It's not—'

'I know. You don't have to defend yourself. I'm just telling you how some will think. They won't hear your name and understand your position, or even look you in the eye. They'll see that ID and think you're here to cause trouble for them. Don't let them see that you're angry.'

'I'm not angry—'

'It's fine – so am I. It's hard to look these girls in the face, see the marks on their arms, and know they've been brought here as slaves. Don't let these people see that, though. They won't understand why you're angry or who you're angry at. The men who would do this aren't a welcome part of this community either but many think one foreigner is bad, so they all are. That's the stigma these people live with, so hide that anger.'

Jessica knew that if Katerina had read her so easily then other people would be able to as well. The truth was that she was raging inside. She'd been up into the early hours, helping to process the girls they'd found, and now, before midday, she was barely half a mile from the pub needing to be calmed down. She wanted to be angry for them but if Katerina said that would be counter-productive then Jessica had to believe her.

'Did you speak to the other girls?' Katerina asked.

'We found a stack of passports in the gloveboxes of the vans, which was one thing. We know who the women are and where they come from, plus it shouldn't be too difficult to help them return.'

'They are scared for their families.'

'I know. We're doing what we can to talk to the police where they come from but it's not easy and we don't have enough people like you who can speak the language.'

'Where are the women now?'

'We have a few secure houses around the city. We've got all the men in custody but not Pavel and we don't know who else could be involved. Hopefully the women will be returning home in the next couple of days but we need to interview everyone first and that's not easy. Like you say, none of them trust us – for all they know, they'll tell us everything and we'll turn them straight back over to those blokes. Some are talking.'

Katerina took another long drag of her cigarette, holding the smoke in her lungs and then exhaling slowly. 'Did you ever smoke?'

'No.'

'You don't know what you're missing.'

'Cancer?'

Katerina laughed. 'That's the problem with you Brits – always worrying about what's going to happen in twenty years and not seeing what's going on in front of you. You could get hit by a bus tomorrow and I'll bet you wish you had a cigarette then.'

'I'd probably be more worried about my punctured lung and broken limbs.'

Katerina laughed again. 'Esther said you were different.'

'Did she?'

'Something like that. Tell me – who are the men you arrested?'

'We don't really know – none of them are British and none are talking. We found the pub because of the text message that Pavel's phone received. The phone that sent it belonged to one of the two drivers, so we've got that. Our tech boys are trying to see what else they can find. The theory is that they brought vulnerable girls in from places all over Europe, then Pavel organised selling them on, taking a cut of the sale prices.'

'The first girl told me she thought she was here to work in a supermarket. She was excited, thinking she was coming over to stack shelves or work on tills. She'd been told she would get free English lessons.'

'We've been taking statements all morning – they're all similar stories. They thought they were coming over to be nannies or to work in a shop. None of them came through the border legally but it's hard to believe someone brought all of them over together. There have to be other people involved who helped to smuggle them across. They'll probably go to ground now we've arrested their mates.'

Katerina dropped her cigarette butt and trod on it. 'These are the lucky ones and they probably don't even realise it. They'll be wondering why you've stopped them being nannies.' She started walking towards the row of shops. 'Come on.'

The first store had the words 'Polski Deli' over the top. Katerina pushed open the door, releasing a wonderful array of meat-related smells.

The shop was small, barely enough room for a small circular table, a counter and the door. Jessica squeezed inside, peering across at the woman eyeing her suspiciously. Katerina said something in what Jessica assumed was Polish and then switched to English: 'Jessica, this is Halina – she makes the best kielbasa in the city.'

Helpfully, Katerina pointed towards the sausages hanging behind the counter to illustrate her point, simultaneously meaning that Jessica didn't have to ask what a kielbasa was.

Halina was young, dark-haired, with matching dark eyes. She wore a white apron and blue latex gloves along with, apparently, a permanent scowl.

'Jessica is all right,' Katerina added. 'She's with me – you can trust her.'

Halina didn't seem convinced.

Katerina nodded towards Jessica, who reached into her pocket and took out one of the few photos they had of Pavel – the mugshot taken when he'd been arrested for driving without a licence. If only someone had checked his credentials then, he could have been long since sent packing.

She passed it across the counter but Halina only offered the briefest of glances before shaking her head.

'Can you look again?' Katerina asked.

Halina scowled at her and then made a point of glaring at the photo before shaking her head once more.

'It's important,' Jessica said, thinking she was helping. Instead, Halina spun to face her, jabbing an accusing finger.

Her English was perfect: 'Where were you when they smashed our windows?'

'Sorry?'

'You should be sorry. Gangs of your kids, hanging around chanting "Polish scum". We called you but there was some other incident you were attending.' She pointed at the window. 'They threw a brick but where were you? Your vans came an hour later – we had to rely on our own men to protect us. And now you need our help . . .'

'I can only apologise – I don't know the specifics but—'

'Go.'

Halina turned back to Katerina. 'Even if I knew who that was, I wouldn't tell. You shouldn't have brought her here.'

With that, Halina picked up a cleaver and took her frustration out on a cut of meat by slamming it down with a squishy thwack.

Jessica exited quickly, Katerina just behind. 'Don't blame her for that,' Katerina said, tucking her blonde hair behind her ears.

'I don't – but finding Pavel helps everyone, not just us.'

'That reaction is the reason I didn't want to take you around this area before. I know you could've come by yourself but you wouldn't have even got as warm a welcome as that. That's why the people you sent out before got nowhere. There are a few pockets of immigrant communities around the city but this is probably your best bet. We can keep going but you're going to get that reaction a lot. I can do the talking if you want.'

'Would it be better if you were on your own?'

Katerina shook her head. 'If I do that, it makes me look like police. It's one thing to do some consulting and help out but I can still fit in around here. The day I start doing this type of thing on my own is the day I stop being any use to you.'

'In other words, you need me for them to get angry at.'

'That too.'

The next shop was a launderette with the word 'scum' spray-painted across the top.

Katerina led Jessica in anyway, greeting the owner in another language and then switching to English. 'Sorina, this is Jessica, she has something to ask you.'

Jessica took out the photograph again but Sorina barely looked at it. 'Do you even know where I'm from?' Jessica couldn't stop her eyes from flicking to Katerina. 'Of course you don't – everyone calls us Poles, wherever we're from. They call us gippos and scum, shout at our children on the way to school. Where are you then? Some of my children speak better English than yours.'

The venom and clarity to her words made Jessica take a step backwards.

'I'm sorry but we really need to find this man, his name's Pavel—'

Sorina didn't even look down a second time: 'I've never seen him.'

'He's suspected of—'

'I don't care. Unless you have washing, then leave.'

The rest of Jessica's morning was spent in much the same way, Katerina trying her best to point out that Jessica wasn't a threat but with the pair of them struggling to get anything approaching a civil answer. In the shops and businesses that were willing to engage, no one seemed to know who Pavel was; everywhere else there were questions about why the police hadn't acted over a multitude of things that Jessica didn't know the answer to. The odd person would appear to recognise Pavel but then shrink away, refusing to elaborate.

Jessica didn't blame any of them. Katerina didn't even officially work for the police and yet she was one of the few people who could go into the shops, know the owners by name and talk to them in whatever dialect they spoke. Jessica barely knew the name of the bloke in the paper shop two streets over from her.

After the fourteenth store and the fourteenth person who didn't know anything about Pavel, Jessica told Katerina she wanted to go back to the station. If she was going to spend an afternoon taking abuse from people, she would much rather it was from her colleagues.

34

After a late night the previous evening, Jessica was steeling herself for another. In collaboration with the Serious Crime Division, they had decided on seventeen flats or possible brothels around the city where they suspected trafficked girls were being used.

Everyone including the superintendent and DCI Topper was expecting at least one of the raids to turn into an embarrassing situation as they burst in upon a woman selling herself perfectly legally to a punter but it was felt not too many prostitutes would be running off to the media any time soon to complain about a police raid. As ever, the underlying social concerns of why a woman might be doing that job were completely secondary to how the force might look in the media if things went wrong.

Jessica put up with the digs about not kneeing anyone in the head, balls or various other parts of the anatomy and then set off in one of the marked police cars. The two uniformed officers she was with chatted about football while she fiddled on her phone, making herself look busy. With seventeen separate raids happening at the same time, officers had been brought in on overtime from all over, with a member of CID 'overseeing' procedures at each site as if uniform weren't capable of barging into a house and arresting a few people.

The superintendent was in a car on the other side of the city with an ITN news crew following the biggest, toughest-looking uniformed officers they could find at the one flat they were utterly certain was being used for trafficking. If something was going to go wrong, then it definitely wouldn't be there.

Jessica read through the 'intelligence' they had on the flat she was heading towards. There was one noise-related complaint from a neighbour, a statement from a landlord saying he was owed rent from 'some foreign type' and three reviews from various websites.

Liam1985: 'Paid £40 for half hour – what a rip-off! With a name like Fiona, I expected a Brit but she was actually called Flora. Dunno where she's from but they sure don't know how to **** a **** over there!!!! LOL. Well, I would be LOLing if she hadn't taken £40. Avoid!'

Dumboandnoddy: 'Thought I'd splash out with £70 for the hole hr – what a ripoff. Fiona/Flora was so skinny that I cud stick my fingers in between her ribs. Def not a size 8. If you like ******* 12yo boys then ull love her. No tits and wudnt let me anywhere nr her ****. Cant even speak English. Bitch.'

Dave4321: 'Can't speak for the other reviewers but I had a gr8 time with Flora. She was a little out ov it but didn't seem to mind me doing anything, so all the better really. Best £40 I've ever spent. 9/10.'

Quite why a site with such explicit content bothered to blank out the ruder words, Jessica wasn't quite sure – but she hoped someone at the SCD was in the process of trying to trace the IP addresses of the comments left.

The door to Flora's flat was along an alley at the back of a row of shops and up a set of metal stairs. All seventeen properties had been scouted earlier in the day with tactical entry squads sent to the places where they might be needed.

The officer parked the car in the shadows around the corner as they waited for everyone else to check in from the other sites. Predictably, the superintendent, his news crew and personal manicurist – or whatever else he had on the go – were the last to arrive at their raid. If he was going to haul himself off the golf course to plan a raid and spend the evening working rather than drinking champagne at a council function, then he was going to look good doing it.

On his word to get into position, Jessica and the two officers climbed out of the car, locked it – a crucial and much overlooked precaution considering the number of laptops they'd had nicked in the past few years – and then headed into the alley at the back of the shops.

The reason Flora's flat hadn't been afforded the luxury of a tactical entry team was mainly because her front door consisted of such thin wood that even Jessica fancied putting her shoulder through it. They double-checked they had the right number – if anyone was going to cock up tonight then it wouldn't be her – and then pressed themselves against the bricks waiting for the final order.

A minute and a half later and it came: 'Go.'

Jessica turned to the biggest officer, who put his size

elevens to good use with the crunching eloquence of splintering wood, and in they went.

The officer with the big feet was a bit carried away, bellowing 'Get down on the floor' at the top of his voice as if they were ambushing terrorists intent on exploding a dirty bomb, rather than a young woman who was 'def not a size 8' and potentially a punter who would be more worried about finding his pants than anything else.

'I'm not messing, get down on the ground!'

Thump, thump, thump.

Jessica entered behind the two larger, male officers. The front door led into a living room where the lights were on but there were no signs of life. The door directly ahead was closed but there was the sound of a woman's voice and some frantic scrambling.

Big Boot Bertie stormed forward, thrusting open the door and repeating himself. Jessica could see the lower half of a bed and a flash of flesh. She caught the eye of the second officer and pointed him towards the other door off to the right.

Jessica followed the first officer into the bedroom, where the woman she assumed was Flora was screaming and punching the officer in the chest. He reeled back but Jessica got to him first, grabbing his wrist with one hand and Flora's with the other. She tumbled forward onto the bed, letting go of the officer but hanging onto Flora for all she was worth. Somewhere in among trying to avoid being bitten, Jessica shouted at the dumbstruck big-booted officer to stop the man who was wearing only a pair of boxer shorts from escaping.

As Big Boot Bertie lumbered towards him, the punter jumped onto the bed, leapt across the officer's back and bolted out of the door. Flora was spitting, swearing, shouting foreign words, biting and scratching but, for the most part, Jessica was avoiding being hit. The officer righted himself and glanced towards Jessica.

'Go!'

As he ran out of the door, Jessica rolled sideways, keeping her grip on Flora but trying not to either hurt the other woman or get clattered herself. She slipped off the bed, avoided Flora's flailing foot, wrenched up the bottom of the duvet – and then threw it forward until the thrashing woman was entirely covered. Then she sat on her.

She took a breath and shouted: 'Did you get him?'

Jessica could hear scrambling from the other side of the door but didn't want to risk moving in case Flora jumped out of the window or something equally stupid.

'Mmmph.'

'What sort of an answer is that? There are two of you and one of him.'

The face of the second officer appeared in the doorway. 'We got him.'

'So what's the problem?'

'He was a bit, er, excited when we caught him.'

'I don't want to know.'

35

Jessica didn't need Pat to tell her that her first point of call the following morning would be DCI Topper's office. He was on the phone as she reached the glass front of his office but waved her inside with a smile. An actual real, non-fake, non-just-for-her-benefit grin. He pointed at the spare seat, still talking into the phone. 'Yes, Sir; thank you, Sir . . . Oh, I totally agree, Sir. I look forward to it . . . Yes, I'll pass the message on.'

He hung up, leant back in his seat and breathed out. This time his faintly Irish-Scottish-something-non-English-accent was lighter than his usual sharp tone: 'That was a hero-gram from Assistant Chief Constable William Aylesbury on behalf of the entire command team. Over the course of the past two nights, we've nicked nine people for people trafficking, five for pimping, four for drugs offences because of what we found in their flats last night, eight for paying for sex with a prostitute under threat of violence. We've also got thirty girls at various stages of being returned home away from people exploiting them. The immigration lot are trying to keep it quiet that they let these girls across in the first place but sod them. That ITN piece is scheduled for tonight and the super says they had a massive result at the place they went to. Even Serious Crime are happy that we didn't blow the cover at any of the other places they're monitoring. This is about as joined-up as we ever get. Everyone's bloody delighted. I even got the kids to school on time this morning.'

'That's good, Sir.'

Jessica waited for the '. . . but where the hell's Pavel' but it never came. Topper was still beaming. He turned around and scrubbed three cases off the whiteboard, meaning it was only two-thirds full of things they hadn't solved. Underneath the board, a canvas bag for life sat with trainers and shorts resting on top. As he spun around, he noticed her watching and patted his belly. 'Got to keep yourself in shape nowadays.'

Jessica couldn't believe she said it but somehow the words popped out anyway. 'We're still looking for Pavel.'

He nodded, although a hint of the grin still remained. 'We're still interviewing our way through everyone from the past two nights. One can only be hopeful. Even if none of them talk, then he's lost many of his lieutenants. We'll get him.'

The fact Topper was sounding so enthusiastic was disconcerting considering Jessica only needed one hand to count the number of positive things he had previously said to her. 'Should I get back to work?'

She motioned towards the door but Topper waved his hand animatedly. 'No, I suppose I owe you something of an apology.'

'Me?'

'You're the one here.'

'Oh.'

'When I was brought into the job, I was introduced to

a lot of new people in a very short period. You were obviously off work following what happened to you but I heard certain things and I suppose that coloured my impression of what you were about. I should have relied on my own opinions instead of listening to others.' He held out his hand for Jessica to shake. 'Can we start again?'

Jessica peered at his face but there was no hint of something deeper going on. His eyes were twinkling, his hair recently washed, the gentle wrinkles making him seem rugged rather than old. She reached forward and shook his hand, then put her arms back by her side, feeling a little silly.

'Can I ask you something, Sir?'

'What?'

'You said that other people had told you things about me – but who?'

He studied her, puffing out his cheeks. 'I probably shouldn't say.' Jessica assumed he was talking about Chief Constable Graham Pomeroy but had no real way of knowing. 'Did you do something to upset the command team?' he asked.

Jessica shook her head. 'I know Assistant Chief Constable Aylesbury fairly well – he used to do your job.'

Topper's eyes flashed away, indicating that it wasn't Aylesbury he meant. 'Never mind – you've done well these past days. If we can kick on and find Pavel, we might be able to put together the final pieces of this and the robbery case. Now wouldn't that be nice?'

'Yes, Sir.'

After a bit more praise, Jessica finally managed to extricate herself and headed down the stairs. Pat had sugar around his mouth and was busy swallowing something as she passed. He held out an arm to get her attention and then treated her to an expert, though rather rancid, display of masticating.

'Sorry,' he eventually said, not sounding it, 'I've got a note from someone called Esther for you – she said to call her. Apparently your phone's off.'

'I was in a meeting.'

'I'm still not your answering service.'

'Judging by the number of messages you take, it seems like you're everyone's answering service.'

Esther had been so worried about security that she refused either to email or text Jessica the address, instead telling her over the phone. Jessica had no clue where she was going but followed Esther's vague instructions about turning right by a petrol station, second left after a pub, going straight on for three-quarters of a mile and then turning left-right-left and looking for number thirty-five.

Except that there wasn't a thirty-five.

Not wanting to call Esther and admit defeat, Jessica retraced her steps, tried right-left-right, and still couldn't find the house. She vaguely remembered this was what things used to be like before satnavs and mobile phones and then finally gave in, calling Esther and realising it was second right after the pub, not left.

The house in which Ana had been put into protective custody was a cosy two-bedroom semi-detached close to a newish housing estate. Esther had been clear that Jessica couldn't bring a marked car and couldn't wear anything that looked vaguely 'policey'. When members of the public thought of 'protective custody', the idea of huge gated houses and patrolling trigger-happy guards came to mind but the truth was generally that it was a normal house in a normal area. Hiding in plain sight was by far the safest policy in almost all cases.

Jessica parked a street away and walked to the address. She knocked on the white uPVC front door and had barely taken her hand away when it was yanked open. A hand reached out, dragged her inside and shut it behind her. Barely a second had passed.

Esther was wearing a pair of jeans and a loose thin top. Her hair was wet and down. The first time Jessica had met her, she'd been staying with a mother who'd lost her child and the casual clothes made Jessica flash back.

'Found it then?' Esther said.

'No thanks to you. How hard is it to figure out which way's left and which is right?'

'I gave you the correct directions – you're the one who can't follow instructions.'

Jessica leant forward and gave her a quick hug. 'Who's here?'

'Ana, Katerina and me. They wanted to leave an officer but it would've drawn more attention because they'd have to swap shifts. We've got panic buttons all over the place plus there are only four people who know for sure that Ana's here – and we're all here now. Plus you'll forget where the house is as soon as you've pulled away, so it's only really three.'

'How's she doing?'

'Good. We sorted out a passport with the Ukrainian Embassy, even though they wanted her to go down to London originally. We talked them out of it when we pointed out she could be in danger but the real reason is that Ana didn't trust any of them. There are a few more bits of paperwork to sort out and then she's flying home on Tuesday or Wednesday next week.'

'Has she been going out?'

'Only into the garden. I've been to get milk and stuff, and Katerina brought some pizza over last night. I heard you had an eventful one.'

'I sat on a prostitute while one of the uniforms I was with had an unfortunate eye-poking incident.'

'Sounds like a normal day then!'

Jessica smiled. 'Can I say hello?'

'That's why you're here – I think Ana's got something to say to you, too.'

Esther led Jessica into the living room where Ana was curled up on the sofa cuddling a cushion while Katerina read a book in an armchair. The television was on quietly: some daytime quiz show with a cheap-looking set and buffoonish contestants.

Ana slipped her bare feet onto the floor as Jessica entered and dropped the cushion. She stood and offered her hand for Jessica to shake, bowing her head. 'Thank you.'

'Er, okay . . .'

'I speak to my sister at home and she's safe.'

Ana sat again and Jessica took a seat next to her. 'That's great. We talked to the police there and they were really accommodating. Well, I say "we", one of our translators did.'

'They're going to help move us when I get back. It's all arranged.'

'Perfect.' Jessica glanced across to Katerina. 'Is it right you're escorting her?'

Katerina looked up from her book, smiling gently. She'd had her hair done since Jessica last saw her, the blonde strands lighter and shorter than they were.

'I couldn't resist the free flight.' She grinned. 'Are you staying? I was about to go out for a run and then I'll pick up something to eat on the way back.'

'No, I've still got work to do.'

Katerina closed her book and pushed herself up from the chair. 'All right – if I don't see you before then thanks for sorting all of this. Good luck finding Pavel.'

She left the room, leaving Jessica and Ana alone. At the mention of Pavel's name, Ana had pulled her legs back up.

'Do you have any idea where he is?' Jessica asked.

Ana shook her head.

'He's not going to get you here. You're perfectly safe and it'll all be over in a few days.'

'I'm sorry.'

'What for?'

Ana held her hands up, showing what was left of her nails. Jessica was suddenly aware of the dull ache at the bottom of her neck from where she had fought with Ana in the flat when Pavel had got away.

Jessica waved her hand: 'It's fine. I know you thought I was coming to hurt you. If my Ukrainian was good enough I'd tell you a story about someone getting poked in the eye by something that wasn't a finger.'

Ana squinted at her, confused, but Jessica shook her head, standing and offering her hand to Ana one final time. 'I'd say it's been good meeting you but . . . well – it'll be nice when you're safe.'

They shook hands again, even though Jessica wasn't entirely convinced Ana knew what she was talking about. She found Esther in the kitchen, said goodbye to her, and then walked back through the streets, Pavel on her mind. Where the hell was he?

Back at the station and things were beginning to wind down for the week. Given his good mood, Jessica had convinced DCI Topper to use his influence to rearrange her rota, giving her the full weekend off. Considering the number of days in a row she'd done something work-related, she was looking forward to being at home. Perhaps she'd put her feet up and spend two days eating pizza and watching some rubbish television? Or perhaps she'd find out if Bex wanted to go somewhere and do something that didn't involve her reading textbooks, cleaning up or baking for a weekend? Perhaps she'd get lucky by going shopping and finding Pavel in the women's section of Selfridges?

As she walked into reception, Pat was bent over the counter breathing deeply.

'Please tell me you're not having a heart attack?' Jessica said.

He heaved himself up. 'Too much custard.'

'I think you're the first person in human history who's ever uttered that sentence.'

Pat picked up a paper bag from under the desk and pushed it towards Jessica. 'You take it. Three-for-two custard doughnuts – they've nearly bloody killed me.'

'How many did you buy?'

'Six.'

'How many did you eat?'

'Five. They're too nice. It's manna from heaven.' He groaned again. 'They're from that bakery down by the Aquatics Centre I told you about.'

Jessica picked up the cake bag and slid the doughnut out. She'd never known Pat willingly give away food before. This was truly a first. She was about to take a bite when she noticed the writing on the bag. Doughnut still in her mouth, she rotated the paper around until the circular logo was facing her. Slowly, she removed the cake from her mouth and put it back on the counter.

'Aren't you going to eat that?' he said.

'Pat, how long ago did this bakery open?'

'I'm not sure, I saw the forum post recommending it a few months ago. It had only just opened then.'

'How many months ago?'

'Three or four?'

'So this bakery opened around four months ago?'

'I suppose. Why?'

Jessica held up the bag: 'Because the person who runs it is called Poppy.'

36

When the priest had first mentioned the name 'Poppy', Jessica knew she'd seen it before somewhere – and there it had been: staring out at her from a crumpled paper bag every time she passed Pat's desk.

With the afternoon wearing on, there was no time to waste. Most similar shops would close at three or four o'clock and likely not reopen until Monday. It was a little after half past two and Jessica had twenty-five minutes to make what was technically a five-minute journey along Stockport Road. In Manchester traffic, especially on a Friday, it could take anything up to an hour.

Jessica dashed outside and raced out of the car park, making the journey in a surprising five minutes. She parked half on the pavement outside the shop next door and took a moment or two to survey the shop front.

Poppy's Bakery had a greengrocer on one side and a pub on the other. It had a white and red awning and the window frames had been painted a bright white some time recently. The shop was narrow with a single window displaying a few leftover cakes and breads. A metal shutter was at the top, ready to be pulled down. There was no sign, simply an A-frame sandwich board on the pavement with the same circular logo that was on the paper bag.

Jessica approached the window and peered inside. The

glare meant she could see little more than what was immediately in front of her but that was enough to notice that
Pat had good reason to keep coming back. Eclairs, chocolate-
dipped shortbreads, strawberry tarts, pink fondant fancies,
mini Victoria sponges, chocolate brownies, fruity iced buns
. . . Jessica was practically drooling against the window
when she remembered what she was supposed to be doing.

The door opened with a satisfying tinkle. Ahead were
two small circular tables surrounded by chairs and a room
at the back with a cooker visible. To her left, a woman was
clearing the cakes and biscuits out of the glass cabinet. She
had dark hair hidden underneath a blue hair net, deep
brown eyes and freckles. It was Rosemary Dean, Pavel's
wife, the woman for whom they'd been searching.

'I'm packing up for the day,' Rosemary said, looking up
and smiling prettily. 'Anything in the window is two-for-
one if you want it.'

'Are you Poppy?'

The woman stood up straighter, her smile shrinking
slightly. 'That's what some people call me.'

'But your real name's Rosemary?'

The smile disappeared as Rosemary dried her hands on
a tea towel. She spoke slowly as she gazed Jessica up and
down. 'Who are you?'

'Where's Pavel?'

The woman's eyes widened as she glanced towards the
front door and then the back room, not that there was
anywhere to go. 'Who?'

'You married him.'

Rosemary started working more quickly, bundling cakes

into boxes. 'I'm sorry, I really have to finish here. You'll have to leave.'

Jessica held her ID out for Rosemary to see. 'It's not as simple as that. We've been looking for you for a little while. And him.'

As Rosemary glanced at the door again, Jessica realised it wasn't because she had a desire to escape, it was because she was scared. Her hand was shaking.

'Do you want me to lock it?' Jessica asked, nodding at the door.

Rosemary caught Jessica's eye, an understanding passing between them. She nodded slightly and then put the box down. Jessica pulled the latch across the front door and dropped the blind. 'Is there somewhere we can talk?'

The other woman's eyes had glazed over and it looked as if she had shrunk by an inch or two. 'I live upstairs.'

Jessica nodded – that partly explained why they hadn't been able to find her. Rosemary led the way into the kitchen, sliding a bolt across the back door, and then opening what at first looked like a cupboard and heading up a set of carpeted stairs.

The flat above was minimal but functional: sofa, armchair, coffee table, television and not much else. Rosemary picked up a notepad from a drawer underneath the television. 'My recipe book,' she said, sitting on the sofa and cradling it to her chest protectively, as if it was a first-born.

Jessica took the chair. 'Who owns all of this?'

'It's on a mortgage. The shop's doing all right and that pays the monthly amounts.'

'Whose name is on the deeds?'

'Mine.'

'Which is . . . ?'

Rosemary sighed. She must have known that it wouldn't take much for Jessica to check. 'It's under Rose Pooley. It was my original name from when I was a kid.'

'Where does Dean come from?'

'My mum got remarried when I was six or seven and I took my stepfather's name. Most of my documents were still for Pooley though. My birth certificate has Pooley on it but my passport has Dean. When we . . . I . . . was sorting out the mortgage for here, I used my birth certificate.'

That explained an awful lot about why she'd been so hard to find. Few realised how easy it was to obtain official documents in a slightly different name based upon various marriages. Jessica had once arrested someone for shoplifting with seven different aliases, all of which the woman had justification to use because her mother had remarried four times and she'd been married twice herself. As well as using her mother's original maiden name, she had a dozen credit cards with different combinations of name. As things went, it wasn't too difficult to deal with – but when people started applying for passports and driving licences with different identities, that's when the police could really have a job on their hands.

'Where does Poppy come from?'

'It was a nickname from when I was a kid. I liked spinach and some of the boys used to call me Popeye, then it sort of evolved. I thought it would be nice for the bakery.'

'What about Adamek?'

Rosemary peered away from Jessica towards the window. 'I've never used that name.'

There was ice in her voice. Not exactly hateful but certainly not the way most people who had been married for five months would talk about their other halves.

'Where did you get the money for the deposit on this place?'

'Do you already know?'

'We can probably find out now that we know about the shop and the name on the deed.'

Rosemary stood and took her apron off. Underneath she was wearing loose dark trousers and a white smock. 'How much do you know?'

'Let's assume nothing.'

The woman shrugged and took a deep breath. She seemed resigned to her fate: 'Pavel needed a way to stay in the country and I wanted to do something with my life that wasn't working in a supermarket. It worked out for each of us.'

'Where is he?'

'I don't know.'

'He's wanted for a suspected murder. It happened a week or so after you got married.'

Rosemary peered away. 'I'm not very good at keeping up with the news.'

'That's not what I asked.'

'What do you want me to say?'

Jessica realised that confessions about who knew what and when wouldn't do much good, not yet anyway.

Rosemary was happily living her life as Poppy, rarely needing to leave the sanctity of the place where she lived and worked. Of course she knew what Pavel was wanted for – and that she should have contacted the police. She'd almost certainly known this day was going to come at some point but figured she would ride it out for as long as she could. She'd not exactly gone into hiding, she had simply waited for someone to put the pieces together and find her.

'This is what I've always wanted,' Rosemary said quietly, peering at her notebook. 'I started writing these recipes when I was a kid. We went on this trip to the lakes for a weekend and there was this little bakery in the middle of the village with all these amazing creations in the window. I've been fascinated ever since and always wanted my own place. When my mum split up with my actual dad, I went off the rails a bit and was a naughty kid. Eventually I grew up but I'd already messed around too much at school and then no one wants to give you a chance. I was at a supermarket and hated that. I went to a few banks about getting a loan but no one was interested. I had full business plans and everything – I knew I could make money – but they didn't want to know. All I needed was a deposit and enough for the equipment.'

'How did you end up meeting a Serbian gangster?'

Rosemary's gaze flickered to Jessica and quickly away again. She didn't want to think that was where the money had come from.

'It sounds awful when you put it like that.'

'I can't stop something being true.'

Rosemary breathed deeply, blinking rapidly. 'A friend of a school friend. That type of thing.'

'What's the friend's name?'

'Does it make much difference?'

'That depends on how involved they are.'

For a few moments, Rosemary said nothing. She pulled off the hairnet and dropped it on the table, letting her long dark hair cascade around her shoulders. In a girl-next-door way, she was very pretty. 'Is there anything wrong with wanting to turn your life around?'

Jessica thought of the young women who were on the brink of being sold to the highest bidder as Pavel watched from the shadows. Of the fear Ana must have had that she was willing to attack Jessica to help him get away. His money came off the back of slavery and desolation – and that was the stuff they knew about. Given he'd probably murdered a drug dealer, there was a strong likelihood he had fingers in other pies too.

'I suppose that depends on how you do it,' Jessica replied. 'If you need money then it depends on whose lives are affected by where it comes from.'

Rosemary nodded but Jessica didn't know if she really understood what Pavel was about. It was obvious she wasn't going to give up her 'friend' without reason, if then.

Jessica continued: 'How did your friend know Pavel?'

'I'd gone to ask if I could borrow some money but it was quite a lot. They said they didn't have it but that they might know someone who did. A few days later, I was given a phone number and it turned out to be Pavel's. We met in this pub in the city centre. He said he needed a proper way to stay in the country and that he was looking to invest in something to make his life easier.'

That was one of the other things Jessica hadn't understood but now it made sense. If all Pavel needed was a game English girl, there were plenty he could have thrown a few hundred quid at to marry him. Spending tens of thousands on a business was unnecessary – except that it gave him a place to help launder his money. Books-wise, so what if a cooker needed repairing every other week? So what if a company was paid to do the cleaning even if Rosemary did it herself? So what if all of the ingredients she used cost a premium? Somehow, that money would find its way back to Pavel. It wasn't simply a marriage he wanted, it was a way to keep his money.

No wonder Rosemary had remained quiet and kept her head down. Jessica had a flash of how disappointed Pat was going to be when this place ended up being closed down.

Rosemary tossed her notebook on the table and slumped back into her seat. 'What happens now?'

'I suppose that depends on a few things – largely on how much you're able to help us.'

'What do you want to know?'

Jessica started to ask something else about Pavel but stopped herself. There was something that had been eating at her for days and this was her best way of finding out for sure. 'Father James.'

'What about him?'

'Did he know you were only getting married to keep Pavel here?'

Rosemary smiled sadly. 'Pavel's a Catholic and said that he wanted things to be done properly. I went along with him because I wanted a place like this. Father James was lovely. I suppose if ever I get a chance to have a proper wedding, it would be nice if it was via someone like him.'

So Jessica had been wrong.

She blinked, holding her eyes closed for a fraction of a second, knowing she needed to move on. She hated reading people incorrectly.

When Jessica opened them again, Rosemary was staring at her. 'Do you know where Pavel is?' Jessica asked.

'I really don't.' Rosemary took a breath, making a decision that she hoped would help her out of the mess she'd got herself into. 'But I know where he's going to be.'

37

Jessica's weekend off was going the way of so many of her other weekends off. It wasn't the 'weekend' part that was the problem, it was more the 'off' bit that she seemed to have trouble with. She could have ignored the logo on Pat's cake bag, coasted through the rest of Friday and then had a gentle two days off in the bath, reading, watching television, going out and doing something with Bex or any number of other activities that normal people got up to when they weren't working. But oh no, she couldn't leave Rosemary until Monday and, as such, her Saturday was already written off.

Greater Manchester Police had staked a few properties out over time, mainly clichéd places like pubs, potential drug dens and the like. No one Jessica could find had ever heard of them staking out a cake shop. Pat was distraught – the fact the bakery could be closed down for money-laundering made his face sink like he'd just been told he'd lost a child.

As Rosemary continued as if it was business as usual, Jessica sat in the flat upstairs watching what was going on below on a series of monitors. This time things had been properly thought out. Alongside Jessica were two members of the tactical firearms squad; waiting in the back yard, hidden in the shed, were two more; across the street in the back of a furniture removal van were another five. Two cameras had been placed in the shop; another was facing the back door; one more faced the front, plus there were three plain-clothed spotters doing laps of the area dressed as joggers and, apparently, a student. What exactly that involved, Jessica wasn't quite sure – presumably looking hungover at this time on a Saturday morning.

Rosemary had told Jessica that Pavel always came around before lunch on Saturday – but that the time could vary. She would give him cash in an envelope, he'd never count it, and then he'd be gone until the next week. Rosemary had been perfectly compliant, allowing the teams to fit their cameras overnight and telling them everything she knew – which wasn't much. They could have arrested her and kept her in the cells but there was little point, so two officers had been placed in her flat overnight and now they were waiting for Pavel to show up.

After opening at nine on the dot, Rosemary had already served a dozen customers ten minutes later. They streamed in to order their usual array of sausage rolls, breakfast barms, pasties or – in one man's case – a dozen eclairs. Also to her credit, Rosemary had gone out of her way to accommodate the officers. On the coffee table in front of Jessica was a plate of chocolate-dipped shortbreads sandwiched together with buttercream, five eclairs and half a breakfast barm. The two tactical firearms officers had made short work of theirs but Jessica could only handle so much egg and bacon in a roll at this time of the morning. Well, that was a lie: she just didn't want to fill up on bread when there were cakes on the go.

Assuming Pavel turned up as expected, Jessica was confident they'd get their man, her only worry being that any of the officers with a gun would be so engrossed by a cream cake that they'd slip and end up shooting themselves or one of their colleagues. Still, more cake for her if that happened.

Jessica guessed that Pavel wouldn't make an appearance while the morning rush was on – it was hard to inconspicuously take an envelope stuffed with cash – so she relaxed onto the sofa, picking her way through the first eclair.

'Big guy on his way.'

The single sentence from one of the spotters made Jessica sit up straight, eyes fixed on the monitor as a 'big guy' tinkled his way into the shop. Jessica leant forward – the man was certainly large but more wide than tall. He had a baseball cap pulled down over his face and a bag for life in each hand.

A tinny voice from the van across the street sounded across the radio: 'Is it him?'

'Wait.'

Jessica peered from one camera to the other, trying to get a clear view. He wasn't taking an envelope, instead he was pointing towards the window. Rosemary picked up a cardboard box and placed two strawberry tarts in it alongside a pair of Easter biscuits.

One of the two tactical firearms officers was waiting by the door to the stairs as the other gazed over Jessica's shoulder. 'What's he doing?'

'It looks like he's stocking up . . . hang on a minute . . .'

Jessica leant in just as the man swivelled to point towards a large chocolate cornflake cake on the main counter. 'It's Fat Pat! He knows we're going to shut the place down so he's buying two of everything.'

She told everyone to rest and then, sure enough, Pat jabbed a flabby finger at pretty much every creation on display, put all of the boxes in his bags for life, paid in cash, and then tugged his baseball cap down before waddling back the way he'd come. Jessica was in half a mind to tell the team in the van outside to snatch him anyway just to teach him a lesson but she figured Topper or the superintendent would have a word instead. Either that or they'd be around his house pronto to help him eat everything before it went off.

An hour passed and everyone's interest started to dip. The two firearms officers were chatting about how United had been 'robbed' by the referee during the week and one of the five officers cooped up in the back of the van was whingeing that his bladder wasn't going to last much longer. Meanwhile, one of the spotters dressed as a jogger was moaning that his legs had gone and that he needed a sit-down. Jessica was having visions of Pavel escaping while one officer was peeing in a bush, hastily trying to pick his gun up, with another dressed as a jogger bent over double saying that he'd already done too much running. Considering the eclairs she'd polished off, Jessica didn't think she'd be doing too much sprinting any time soon either.

'Something's happening.'

The two words were barely a whisper but came from

the pair of officers crammed into the rickety wooden shed in the yard at the back of the shop.

Jessica turned to the camera showing the rear, where a figure in a large heavy coat was standing hood up, with his hands in his pockets. From his size, it could easily be Pavel but he was facing away, peering towards the shed. Had he heard the whisper?

The two officers in the room with her stepped towards the door but Jessica hissed at them to wait. If it was Pavel, he had somehow stridden past the people supposedly keeping an eye out for him and was only a few metres from the gate at the back. Any loud noise could send him scarpering again.

The figure continued to stare towards the shed in a bizarre stand-off between man and slightly rotting wood. After a couple of seconds, he reached into the pocket of his coat and took the two steps towards it. He could have a gun, a knife, anything. Jessica held the radio close to her mouth, waiting . . . hoping a late call didn't lead to a situation where someone was harmed, praying that the armed officers didn't get twitchy and shoot him for being too close.

At the last moment, the figure moved to the right of the shed where he lifted the lid of a wheelie bin and dropped a host of food wrappers inside. If it was Pavel, he might be a people trafficker, pimp, thief, murderer and any number of other things – but apparently he wasn't a litter bug.

He opened the back door without knocking and then headed through the kitchen into the main part of the shop, pulling his hood down and ruffling his hair.

Pavel.

'Team one go.'

Jessica heard the opening of van doors and nodded to the armed officers. 'Don't sodding shoot him,' then into the radio: 'Team two go.'

Crash, bang, thump, thump, thump. 'Get on the floor', shouty-shout-shout.

Jessica watched on the monitor as Pavel turned a full circle, definitely not getting on the floor, despite the armed officers in front of and behind him.

More shouting.

Jessica headed carefully down the stairs, pressing between the four officers in the doorway of the kitchen, guns at the ready.

Pavel grinned as he saw her, recognition in his face. 'You no shoot?'

He took a step towards the counter. Jessica could see Rosemary on the other side, lying on the floor, hands on her head, body shaking.

'Get on the floor, Pavel,' Jessica said.

Another step until he was resting against the glass of the counter. The coat made him look even bigger than he actually was. His forearms were like joints of gammon. He smiled even wider: 'You shoot?'

Jessica didn't know if he was goading them into shooting him but he certainly didn't seem too bothered. Space was tight with four gunmen in one doorway, five in the other and her trying to keep a distance from Pavel while also making sure both sides had a clear shot just in case. Over the shoulders of the officers in the door, Jessica could see pedestrians beginning to mass and point. This was the last thing they needed.

'On. The. Floor.'

As he continued smiling, Jessica could see a golden tooth glinting towards the back of the mouth.

'Shoot,' Pavel said with a grin, egging them on.

Jessica didn't want to say 'don't shoot' out loud but she hoped the officers would know well enough. They bloody should, considering the amount of forms they had to fill in for every bullet fired. One of the officers close to the front door lowered his gun and took a step forward, reaching for his handcuffs. Behind him, the other four tensed, weapons still focused on Pavel.

'You heard the lady,' he said firmly.

Jessica had long suspected the firearms lot presumed they were one step away from being in an action film and that confirmed it. If he arrested Pavel and followed it up with a 'You're welcome, Ma'am', she'd show him why she was being called Ball-breaker around the station.

Pavel glanced from Jessica to the officer and back again, knowing there was nowhere to go, that he was heavily outnumbered, and that they weren't going to shoot for the sake of it.

In a flash of movement, he reached towards the counter, picking up the large Victoria sponge and hurling it over his shoulder just as the officer from the front door rugby-tackled him. Three more piled in, wrenching his arms backwards and cuffing him. One rested on his legs while another knelt in the crook of his back.

Considering no one had been shot and one of their

most-wanted was in custody, on the surface it couldn't have gone much better. Unfortunately for Jessica, the first sniggers began as soon as the officer who had rugby-tackled Pavel looked up to see if she wanted to read the caution.

As she picked the sponge, icing and jam out of her eyes, Jessica told the officer he could do it.

38

Jessica glanced up at the red light underneath the camera and then peered across the table in the interview room. After twenty minutes in the station's shower, she was pretty sure she'd got all of the cake out of her hair but there was still a slightly sugary smell, the origins of which she couldn't quite figure out.

Pavel was cuffed to the table but it still felt as if he could wrench his way free Hollywood-style if he really tried. Someone had mentioned something about needing specially enlarged cuffs to fit his wrists, which hardly made Jessica feel any better. His sleeves were rolled up, exposing broad, hairy arms that looked like giant caterpillars. His vast shoulders were hunched forward with that too-small head facing the table.

'Is your name Pavel Adamek?' Jessica asked.

His reply was thick with accent but perfectly clear: 'I do not speak English.'

'Were you born in Serbia?'

'I do not speak English.'

'If that's true, we're obliged to get you a translator. Is that what you want?'

'I do not speak English.'

Two hours later and they were back in the same positions, this time with a dark-haired woman sitting next to Pavel. She'd moved the chair away to give herself a little space but he was so big that it was almost impossible unless she swapped to the other side of the table.

Jessica glanced towards the translator and then back at Pavel.

'Is your name Pavel Adamek?'

'I do not speak English.'

The woman translated, ending with the words 'Pavel Adamek'.

Pavel replied in a language that sounded similar but the translator turned to Jessica with an apologetic sigh: 'He says he doesn't speak English.'

'Were you born in Serbia?'

'I do not speak English.'

The translator tried again only to be met by something that sounded like: 'Ya knee go for rim English ski.'

She turned to Jessica: 'He said he—'

'I get it.' Jessica wasn't quite sure what to do yet persisted anyway: 'Did you come to the UK illegally?'

'I do not speak English . . . Ya knee go for rim English ski.'

'Did you marry Rosemary Dean in order to stay here?'

'I do not speak English . . . Ya knee go for rim English ski.'

'It's going to be a long day if that's all you've got to say.'

'I do no—'

'Yeah, yeah, you enjoy rimming on a ski slope and you don't speak English. I get it. I used to go out with a guy like this – not the rimming. The moment you asked him to do the washing up or anything really, he forgot which language he spoke.'

Pavel didn't move. 'I do not speak English.'

'You might not speak the language but you definitely understand it – so you can sit there refusing to talk and I'll tell you what's going to happen. First—' The translator cut in but Jessica held a hand up to stop her. 'First, we're going to test the swab we took to confirm for absolute certain that samples of your skin were found under the nails of the drug dealer you beat to death. It will come back positive and you will go to jail for it whether or not you speak English. Second, you'll be charged with entering the UK illegally. There's also every chance we'll be able to charge you with false representation offences, such as getting a priest to marry you without him knowing you weren't allowed to be here. We've got enough to charge you for money-laundering, threats, exploitation under the Sexual Offences Act, people trafficking . . . it's quite a shopping list.'

'I do not speak English.'

'I want to ask you about the burglaries you were charged for in Serbia.'

'I do not speak English.'

'Who did you tell over here?'

'I do not speak English.'

'Was it members of your gang or someone else?'

He peered up from the table for the first time, staring her straight in the eyes. His were grey and emotionless. 'I do not speak English.'

'Who was the man with the local accent?'

'I do not—'

Jessica slumped back into her seat, defeated.

'—speak English.'

Jessica sat in the station's canteen, machine-made tea in a plastic cup, man-made egg on toast uneaten on a plate. Well, there was probably a chicken involved somewhere but the man behind the counter had certainly fried it.

Across the table, someone squeaked a chair across the floor and then slid in. 'All right?'

DC Dave Rowlands was looking tired, bags under his eyes, hair flat, and a general sagginess to his face that was otherwise hard to describe.

'Do you want egg on toast?'

'Go on then.'

Jessica slid the plate across the table and handed him the knife and fork.

'How's life?' she asked.

'I've got to get away from Franks. The guy's a lunatic. Because you were involved in all those arrests this week, he keeps saying you've got one over him and we need to catch up. He's one step away from us going door-to-door to ask if anyone's committed a crime. Plus he keeps disappearing. One minute, he'll be there asking why you've not arrested someone, the next he's gone for an hour.'

'He probably sneaks out to Whitworth Park to sniff the seats in the public toilets.'

Rowlands swallowed some of the toast and smiled. 'How was the cake?'

'For crying out loud – how does anyone ever get

anything done around here? The minute something happens, the gossip merchants are out in force.'

'That doesn't answer the question.'

'Fine – the cake *would* have been good if I wasn't wearing half of it. I had to walk onto the street covered in it and then I was in the back of one of the cars returning here.'

'Someone with a camera phone must've got a picture of that.'

'They'd better bloody not have done.'

'What about your Serbian bloke?'

'He does not speak English.'

Dave reached across and had a sip of Jessica's tea. 'I thought he'd been here for a while.'

'Oh, he has. All I could get him to say was that he didn't speak the language. Then he told the translator the exact same thing. There are more insightful things written on the walls of the women's toilets.'

'Like what?'

'Never you mind. Anyway, the point is that we've got him for about half-a-dozen charges – but he won't say a word about the robberies.'

'Have you got anything to link him?'

'Only the fact that his criminal record in Serbia has the exact type of home invasions on it. Not just similar – they're the same. It can't be a coincidence and yet if someone that size broke into your house, you'd remember it, wouldn't you? Even if he didn't speak.'

'So it wasn't him?'

Jessica took her tea back and drank the rest in one as Dave sliced into the yolk, sending the yellow liquid running pleasingly across the plate.

'It was and it wasn't,' Jessica replied, 'but we're not going to get it from him. I think he told someone what he'd been up to in Serbia and they took his idea and ran with it.'

'Who?'

'If I knew that, I wouldn't be sat here watching you eat my lunch, would I?'

Dave delved into his pocket. 'Have you got fifty pence?'

'What for?'

'Another tea.'

Jessica stood and fished in her pocket. 'Somewhere, I . . .' She stopped, a thought suddenly dropping into her mind.

'What?' Rowlands asked.

'Rosemary.'

'Who?'

'She said she'd gone to ask her friend for money but she was after thousands.'

'You're talking to yourself, Jess.'

Jessica sat back down. 'If you wanted thousands of pounds, tens of thousands, you wouldn't go to a normal mate, would you? You'd go to someone you knew had cash who might be willing to give it away. Or at least lend it. Rosemary said she was a naughty child after her parents broke up. I wonder which school she went to . . .'

Jessica was halfway towards the door when she stopped,

spun, and strode back to the table. She planted a fifty-pence piece next to the plate, kissed Dave on the forehead and muttered 'I miss you', before rushing off to her office.

39

The collection of items on the driveways around Martin Teague's house was down to just the one skip, although there were still three cars each with a wheel missing, the row of rusting motorbikes, the vandalised green telephone exchange box, garages with paint peeling, scrap and old number plates. In addition, just to make the area feel more welcoming, someone had used a black marker pen to draw a penis onto the exchange box.

Welcome to Manchester.

As she rang the bell next to the cherry wood double-glazed door, Jessica could hear Joy Division thundering out from the inside, not sounding particularly joyful.

She thumped on the doorframe, then the window, then tried the doorbell again. Eventually, the music went quiet and Teague opened the door, wearing what appeared to be the same dressing gown she'd seen him in last time: 'For God's sake – that bitch next door is lying to you,' he thundered. 'We weren't even arguing – we just had a few mates over. Is that a crime now?'

'Can I come in?' Jessica asked.

Teague didn't move, blocking the door: 'Are you actually asking this time?'

'You remember those words that just came out of my

mouth; the bit where I said "Can I come in?" – that was me asking.'

'Suit your sodding self.'

Teague stood to the side as Jessica wound her way through the house into the living room. A couple of the magazines seemed different but there were still music videos playing silently on the television and the entire place had a morbid, desolate feel to it.

'There are no tea bags so you can get stuffed,' Teague said as he sat.

'Charming. You're not doing that reality TV thing where they host dinner parties, are you?'

'What?'

'Thought not. Anyway – I've got a question for you.'

'What?'

'How do you know Pavel Adamek?'

'Who?'

Teague didn't blink and neither did Jessica. 'Bloody hell: for someone who's been arrested as many times as you, you could at least string it out a bit. "Pavel who?", "I don't know an Adamek", that kind of thing. I was expecting a good hour out of this.'

Teague stared at her as if she was speaking a foreign language. Not another one . . .

'Okay, I'll make it easy for you,' Jessica said. 'It's called word association. I say something and you reply with the first thing that pops into your head. Here goes: Pavel Adamek.'

'Who?'

'Fine, if you're not going to play along, how about Rosemary Dean?'

Teague had the same fixed, emotionless expression on his face: 'Who?'

'Oh, for f—. Look, you can't deny knowing her – you went to school together. I checked and everything.'

Teague's eyebrows met in the middle as he screwed his features up. 'Rosie Dean?'

'If that's what you call her. When was the last time you spoke?'

He shrugged. 'Rosie? I dunno. Ages.'

'Rosemary was looking for money to start a business. She couldn't get money from a bank, so she thought to herself, "Now who do I know with nine point eight million lying around?" Mistakenly, she thought you had money left, so she popped around for a brew and asked if you could lend her some. Perhaps she had a business plan with her?'

Jessica still hadn't been able to get Rosemary to talk about her friend but there had been enough recognition when the woman was asked about Martin Teague that she knew she was onto something.

'Oh, aye, I do remember,' Teague replied, scratching his head. 'It was a little while ago – I don't think she'd seen the papers. She phoned up and asked if I could help but all my money had gone.'

'Right, so you told her you had no cash but you knew someone who might be able to help – and that's when Pavel Adamek's name came up.'

'I don't know who that is!'

315

'Bollocks don't you. Look, I get it – you grew up with nothing, suddenly had the world at your feet, and then lost everything again. You were looking to get it back. Someone like you who's been in prison must have a few street contacts, so you put the word out asking if there was work about. Someone mentioned Pavel and away you went. You sent Rosemary his way to help him out and in return you had a cosy little chat about money-making schemes.'

Teague waved the back of his hand towards her. 'You're crazy.'

'I've been called worse. Anyway, we both know what happened next – do I have to spell it out?'

'Spell what out?'

'You hooked up with a couple of your old street pals, perhaps even someone Pavel knows, and you went back to the area where your old mansion was to rob a few houses. You knew the area because you used to drive around there. You figured it'd be an easy target – go for those with money and possessions but not the super-rich because their security would be too high. It was a good plan but there wasn't as much cash as you thought. You didn't know what to do with the jewellery because it's too hard to sell for any real amount of money so you panicked a bit. You ended up delivering smallish amounts of money to all sorts of charities, making people think you were a good guy.'

Teague was shaking his head. 'I don't know what you're on about.'

'If you won't admit you know Pavel then at least tell me where the jewellery is.'

'What jewellery?'

Jessica sighed. 'All right, sod this. At this exact moment, there are some big bastards in your garden with some huge feet and a massive battering ram – and that's not even a euphemism. You can either let them in, or they'll break in anyway.' She reached into her pocket and passed the warrant across. 'Don't even ask what I went through to get that on a Saturday.'

Teague took the page, skimmed the top line and then stared across at her open-mouthed, saying nothing.

Jessica shook her head, stood, walked into the hallway and opened the front door, telling the first officer to follow her. She went up the steps into the final bedroom she'd sneaked a peek at the previous time she'd been. The roll of carpet was still pushed to the side, although the hammer that had been resting on top of the bare floorboards was gone.

'Under there,' Jessica said, nodding at the naked wood.

The officer with the crowbar strode forward confidently, sticking the flat end in between two of the boards and wrenching it upwards. Jessica stood and watched as five, six, seven, eight more were pulled away. The officer got down onto all fours and peered both ways underneath the floor.

'Anything?' Jessica asked.

He twisted to stare up at her.

'Not even a stray pound coin.'

40

Sunday: Jessica's second 'day off' in a row spent at the station. It was fair to say Saturday had been a mixed success. Topper had called her to offer his congratulations on how smoothly the arrest of Pavel had gone, missing out the flying cake part, and then asked why exactly she'd arrested Martin Teague and why he'd vouched for a warrant early on a Saturday afternoon. She repeated everything she'd told him at the time and clarified that Rosemary still wouldn't talk about how she'd met Pavel and was threatening to withdraw all cooperation if they kept pushing her. He'd made a non-committal 'hmmm' sound and then initially asked to be kept up to date if anything changed, before deciding he was coming in anyway. It sounded to Jessica as if he wanted to get away from the kids for a day.

Pavel was going to spend the weekend in the cells underneath Bootle Street Police Station ahead of going before magistrates on Monday. The chances of him getting bail were as close to zero as anyone's had ever been and, given the fact he refused to say anything other than 'I do not speak English', there was little else they could do, other than hand over what they had to the Crown Prosecution Service and let them sort out what they wanted to pin on him. For all the effort they'd gone to in order to find him, the outcome was quite the anti-climax.

Jessica sat in the interview room, Archie at her side, Teague and his solicitor across the table. Jessica recognised the legal guy – he worked for one of the cheaper practices in the centre, talking a reasonable game but generally not delivering. That's what happened when a legal firm charged so little that all the scroats could afford them.

Teague had already offered a string of denials about practically everything before Jessica nudged Archie with her knee. He leant forward, top lip curled. 'Where's the money, Martin?'

'What money?'

'Where is it?'

Small wisps of hair had begun to grow on Teague's otherwise shaved head and his red face looked more bloated than ever, the loose skin on his cheeks hanging like a basset hound's. 'You'll have to tell me what money before I can tell you where it is.'

'What about the jewellery?'

'What jewellery?'

Archie slipped a sheet of paper out from a cardboard wallet and reeled off the list of stolen items, adding, 'Where is it?'

'I don't know where any of it is.'

'That's such shite. Shall we get some of the robbery victims in and see if they recognise your voice? How about we rip up the rest of the floorboards in your house? Or we go back to your old mansion and see if it's being hidden there? I'm sure there's a big list of places for us to look.'

'I haven't stolen anything!' Teague turned to his solicitor. 'They can't fit me up for this, can they? I saw that shite on the telly about the Slasher.'

The solicitor leant across the table. 'Are you going to put any specific allegations to my client? This is all conjecture and guesswork. You have some vague associations between Mr Teague and people he insists he doesn't know, then someone from his old school who I gather hasn't actually implicated him in anything. Then there's missing money and jewellery that you can't find. He's already spent a night in the cells, much to the dismay of his distraught wife. From what I can tell, you don't actually have anything that implicates him, despite arresting a wide selection of his friends. Could I perhaps suggest that this is more of a fishing expedition than anything serious . . . ?'

The smug . . . fellow.

Jessica took the folder from Archie and removed the page with the details of the first robbery, asking Teague where he was when it had happened.

'I can't remember – it was weeks ago. Almost certainly at home.'

'By yourself?'

'Tania would've been there.'

His story was the same for the second and third robberies – Tania would apparently give him an alibi. For the third one he said he thought there was football on the television. Archie gave her a look to confirm it but that didn't prove Teague had been at home watching it, simply that he knew it was on.

As for Tania, how reliable her testimony could be given that they were married was questionable but she was the next person on Jessica's list to drag in anyway.

The fruitless interview drew to a close, with Teague and his haughty solicitor disappearing back downstairs to the cells.

Jessica told Archie she'd catch up with him later and then went to find the newly arrived DCI Topper in his office. He was dressed down in a loose-fitting pair of trousers and a red and blue stripy jumper. He was smiling but it felt slightly forced. 'How's the weekend off going?' he asked.

'Much like the rest of the time off I take.'

'Did you get anything from Teague?'

'Sod all. We've been to every house that's even remotely connected to him overnight and not found anything that even looks like stolen jewellery. There are no lock-ups, no storage units, no anything in his name either. We've had his mates in – the street ones he grew up with and the ones we know he's in contact with. There are a few stories about the types of thing they got up to when he had money – racing cars around his garden, that sort of thing. There are four that fit the profiles of the robbers perfectly in terms of height and weight but it's not easy to prove anything with the lack of forensics and the fact only one of them spoke. There were only four robbers and, if Teague was one of them, then they can't all be involved but we figured there was no harm in getting them all in. They're all local, so any of them could be the main robber from the accent but we can't charge anyone based solely on that.'

'What are they saying?'

'"No comment" – that's it. Over and over, all four of them. "What's your name?" – "No comment". "How do you know Martin Teague?" – "No comment". We can't even start to check alibis because no one's given us one, they just no-comment.'

'That tells its own story.'

'True – but it's still not enough for the CPS to get excited about.'

'Also true. What about Martin?'

'He's talking – but he's denying everything. He says he doesn't know Pavel, he didn't put Rosemary in contact with him, he's not robbed anywhere, and so on.'

'Rosemary?'

'She's gone a bit quiet since she got a solicitor. I think it's dawned on her that her shop is going to be shut down for the money-laundering regardless of what she tells us. Cooperating can only get you so far and I don't think she wants to testify against Pavel anyway. I suspect it's all been done cleverly enough to keep her off the hook. She'll say she didn't know where Pavel's money came from and that the cash "donations" every Saturday morning were simply to pay back the loan. She can argue that she didn't know the repairman she paid to look at the cooker every week was one of his, and so on. She'll probably just about avoid prison and then have to start again. If she keeps talking, she's only going to get herself into more trouble.'

Topper smiled knowingly: 'That's what happens when you hire a proper solicitor – they tell you to shut up.'

'Quite.'

'I'm beginning to see why DCI Cole retired. You have quite the different class of criminal here compared to where I'm from.' Jessica was about to ask what exactly he was used to but he moved on. 'What's your thinking?'

'About Teague?'

'For the robberies.'

'The basics fit: the motive that he wants his money back, or at least some of it, his alibi's pretty weak regardless of what his wife might say, the descriptions we have of the robbers are just about right.'

'It's not going to be enough.'

'I know.'

'You need to find the money or the jewellery.'

'We're still trying to track down anywhere else he might have connections to. A few of the houses he bought at auction haven't been resold yet.'

Topper kept his lips tight, not having to say it because Jessica knew: if she didn't get her skates on, they were going to have to release Teague – and if he went to the media claiming wrongful arrest, given how well-known to them he was, all hell would break loose.

'What are you going to do next?' he asked.

'His wife Tania is downstairs. She's his alibi but we've been so busy listening to his friends say "no comment" that we've not got to her yet. First, I'm going to check what she was up to on the nights of the robberies.'

41

Tania Teague wasn't exactly looking her best. The heels, tight jeans and tighter jumper were all still in evidence but her dark roots were beginning to peek through her blonde hair that hadn't been straightened in a little while, instead becoming frizzy and free. With a lack of make-up, she looked quite different to the woman who had click-clacked her way into the living room the first time Jessica had met her.

Tania was sitting in the interview room, with the same solicitor as her husband had had. He was beginning to seem a little bored by spending an entire Sunday at Longsight Police Station. In fairness to him, it wouldn't make too many people's top-ten list of where to spend a weekend.

Jessica ran through a few general questions about Martin's behaviour over the previous weeks, receiving rather non-committal replies, before she got down to the actual reason for giving up her Sunday afternoon. She removed the details of the first robbery from the cardboard wallet again and read Tania the date. 'Where were you on that evening?'

The woman exchanged a glance with the solicitor. 'It's hard to know. Do you remember exactly where you were weeks later?'

'Pretty much – I'm usually either here or home, so it's not hard.'

Tania smiled sweetly. 'Good point. In that case, I was probably at home. I am most evenings.'

Jessica checked the next two robbery dates with her but Tania said the same was true, adding for the third one: 'I think he was watching football that evening.'

'Are you confirming for sure that you were with your husband on the night of all three robberies?'

Tania looked to her solicitor and back again, nodding. 'I'm not sure where else I'd be.'

It wasn't quite definitive but it seemed to be as far as she was going to go. 'When I was first at your house, Martin was complaining that you were always at the gym.'

'He does exaggerate.'

'I tripped over your gym bag when I was there. It had the name of the gym on the side, so I checked with them earlier. They were able to give me the exact dates and times when you used your ID card to check in.'

Her face scrunched up: 'Oh.'

'So I know that you weren't at home with your husband on any of the occasions he needed an alibi. For the third one, you would have arrived back while he was still out – but this means that any alibi you've given him is utterly worthless.'

Tania turned back to the solicitor but he was writing something on a pad.

'I suppose I could have been mistaken – it's difficult to remember where you are all the time . . . I still don't see why you think it's Martin, though. You've been in our house, causing a mess, ripping things up. Are you going to put it all back together again? There's nothing there.'

Jessica nodded upwards towards the camera. 'If I were you, I'd be more worried about the lies you just told while under caution.'

'Hey, I—'

Tania's solicitor cut in: 'Her exact words were that she wasn't sure where else she'd be if she wasn't at home. She didn't lie, she simply didn't know. Any right-thinking person would agree. You'd already found out where she was, so there was no need to goad her into making a mistake.'

'When I was at your house that time,' Jessica continued, focusing back on Tania, 'you said that your husband missed the money. Your exact words were: "It wasn't me who spent all the money and it's not me who's missing it". Do you remember that?'

Tania was running her fingers through her hair, trying to pull it straight. 'Vaguely. It sounds like something I'd say.'

'Why?'

The solicitor didn't offer anything, so Tania answered. 'Because he *does* miss the money. Life's very different without it. I've just gone home but he's lost everything. You can't think the rollercoaster, the cinema, or any of the cars were anything to do with me.'

'Is Pavel Adamek one of your husband's friends?'

'I've never heard of him.' Jessica took out a photo of Pavel and held it up. Tania peered closely but shook her head: 'I've never seen him either.'

'Be honest – the night of the third robbery, when you got home from the gym, was your husband there?'

'Of course he was.'

'You know any alibi you give him now is useless. You might as well tell the truth.'

'I don't care what you say – he was there.'

She would say that, of course, but Jessica had to ask. It counted for little now anyway given her previous 'mistake'.

'Did you know your husband was breaking into places and robbing the owners?'

Tania's solicitor leant forward. 'Don't answer that. My client has no knowledge of what you're talking about, be it anything her husband may or may not have done, or whether she knew about any of it.'

'In which other places could he be hiding the money?'

'She's not answering that either. Mrs Teague has told you what she knows.'

And on they went. Now that the solicitor had found his voice, he only allowed Tania to answer one question in every five or six and only then for basic clarifications, nothing serious. Given that she wasn't under arrest, or even suspicion, there wasn't much else they could do. In between the interruptions and missed questions, Jessica had done little other than establish that Tania apparently knew nothing about anything in regards to what her husband may or may not have been up to.

As she ended the interview, Jessica tried one final track, catching Tania's eye as she was leaving the interview room, away from the camera and recording device. 'You do realise how serious this all is? It's not just someone stealing a few quid from people that can afford it – this involves people having guns shoved in their faces, kids being traumatised. This has changed lives.'

The lawyer clicked a finger in Jessica's face, making her want to bite it off.

'Tania . . .' Jessica said.

'What?'

'You must know something was up. This was all going on under your nose, you can't be completely blind to it.'

The lawyer stood in front of Jessica this time, backing Tania into the corridor: 'If you want to talk to her, you're going to have to do so properly. This is utterly inappropriate.'

'Tania . . .'

The lawyer grabbed his client's wrist and began to walk away but Tania stopped, freeing herself and staring along the corridor towards Jessica. 'I don't know what you want me to say. All I know is that before he lost his money, he wanted to buy his childhood house.'

She spun, batted away her solicitor's arm and click-clacked her way towards reception.

42

Two days later, Jessica walked into reception, just as Pat was biting into a brownie. 'You mmmfly eckd mmff life,' he said, mouth full.

'That's disgusting.'

Pat swallowed but there were still bits of brown mush in between his teeth. 'I said you nearly wrecked my life. Thank God I had a bit of freezer space.'

'Yeah, and you nearly got yourself shot by walking into somewhere we were keeping an armed watch over.'

'It was an accident – I mixed up the days!'

'You've had all this time since and that's the best excuse you could come up with?'

He took another bite and scowled at her, eyes narrow and accusing. Jessica headed past him towards the stairs to DCI Topper's office. His door was already open but she closed it behind her. As she was sitting, he pointed to the whiteboard behind him which, for the first time since Jessica had returned to work, had a lot more blank space than black handwriting on it. Underneath, the same canvas bag for life rested with a pair of too-short shorts on top.

'Wonderful sight, isn't it,' he said. Jessica assumed he meant the board, not the shorts. 'Do you want the good news or the . . . oh, forget that – we'll start with the good news. First, how was your day off?'

It was true: Jessica had actually taken the Monday off.

'Good, Sir. I watched a lot of TV. I hear it was busy here.'

'Quite – as you know, we found the remaining banknotes that hadn't been given away to charity hidden in the fireplace of Martin Teague's childhood home. It was scheduled to be demolished in the next three months, which I don't think he even knew about. With that and his lack of alibi, the CPS are looking good to go forward.'

Jessica replied 'great' but she didn't feel it. The day off had given her time away from the case, time to think, and she knew there were things she wasn't happy about.

Topper continued unabated, still smiling. 'That's not all – we had the results back from Bradford Park this morning. We've got positive results from three of Martin's friends to the banknotes, either fingerprints or skin samples. Whatever they might claim, despite their "no comment"s, we know they handled the stolen money.'

'Oh.'

That was news to Jessica.

'That's not all – one of the three works for a private security firm. When we arrested him, we started going through his books and he has a receipt for an old police-issue battering ram that was bought at auction along with a job lot of various policing items. Quite how it ended up for sale, we don't know but it also gives us an idea of how they got into the house and knew about things like disabling panic buttons, alarms and cameras. This guy's company actually installs them.'

Jessica was genuinely surprised. Considering this had

all happened on her day off, she wondered if she should stay at home more often.

'Wow – things have moved on a lot.'

'They're still no-commenting but it can't be long before one of them turns when they realise how long they're going to go away for. They're back downstairs with their solicitors. That third off a sentence for confessing must seem pretty welcoming right now.'

'Did we find all of the money?'

'More or less. It's a few thousand short but we always suspected a few charities who were donated money might have simply sat on it. Martin Teague's still denying everything.'

'Are his fingerprints on the money?'

'No . . . but he has no alibi and they're his friends. Plus it's his motive, of course. There is a problem, though.'

'What?'

'We found a fourth set of prints on the money but they're not his.'

'Whose are they?'

'Another of his old school friends. He's got a few things on his record, so we matched it to him straight away. We've got a warrant out and are currently looking for him.'

'But there were only four robbers – so does that mean it's the four we've got? Or that Teague was masterminding things? Or that they took it in turns?'

Topper shrugged. 'We don't know. Until someone starts talking, we're only going to be guessing. Teague has to be in there somewhere, though – he's the link from Pavel to the others.'

'What's going on with Pavel?'

'He was in court yesterday and remanded without entering a plea. Apparently the court solicitor couldn't get a word out of him. He knows what we've got on him and if he starts talking, he might talk his way into more trouble. He'll get sent down, serve six to twelve months in one of our jails and then the Home Office will send him back to Serbia to serve the rest because our jails are too full. Of course, what happens when he's under another country's jurisdiction is anyone's guess. If he knows the right people, he could have quite the cushy existence when he gets away from here.'

'What about the jewellery?'

Topper spun a quarter-turn in his seat. 'Aah, well, that's where it's not all wrapped up too tidily. We don't have a trace of any of that.'

That was what had been playing on Jessica's mind for the day she was off.

'When I was in London, that Richard Froggatt guy told me his gang had given away money to disguise the reality of what had gone on. I know we've recovered pretty much all of the cash – but that's nowhere near everything that was stolen. The money was in the jewels.'

'That's what we're trying to get out of the men we have in custody.'

'But you said it for yourself about Pavel – he doesn't want to get himself in any more trouble. They could say nothing the whole way through and then claim they were simply renovating the Teagues' original house and that's how their prints ended up on those notes. Or that it's profits from the security company but they don't trust banks so their friend, Martin Teague, told them to hide it at the house.'

'That's nonsense.'

'Of course it is but you only need to convince two or three jurors and the whole thing falls apart. Even if they get sent down, they'd be out before they were really old men. So they sit tight, say nothing, and get a share when they get out.'

'In real terms, it's thousands not millions. That's not a lot to go to prison for.'

Jessica sighed, focusing on Topper's whiteboard and then letting her eyes relax again. She'd spent the whole of the previous day thinking about things like this. 'True – but we caught them early. This could have been ten robberies before we got them, or more. The principle of shutting up and letting a jury decide would be a sound one regardless. You know how stupid people can be when they hear the words "beyond all reasonable doubt". Suddenly a string of half-a-dozen coincidences that wouldn't convince anyone with half a brain is doubt enough.'

'So where's the jewellery? Could they have pawned off small amounts at different places all around the country?'

Jessica shook her head. 'I made a few phone calls yesterday—'

'I thought you were off all day?'

She held his smile. 'I was. Anyway, my point is that pawnbrokers only pay perhaps twenty-five to thirty-five per cent of what something's worth. Our robbers need to be selling direct to people, not via a middle man.'

'Car boots?'

'Too obvious and too easy to be caught.'

'So what are you thinking?'

Jessica blew out hard, making a braying sound with her lips. 'It's too clean, isn't it? Lottery winner wants money back, takes idea from Serbian gangster.'

'It was your theory!' Topper was smiling but there was a seriousness to him as well.

'I know . . . I think I've talked myself out of it.'

'But there's evidence.'

Jessica clucked her tongue. 'Can we get Archie up here?'

'Constable Davey? If you think it'll do some good.'

Topper reached for his phone but Jessica stood. 'I'll get him.'

She headed down the stairs through to the main floor where Archie was sitting on the corner of Rowlands's desk, chatting. As Dave spotted her, he nodded and Archie stood and spun around, looking guilty.

'Were you just talking about me?' Jessica asked.

Dave replied with a half-smile: 'The whole world doesn't revolve around you, Jess.'

She eyed the pair of them suspiciously, not entirely pleased at the fact they could be friends again. When Archie had first joined, Dave had followed him around and they'd been as thick as thieves. Things had changed now Rowlands was working with DI Franks.

'Topper wants you upstairs, Arch.'

'Why?'

'Because he does.'

'You're a bit grumpy,' Dave said, laughing.

She gave him her best glare and then headed away with Archie at her side.

'What does he *actually* want?' Archie asked.

'It's me really. I've got a question to ask you.'

'In front of him?'

'Yes.'

'Why me?'

Jessica stopped and pulled him towards a closed doorway, lowering her voice. 'If I tell you, do you promise not to be offended?'

He chewed his bottom lip. 'Depends what it is.'

'It's sort of bad but not really bad if that makes sense.'

'Er . . .'

'I mean it affectionately.'

'Go on then.'

'You won't be offended?'

He shrugged. 'Whatever it is, I've probably heard worse.'

She lowered her voice even further, looking both ways along the corridor to ensure there was no one there. 'It's just you're a bit of a . . . I'm not sure of the best word . . . you're a . . . scally, a chav, a lad. Whichever one you prefer.'

He stood up on his tip-toes until he was somewhere close to the five foot eight he told everyone he was and puffed his chest out. 'Aye, fair enough.'

'You don't mind?'

'Nah, "lad" is a good shout. Dunno about "scally", like. That's what we call Scousers.'

'Right . . .'

'What do you need to ask me in front of Topper?'

'I'd rather not say anything else until we're upstairs. I need your response to be real.'

He shrugged again, sinking back to his actual height. 'A'ight, let's go then.'

Moments later, the pair of them were sitting across the desk from DCI Topper in his office, the two men looking expectantly at Jessica.

'Go on then,' Archie said.

She whispered him a silent 'sorry', and then asked: 'What was the worst thing you ever did as a kid?' Archie glanced sideways at the DCI, who had his attention on Jessica. 'Trust me,' Jessica said.

Topper turned to Archie. 'You don't have to answer.'

He shook his head. 'Nah, it's fine. I was a bit of a, well . . . *lad* . . . when I was a young'un. A right little terror according to my mum, God rest her soul. All right, I'm not proud of this, mind.' He turned to face Topper himself. 'I'm not going to get in trouble or anything, am I?'

'Did you murder anyone?'

'Oh, God no – it's nothing like that.'

'Probably not then.'

'Right, well, there was this little paper shop at the end of my road. This old fella ran it – lovely guy: he'd been doing it for donkey's years. I used to do a paper round but then I started nicking odd things: chocolate bars, sweets, pens. I've always felt really bad about it because it was this

336

tiny place and he was really good to me. He can't have been making much money from it, he just liked seeing people. He had this little black and white TV above the door that he'd watch when it was quiet. Either that or he'd listen to the cricket on the radio. Even when I stopped delivering papers, he'd always say hello and he knew my name. I kept wanting to say sorry but he died one Christmas and it never happened. The shop's gone now – they converted it into flats.'

He turned away, genuinely moved. Even Jessica felt a small prickling behind her eyes as well as guilt that she'd made him share it in front of the DCI. It wasn't really fair but he'd done it because he trusted her.

'Sorry . . .' Jessica said.

'It's all right. I was a little shite then.'

'Okay, say some of your mates knew what you'd been up to and the police were involved. Would they have given you up?'

'Never.'

'What if it meant them taking the fall for it?'

'Oh, they'd have done that. They'd have taken all the stick off their parents, all the trouble – whatever it took.'

'Why?'

He shrugged. 'That's what it's like when you're mates. I'd have done the same for them.'

'What about now?'

Archie glanced at Topper and back to her. 'Well, within reason. They know what my job is. It's not like any of us are going around getting into rucks or kicking off or anything. Half of them have kids nowadays.'

Jessica turned to Topper, wondering if he knew what she was getting at. He peered from her to Archie and back again, then shrugged. 'What?'

'Martin Teague and his mates come from a couple of streets over from Arch. They'll be exactly the same. They'd rather go down than drop one of their mates in it – except that Teague's not doing that at all. They're all saying "no comment" but from the time I went to his house to arrest him, all he's said is that he doesn't know Pavel, that he doesn't know anything about robberies, money or jewellery.'

'So you think that because he's denying it, he's telling the truth?'

'If he knew what was going on, he'd be no-commenting too. It'd be the code he grew up with, they all grew up with – don't grass. If he knew the robberies were some-thing to do with his pals, he'd be shutting his mouth.'

'That's a bizarre reverse kind of thinking.'

Jessica's eye was drawn back to the pair of shorts on top of Topper's bag underneath the whiteboard. 'I'm sorry, Sir, I've got to ask, why do you bring your training kit to work?'

He turned around, glancing at the bag and then back to Jessica, not annoyed, just confused.

'Why?'

'Indulge me.'

'It's easier to come straight here after the gym. I leave my things out to, ahem, dry off. Is that all right with you?'

Jessica checked her watch. It took her a while to reply as she battled the sinking feeling of horror. 'I think I've made a terrible mistake.'

43

Jessica pressed her foot onto the accelerator and shot across the junction, sirens blazing. Archie was in the passenger's seat, hanging onto his seatbelt with both hands.

'I still don't get iiiiiiiiiiittttttttt—' he said as Jessica took a corner.

'What's not to get?'

'Who robbed the houses?'

'Teague's mates – we've got their prints on the money.'

'But not Teague?'

'No.'

'Or Pavel?'

'No.'

Jessica rocketed onto the M60, keeping one eye on the outside lane as cars moved to one side. She only had one junction before she turned onto the M56.

Archie let go of the seatbelt and leant on the door. 'Whooooooooooa.'

'You're putting me off.'

'Why are you going so fast?'

'Because I want to deal with this. It'll be better if it's me, honestly.'

'You would say that.'

'That's because I'm right.'

Jessica swerved between two cars and took the exit onto the M56.

Archie regained his breath and continued. 'And you got all of this from Topper's dirty laundry?'

'Sort of. It's more than that. I'll tell you later.'

Jessica screamed along the motorway, bumped her way up the exit ramp, rammed the car into the left lane, fizzed across two roundabouts, and then accelerated until she was outside the Terminal One departures area at Manchester Airport. She came to a halt with a screech, then told Archie to wait by the car. He didn't look particularly happy at Jessica's explanation that it had to be her by herself but didn't argue.

A security officer was already waiting for her, escorting Jessica through five sets of heavy doors before leading her into the departures lounge. She assured him she'd take it from there, knowing there would be other officers nearby if she needed them.

Jessica peered up at the board: the flight to Kiev was leaving in an hour and a quarter, with a gate number already assigned.

She slowed to a walk and caught her breath. It was such a stupid hunch that she knew it was right. She moved slowly along the line of departure gates, past the prize-draw car that was apparently a feature of every airport in the Western world, despite the fact Jessica had never heard of anyone who'd ever won one, past the screaming kids, the stag party wearing shorts, the hen party who were already pissed, the couple all but making a baby in a pair of seats behind a pillar, the shuffling, creepy-looking cleaner, the businessman wheeling his suitcase behind him even though it couldn't have weighed too much for him to carry, and everyone else ready to jet away to wherever they were going.

Even from a distance, Jessica spotted the two blonde women sitting next to each other, one of them reading, the other wearing dark sunglasses and gazing aimlessly towards the window.

Jessica manoeuvred her way through the crowd until she was sitting in the seat opposite them, barely a metre away.

Ana noticed her first. 'Oh, hi, it's you – why are you here?'

Jessica smiled at her. 'You're nearly home, Ana.'

'I know . . .'

Katerina peered up from her book, studying Jessica, her face hard to read. 'Are you here to wish us goodbye?' she asked.

'Something like that.'

Jessica glanced towards the end of the row of seats where two officers were standing with guns across their fronts, doing a terrible job of looking casual.

Ana looked between the two women. 'What's going on?'

Katerina said something in a language Jessica didn't understand. Jessica kept her eyes on Katerina but spoke to Ana. 'What did she say?'

'To keep calm.'

Jessica continued to stare at Katerina. 'Ana, I want you to pick up your bag and go and stand close to the gate.'

'Why?'

'Because if you want to go home today, that's the only way it's going to happen.'

The two women exchanged words that weren't in English and then Ana picked up her bag and walked past Jessica. There were half-a-dozen seats free on either side of Jessica and Katerina: no one to overhear.

'Just so you know,' Jessica said, 'it was the towel that did it. When it flew off your back seat and hit me in the back of the head, I noticed the logo from your gym. I'd seen it before but it didn't mean anything to me at the time. Then you talked about going for a run when you were at the safe house.'

Katerina's eyes flickered to the right where another pair of armed guards had emerged. She laughed slightly, humourlessly. 'Perhaps I should drive more carefully next time.'

Jessica leant forward and pushed the woman's long sleeve up to reveal a row of glittering, expensive-looking bracelets. 'I could probably say the same.'

44

Katerina squirmed uncomfortably on her seat in the interview room, muttering things in a foreign language to her solicitor. Jessica watched through the observation window, saying nothing, even though DCI Topper could barely contain himself: 'You figured this out because of my gym kit?'

'Sort of . . . not really. Sometimes my mind works in weird ways. It just needs a shunt here and there.'

'That's some shunt. Do you want to come around and do my laundry in case it gives you any other ideas?'

'Very funny.'

'Do you mind if I sit in?'

Jessica shrugged and laughed. 'You're the chief inspector. You don't need to ask.'

'I am asking. I know we didn't get off to the best of starts.'

'That was my fault too. I have a habit of . . . rubbing people up the wrong way.' Jessica turned to face him. 'Shall we do this?'

'Lead the way.'

Jessica exited into the corridor and then entered the interview room properly. She poured herself and DCI Topper some water and then sat, making the introductions for the purposes of the recordings before downing her drink in one.

'That was close, wasn't it?' Jessica said.

Katerina had a strange sort of half-smile on her face: forbidding, resigned. 'Not close enough.'

'For the purposes of the tape, we've been looking for somewhere in the region of three hundred thousand pounds in stolen jewellery. When you were arrested at the airport, Katerina, you had around half of that amount on your person ready to be taken to the Ukraine, or wherever you were heading after leaving Ana. That's the thing with jewellery – no one really knows what it's worth at a glance, so the security staff were happy to wave you through. Because it's quality over quantity, you didn't even need to be carrying that much.'

The solicitor cut in: 'Is that a question?'

'No, I'm simply clarifying things so that if you ever listen to your copy of the tape, there's no doubt what I'm referring to. I suppose the first question is where the rest of the jewellery is.'

Katerina shrugged. 'You tell me.'

'Who has it?'

'You tell me.'

Jessica was pretty sure she knew anyway. She slid the photograph across the table. 'Do you know who this person is?'

Katerina didn't look at it: 'No.'

'I know that you do.'

'I don't know.'

Jessica left it face-up on the table. 'Before we get into things, when we were going around the shops in Cheetham

Hill and everyone was so reluctant to talk to us – to me, you said something to them in their own language before you let me speak. Were you telling them not to talk to me?'

Katerina smiled: 'The whole world doesn't revolve around you.'

'That's not an answer.'

'Perhaps I was saying hello and the rest is all in your mind. Maybe they just don't like you?'

'But it wasn't that, was it? You were telling them not to say anything to me.'

Katerina smirked more widely. 'You English and Americans; colonising the world and not even bothering to learn how to say hello. Perhaps you shouldn't be so ignorant of everyone else's culture. Maybe then you'd be able to understand what's being said.'

Jessica continued to stare at her but Katerina wasn't going to give a definitive answer: perhaps the shop owners hadn't liked Jessica and that was that.

'How do you know Pavel Adamek?' Jessica asked.

'Through you.'

'I know that's a lie – you're why he wasn't in the pub car park even when it was him who'd received the text message about being there in the first place. I called Esther and Esther called you asking for help – except that it was so late in the day that you didn't have time to tip him off properly to stop the whole thing. In the end, you only managed to text him, or call him quickly, something that stopped him being there with the rest of the men.'

'Think what you want.'

'Is it because Montenegro and Serbia are close? Or you lived in Serbia? Is that how you know him?'

'You know nothing about the history of our countries.'

'Tell me how you know him – did he come to you over here because he knew you were working for the police or was it something else?'

'You seem to know a lot, you tell me.'

'Just tell me.'

Katerina blinked and suddenly her eyes were locked to Jessica's. 'It's not just Ana who has people she cares about.'

DCI Topper sat up straighter as they finally got an answer other than flat denial but Jessica stayed where she was, speaking deliberately and trying to sound as open as she could. 'If that's the case, we can contact the police in Montenegro, or wherever your family are.'

'The fact you don't even know where my family live should tell you all you need to know about what I think of your protection offer. They could be living next door to you and you wouldn't even know.'

It was true: Katerina was Montenegrin but that didn't mean that was where her family lived. No one had even bothered to find out, so it was no wonder she was hostile.

'If you tell us what you know about Pavel, then—'

'Pavel who?'

Jessica stopped and pointed at the photograph. 'How about this person?'

Katerina glanced down but peered back up, smiling. 'I don't know who that is.'

'You do. You had Pavel's half of the jewels and were taking them to the Ukraine. Someone would have either taken them from you there, or you'd have flown on to Serbia. Perhaps you were getting a cut? Perhaps you owed Pavel something? Perhaps he's got your family? His people would deal with selling them on. If you don't tell us, there's nothing we can do.'

Katerina shrugged. 'Then there's nothing you can do.'

Jessica patted the photograph one more time. 'All you have to do is say the name, then we'll know for sure where the other half of the jewellery ended up.'

Katerina shook her head.

Jessica stood and picked up the photograph. 'More fool you, then. This is Tania Teague and at half past nine last night, she took a flight to the Cayman Islands with one hundred and fifty grand's worth of jewellery and who knows what else on her. While she's sunning herself in the Caribbean, you're going to be living in a cell. Congratulations. I've heard the food's shite.'

45

Jessica sat in DCI Topper's office with Assistant Chief Constable William Aylesbury at her side. He was stirring his tea, scraping the spoon along the bottom of the mug in an increasingly annoying way. If anything, Aylesbury was looking younger than when he'd been DCI. He was wearing a navy blue jumper with knitted cables that made him look thin, plus matching dark trousers. His hair had apparently stopped going grey without even having that dodgy dyed look about it. He seemed every inch the retired country gentleman – except he was part of Greater Manchester Police's command team.

'This is exceptional work,' he said in between bites of a Battenberg slice. Somehow, whenever the superintendent or anyone else senior was in the station, someone found a packet of biscuits or a cake. Aylesbury was eating the marzipan from around the edge, leaving the cakey centre for last.

Jessica was leaning back in her chair, staring at the ceiling. The bright white lights were making green shapes appear in her vision. She didn't feel 'exceptional'.

'Tania played me completely,' she said, still looking into the lights.

Scrape, scrape, scrape. How much stirring did one cup of tea need? And how come they were constantly left with sludge from the machine, yet someone magicked up a proper mug if anyone important turned up?

'Now, now,' Aylesbury said, 'anyone could have been taken in. We've got Pavel Adamek, who's wanted for all sorts of things; we've got the gang of robbers, plus fingerprints on the stolen money; we've recovered half of the stolen jewellery. That's a pretty good result.'

'What am I going to say in the press conference when they ask about the mastermind?'

'Feel free to leave the talking to those of us who are more . . . comfortable in front of the camera. I know it's not your thing.'

Jessica peered back down, blinking away the green and pink stars. Aylesbury was eating the cake square by square. 'With respect, Sir, I've not written everything up yet, so you might struggle to give information if you don't know it.'

He popped more of the cake into his mouth and grinned. 'So tell me.'

Jessica sighed. Again. She was doing a lot of that recently. Saying it all out loud made her feel stupider for allowing Tania to run rings around her.

'It was a daft thing, really.' She nodded towards the canvas bag still under the whiteboard. 'I saw the guv's gym stuff and it jogged my mind. When I'd been out with Katerina around Cheetham Hill, she had a towel on the back seat of her car that had a gym logo on it. I was at Martin and Tania Teague's house and she had a gym bag with the same logo. I don't know who approached who first but I guess they were talking in the changing rooms or somewhere like that at some point, the way that people do.'

Aylesbury interrupted: 'The way that *women* do!'

No one laughed, so Jessica continued: 'Tania would have said that one of her husband's friends – Rosemary – had come to them looking to borrow thousands of pounds. She might have joked about it but Katerina already knew Pavel was looking for someone to marry to try to stay here. I don't know how they knew each other but I strongly suspect Pavel came to her. She told me that the dialects are similar and they come from adjacent countries. Perhaps he found out a few things about her first and threatened her family, or maybe that came later? Either way, Katerina began doing odds and ends for him. With her work for us around the local immigrant community, she'd have been very useful to him.'

Aylesbury took another slice of Battenberg from the plate and began nibbling around the edges a little like a rabbit.

'I should have seen it,' Jessica continued. 'It was never Martin who was money-obsessed. He was an idiot with it. He spent whatever he had whether it was nine quid or nine million. He didn't care. When I was there, he had his feet up, a beer by his side, his mates around. That's all he was ever bothered about. Tania was the one who liked the nice things in life – it was obvious with her choice of clothes, even the way she held herself, but I was so focused on him that I wasn't even looking. When she had an inkling of what was going on in my head, she fed me the line: "It wasn't me who spent all the money and it's not me who's missing it". Martin didn't react because he was trying not to argue with her but she'd said it for my benefit anyway. She's the smart one, Martin's the street kid who picked the right numbers.'

Aylesbury was peeling away the marzipan again. 'It wasn't her who did the robberies though.'

'Of course not. Perhaps by accident, Katerina introduced Tania to Pavel. Katerina thought it was because Pavel was after a wife but Tania was way too clever for that. She wanted to get her fortune back, so she was talking to Pavel about ways they could make money quickly. That's when he told her about the scheme he eventually got caught for in Serbia. Because she and Martin had lived in a rich area with their lottery winnings, Tania knew exactly who to rob – not their immediate neighbours, the ones a little lower down the social ladder. All she had to do was rope in a few people. Her husband was out – he was stupid enough to blow almost ten million in the first place – but they were childhood sweethearts. He hired an island and flew her and all their friends there. Because they'd all grown up together, she knew his friends as well as she knew Martin. She'd have known how to press their buttons; perhaps flirt a bit, perhaps say what a perfect plan she had, promise them money, riches, whatever. They'd have all seen their mate spend ten million and wanted a bit for themselves. Suddenly she was offering them their own windfall. All they had to do was follow exactly what she said and keep their mouths shut. As for Pavel, to keep him quiet, he was getting a percentage.'

Aylesbury frowned as a blob of jam dropped onto the floor. 'Very clever.'

'The first house might have been a surprise. They couldn't take big items because that's how you get caught. Cash, jewellery, anything shiny, in-out, don't hang around. Tania might not have expected so many bracelets or necklaces but then they were left with a problem of how to get rid of it. Pavel had the answer because he has contacts at home from his old jobs. It'd be too risky to go abroad after every robbery, so once they had enough jewellery stockpiled, someone flies out of the country keeping it in plain sight, passes it over to Pavel's men and then it's converted back to money again. They didn't know what to do with the cash in case it was marked but there wasn't much there relatively speaking. I suppose it was Tania's idea to give it away because it was all about the jewellery anyway. It made us look silly, took the attention away from what they were actually doing, and still left a few thousand hidden away. If it turned out the notes were marked, or there was something else traceable about them, we would have said when people started giving them away. We'd have fallen right into their hands and told people to check the serial numbers, that sort of thing. As it was, by doing nothing, we told Tania and her gang it was fine to spend.'

'She even told you where the house was, I gather.' Aylesbury hadn't said it critically but Jessica took it that way.

'I thought I was being smart by appealing to her conscience but she'd deliberately wound me up to get to that point. She didn't care if her husband was implicated but knew we probably didn't have enough on him other-wise, so she pointed us in the right direction. It wouldn't surprise me if she engineered being at the gym on the night of the robberies, knowing she wouldn't be able to give Martin a proper alibi. That way she could offer the pretence of being the supporting wife, all the while doing her best to make him look guilty.'

Aylesbury was on a roll of clichés and casual sexism. 'Hell hath no fury like a woman scorned, I suppose.'

'I don't know about that, Sir, but perhaps if you ever win nine point eight million quid, you should put a million to one side for your wife to spend as she sees fit.'

He brayed, not noticing DCI Topper's withering stare. 'Quite, quite. I'll bear that in mind. She'd probably blow it in a week on shoes.'

DCI Topper interrupted the laughter, talking directly to Jessica. 'We know Tania got off the flight in the Cayman Islands last night but have no idea where she went after that. Her poor dog—'

'Tinkerbell.'

'Yes. We found her roaming their house by herself. We had to call the RSPCA in to take her.'

He turned back to Aylesbury and passed him the photo-graph Jessica had shown to Katerina in the interview room. It was a CCTV image, showing Tania shortly after passing through airport security, reattaching a sparkling bracelet to her wrist.

Aylesbury glanced at it and nodded. 'The chief con-stable's been talking to Interpol. We'll catch her.'

Jessica didn't want to disagree but knew that Tania

wasn't stupid enough to get caught so late in the game. She would have kept her half of the loot somewhere close, bided her time, and then, when things had started to fall apart, her plans would have gone into action. Within an hour or so of getting off the plane, she'd have been on a boat somewhere. One hundred and fifty thousand pounds in jewellery wasn't much in the long run but she was smart and probably had other amounts squirrelled away somewhere.

Aylesbury grabbed one more slice of cake and got to his feet. 'Come, they'll be waiting for us downstairs. Leave it with me: I'll play down the Tania thing as much as possible. This is a massive success. Everyone here deserves the highest praise.'

DCI Topper caught Jessica's eye behind Aylesbury's back as the assistant chief constable turned to leave. He didn't need to say it because the raise of an eyebrow was enough: 'Don't get involved.'

He was right, except Jessica still had to find a few minutes to call Esther and tell her what Katerina had done. They were colleagues, after all.

Jessica closed her mouth and followed Aylesbury down the stairs and through the corridors towards the Press Pad. In the passage ahead, runners and technicians were racing up and down checking cables and strength of reception. Given the Robin Hood element that had been reported by practically every media outlet in the country, the revelation that the case had been solved was going to attract massive attention. Topper kept a hand on the bottom of Jessica's back as they moved along, pressing gently, not intimately. It felt like he could read her mind, knowing she wanted to do a runner. In the space of a few days, she'd gone from hating him to thinking he was one of the few people who understood how she worked.

Aylesbury led them into a side office and it was only then that Jessica knew she couldn't go through with it. Chief Constable Graham Pomeroy was sitting in a chair talking to someone on his phone, enormous rolls of fat bursting out through a shirt that was tucked into his trousers and hanging on literally by threads. His cheeks were overhanging his jaw, his chins blubbering into one. The last time she'd seen him in person was at a press conference and he was disgusting then. It wasn't even his appearance, it was what she knew about him. What she *thought* he and his group of friends knew about the way her car had blown up with Adam inside.

He acknowledged the three of them with a nod, said goodbye to whoever he was talking to and then hung up. When she'd last seen Pomeroy, he'd barely nodded at her, not really knowing who she was; now he had eyes only for Jessica, stretching out his piggy hand for her to shake.

Jessica remained where she was, partially behind Topper. 'I've not been feeling well,' she said. 'I wouldn't want to pass on any germs.'

Pomeroy stopped where he was, hand still outstretched. Topper saved her by reaching forward and shaking it vigorously. 'I have no such problems, Sir. Thank you for coming.'

Unable to ignore the chief inspector, Pomeroy turned to Topper, a disingenuous grin appearing on his face.

'Quite, an excellent result – almost perfect. Interpol are very confident about wrapping things up.'

Jessica took another half-step sideways so that Topper was almost completely blocking Pomeroy from even looking at her.

'Much of the credit has to go to Inspector Daniel,' Topper said.

Pomeroy's gaze flickered around the DCI until Jessica had no choice but to look at him. 'Excellent, excellent. That inquisitive mind is such a praiseworthy thing . . .' He let the words hang, the meaning clear to Jessica, even if it was lost on the other two. 'And you'll be joining us at the press conference? I'm sure there'll be a lot of questions.'

Jessica shook her head. 'I should probably go home. I think I've eaten something a bit ropey.'

Aylesbury cackled with laughter. 'I suppose the canteen here hasn't improved since I left.'

No one else joined in.

Jessica took two more sidesteps until she was next to the door. She had one hand on the knob when she heard Pomeroy's voice behind her: 'Oh, Inspector Daniel . . .'

She didn't turn, not wanting to look at him again. 'What?'

'Drive carefully.'

46

'Drive carefully . . .'

Jessica's eyelids flickered open slowly, her eyes searching through the darkness towards the square green digits of the clock in Archie's bedroom: 02.41.

Again.

Was she dreaming? This had happened before, hadn't it? The alcohol, Archie, the bed, 02.41?

She slipped out of the covers, standing and letting her eyes adjust to the gloom. Archie was sleeping on his front again, naked except for one of his legs underneath the sheet. She ran her hand along the floor until she found her clothes and had reached the door by the time his voice filtered through the room. 'Are you ever going to stay the night?'

Jessica stopped, one hand on the cool metal of the handle. 'No.'

'Why?'

'You know why.'

She could hear him moving into a sitting position. 'You know the story about nicking things from the man with the corner shop at the end of my road – I've never told anyone that. If it hadn't have been for you, I never would have done.'

Jessica shivered, not because of the cold. 'What do you want me to say?'

He gulped. 'I don't know. I just wanted you to know.'

'I have to go.'

This time, she had the door half-open before he responded. 'Jess . . .'

'What?'

'I had fun this evening.'

She paused, wanting to pick her words but in the end it came out the same as it would have done if she had replied without thinking. 'Me too.'

'Are we going to do this again?'

'Maybe.'

'At yours?'

'No.'

'Are we going to tell anyone?'

'No.'

They waited in silence for a few moments. She could hear him breathing across the room, practically hear his thoughts.

In the end, Jessica broke the impasse: 'Go back to sleep, Arch. I'll see you tomorrow.'

She didn't want to wait for a reply but it came anyway, his voice barely a whimper. 'Is this enough?'

'Is what enough?'

'This. Leaving at silly hours of the morning, not sleeping, pretending we barely know each other during the day.'

Jessica turned, holding onto her clothes with one hand.

She whispered her reply before closing the door and heading to the sofa to get changed: 'It's this or nothing.'

Jessica padded through the corridors, trying not to make her feet echo too much on the hard floor. Lights turned on overhead as she walked, as if controlled by an omnipresent Big Brother tracking her progress, rather than a simple movement detector.

She should have stopped at the hospital's front desk to ask permission to be here but she would only have been turned away. Ultimately, who cared if she turned up at almost four in the morning? Her eyes felt heavy, her hair was all over the place and she knew she looked a mess.

Had she driven drunk? Perhaps – she'd finished drinking hours ago but maybe there was something still in her system. What was she becoming?

Pad, pad, pad, pad.

There were only a few people in the corridors, so it was easy enough not to make eye contact. Keep your head down and walk. Most of the people not sleeping at this time of the night were lunatics anyway and Jessica was right there with them, following the black line of tape on the floor.

Pad, pad, pad, pad.

Eventually she arrived at the door: a dead end in a place where only the dead belonged. She pushed the door open and crept inside, hearing the whoosh of the machinery. For a moment, she stayed where she was, listening: a thunk and a hiss on endless repeat.

Jessica took a deep breath and stepped forward, away

from the shadows into the dim light, moving the chair around and settling next to the bed. She closed her eyes, breathing slowly.

Thunk-hiss. Thunk-hiss.

She hadn't been here in a few weeks because she couldn't face it, not after that month where she'd barely left this place.

Couldn't face him.

When Jessica opened her eyes again, she was staring directly at Adam's broken, swollen, patchy skin. The heat from the car blaze had literally roasted him to the point where the skin was dripping from his body. He'd never woken and couldn't breathe for himself; yet somehow he was still here, still alive, having a machine maintain whatever life was left in his body. His eyes were taped closed, his chest rising and falling only when the machine made it happen.

Thunk-hiss. Thunk-hiss.

Jessica slipped his hand out from under the blanket, running her thumb across the area where they had managed to graft the skin. She could feel the bumps and scrapes, see the patchwork of different colours blending into one another.

The tears hit the floor before she even knew they were coming, her single word of apology forever lost among the sobs. She'd said it enough anyway, over and over. One word that made no difference because he was here because of her.

'Sorry.'

DOWN AMONG THE DEAD MEN

Kerry Wilkinson

Money can't buy everything . . .

Jason Green's life is changed for good after he is saved from a mugging by crime boss Harry Irwell. From there, he is drawn into Manchester's underworld, where stomping into a newsagents and smashing the place up is as normal as making a cup of tea.

But Jason isn't a casual thug. Fast cars and flash clothes don't appeal – he's biding his time and saving his money, waiting for the perfect moment to make a move.

That is until a woman walks into his life offering one thing that money can't buy – salvation.

OUT NOW

SOMETHING WICKED

Kerry Wilkinson

*There's nothing worse than watching your child
walk out the front door, never to return . . .*

Nicholas Carr disappeared on his eighteenth birthday and
the world has moved on. His girlfriend is off at university,
his friends now have jobs and the police are busy dealing
with the usual gallery of thieves and drunks.

But his father, Richard, can't forget the three fingers
the police dug up from a sodden Manchester wood. What
happened to Nicholas on the night he disappeared, and
why did he never return home?

A private investigator is Richard's last hope – but Andrew
Hunter has his own problems. There's something about his
assistant that isn't quite right. Jenny's brilliant but reckless,
and he can't figure out what she gets from working for him.
By the time he discovers who's a danger and who's not, it
might all be too late . . .